NORTH COUNTRY HONEYMOON

A Kate Killoy Mystery

Previous Kate Killoy Mysteries

Fashion Goes to the Dogs

Puppy Pursuit

National Specialty

Search

Check them out by visiting www.PeggyGaffney.com

I look forward to bringing you more adventures with Kate and Harry next year.

North Country Honeymoon

-A Kate Killoy Mystery-

Suspense for the Dog Lover

by

Peggy Gaffney

Kanine Books

2019

NORTH COUNTRY HONEYMOON

A Kate Killoy Mystery

ISBN-13: 978-0-9770412-6-8

Cover art by Peggy Gaffney
Edited by Sandra McDonough
Interior design by Peggy Gaffney

www..peggygaffney.com

Give feedback on the book at:
gaffney@kanineknits.com

Twitter: @PeggyGaffney

First Edition
Kanine Books
Printed in the U.S.A

DEDICATION

For my son Sean
and
Dillon, Quinn, and all my Samoyed dogs down
through the years.
You are my inspiration.

Acknowledgment

My many thanks to my super editor Sandy McDonough, a dear friend who cheers me on and encourages me to write the stories of Kate and Harry and the wonderful Samoyeds we both love. I thank my son who serves as the person I bounce ideas off and who is there with encouragement when I am frustrated. And of course a special thank you to my readers who have taken to heart Kate, Harry, Dillon, Quinn and the people and dogs who populate the Kate Killoy Mysteries.

Cast of Characters

Kate Killoy Foyle - Dog trainer, Show dog handler, Knitting designer, The bride
Harry Foyle - Owner of cyber security company, Former FBI, The groom. New owner of the great house called "Camp"
Helen & Otto Marks - Caretakers at "Camp" where honeymoon takes place
Officer Calub Jones - Bolton police officer
Lt. Gil St. Amand - Bolton police detective in charge of murder case
Sgt. George Braxton - Bolton police sergeant and Gil's partner, Former dog show friend of Kate Killoy. He shows Malamutes
Officer Joe Magyar - Bolton police officer
Vivian Durgin - Former owner of "Camp", Cousin of Ann Durgin Killoy, Great Aunt to Kate Killoy
Ann Durgin Killoy - Cousin of Vivian Durgin, Grandmother to both Kate and Tom Killoy
Tom Killoy - Brother of Kate Killoy
Gwyn Braxton - Bolton Forensic Pathologist, Cousin of George Braxton, Childhood friend of Kate Killoy
Deshi "Des" Xiang - FBI Agent, Friend of Kate, Harry and Maeve Donovan
Oliver Bailey - FBI Agent, retired
Count Grigori Baturin - Russian expatriate

Mrs. Jansen "Evangeline Durgin" DeBeer - Aunt to Vivian Durgin and Ann Durgin Killoy
Maeve Killoy Donovan - Kate's great-aunt, Ann's sister-in-law, Former MI 5 retired.
Padraig Donovan - Maeve's husband and Ann's brother-in-law, Kate's great-uncle
Mikolas Castellanos - Brother of murder victim
Demetre Papadopoulos - Greek Consul based in NYC
Norman Messier - Metropolitan Museum of Art director in charge of exhibit of Iolanthe's Treasure

and

Kate's Samoyed Dogs - Liam, Dillon, Quinn

-1-

Sunday Early Morning

Dawn was still a long way off when Harry Foyle quietly loaded three Samoyed dogs, their food, their toys, and one, very sleepy and beautiful bride into his car. He wanted an early start on their honeymoon. The extra-long minivan held the three Samoyed dogs in crates, their luggage and everything needed for the next two weeks. He'd gotten this car to replace his sedan as he was determined to travel with Kate when she showed her dogs. It came with more bells and whistles than he could imagine. This morning he was also determined to get on the road before dawn to avoid both heavy traffic and any stunt to embarrass them that Kate's brothers could dream up.

Glancing over at Kate, he was glad that he'd remembered

the pillows and blankets. The last twenty-four hours had been exhausting, both for their horrors and delights. She had barely gotten any sleep the night before the wedding when a killer shot at her through her window. This was followed by the attempt on their lives during the wedding. Last night, following the wedding, neither of them had gotten much sleep, but that had been much more enjoyable.

Before they had reached Route 8, she was sound asleep. He leaned over and tucked the blanket over her shoulder, and noticed that she curled even tighter into her cocoon. Today's drive was about three hours long, but since it was mostly interstate, and it was Sunday morning, it should go smoothly. They would head northwest through Connecticut until they hit the Massachusetts Turnpike at Lee then transition onto the New York Thruway toward Albany and from there, make a straight run up the Northway into the Adirondacks and their destination.

Kate had no idea where they were going. The choice of destination was decided after her grandmother, Ann, told him about Kate's childhood dream. When he saw the place, it was obvious that would be the perfect honeymoon spot and bridal gift.

Months ago, while Kate was off in New York City with her cousin Agnes, arranging for her second annual fashion show which ran in conjunction with the dog show in February, Ann invited him to dinner. They talked about the upcoming wedding and she asked where they were going to honeymoon. Harry confessed he hadn't a clue. He wanted their honeymoon to be perfect but knew that traditional trips to resorts wouldn't work for his bride. Ann smiled and said that she might have an idea. That's when she told him about Kate's castle.

"When Kate and Agnes were young and showing dogs, her father and grandfather would take them on the Adirondack dog show circuit. And every year, that trip would include a side trip to stay overnight at what Ann's family called Camp but what Kate referred to as her castle. She explained that her grandfather, James Durgin, who was a financier, had built a grand home in the Adirondacks on Lake George in 1878. Many of the wealthy families were doing so. They would bring in famous architects to design palatial homes out of native materials.

"Our architect was not famous. He was a cousin who did a really wonderful job. Remember: this was a time before income tax, so the wealthy had a lot of money to spend. There was also a tradition among the better-off classes that this beautiful part of the country should be preserved for future generations."

"How big are we talking about?" he'd asked.

Ann laughed and explained, "There are a dozen bedrooms, nine bathrooms, a game room, a sitting room, a library, a ballroom, an indoor swimming pool, numerous patios, two private cabins, a dock, and a boathouse, plus many other smaller rooms which were used by staff when I was young. What enchanted the girls were the bedrooms located in the towers, one at each end of the front facade. The idea of a circular bedroom with a bed in the middle of the room where a princess could lie in bed and look out windows in all directions enchanted Kate.

"A covered porch extends from the south side of the house, around these towers and then runs back along the north side. When I was growing up, the porch was a playground on rainy summer days when we could race each other, play shuffleboard, or just collapse into one of the Adirondack chairs or on the hanging porch swings and read. It was heaven for both kids and grownups."

"And this house is still in the family?"

"Yes and no. Yes, because it is still there and is owned by my cousin whose father, being the oldest of my grandfather's sons, inherited it. However, since the rest of the family didn't marry into such healthy Irish stock as I did, the number of descendants from all my uncles is just my one cousin. She is now in her eighties and not in the best of health. Vivian's been living at Camp for the last thirty years. She sold her house in Manhattan, which she said had become too noisy with all the traffic and moved up to the mountains. She has a very lovely couple who cares for her and does their best keeping up the large house, but Vivian is reaching the age where she needs round-the-clock care.

" When I last spoke to her, she became almost hysterical when I suggested that she just sell it. She kept repeating 'I promised, I promised.' She refuses to leave because she promised her father that Camp would always remain in the family."

Harry sat and thought. He and Kate were building their home and construction would begin the Monday following the wedding. He'd budgeted for that. However,depending on what kind of money they wanted for Camp, he might be able to afford that as well. Only Sadie knew how much he was worth since he'd been keeping his wealth a secret even from Kate.

He'd been chosen as a ten-year-old child to travel across the country and study with college students at Caltech in a program for math geniuses Though his education was fantastic, he spent most of his childhood feeling lonely. The game of playing the stock market had kept him from feeling abandoned. He had begun investing when he'd taken his first course in the math on how the stock market works. Harry had eventually made friends who were, for the most part, much older than he, but life had worked out and his little hobby led him to earn his first million by age twelve. He'd continued playing, investing only money he could afford to lose. But he rarely lost. This meant that he and Kate wouldn't need to worry, nor would their children. He and Ann spoke some more. Then she called her cousin Vivian and arranged for a visit the following day.

The house was a wonder: from rampant lions on the stone gate posts to the long drive through a forest of evergreens to the stunning vista of a house that seemed to grow from its natural surroundings. The drive swung around and ran to a covered entrance. He could easily see why Kate thought it a castle. The drive then continued to on a carriage house which at one time must have held numerous carriages as well as stalls for horses. The place made a statement—that of old money tastefully spent.

Otto Marks and his wife Helen had been caring for Vivian for at least thirty years since she moved into Camp permanently. Otto was able to connect Harry with someone to inspect the house and go over exactly what repairs it needed. Helen had a nephew who owned a construction business two towns over who could do the work.

Once the inspection was complete, Harry met with Vivian's lawyers to take care of the transfer of title and then with Helen's nephew to begin the updates and repairs. Vivian

Durgin moved into a lovely care facility nearby, content that Camp would remain in the family.

Harry smiled remembering how he got Kate's signature on the deed without spoiling the surprise. He took her to Boston telling her she had to meet with his lawyer to sign all the wills and other papers before the wedding, especially with people shooting at them all the time. This would guarantee the safety of his business and her dogs and business, but most of all their future children. She was so distracted by her cousin's fussing over the wedding and the amount of work she had to get out-of-the-way first, that she just signed what was put before her. He'd buried the deed in the middle of the stack of papers.

The day had been wonderful. Since they were in Boston, they pretended to be tourists, exploring the Freedom Trail, and visiting the Old North Church. So much history still lived in that small area of Boston. Even though he had lived in Boston for years, it was Harry's first time to explore these sights.

He clicked a button and a dashboard screen showed the view of the inside of the car from an overhead camera. Three dogs lay sleeping peacefully in their crates. He decided he was going to love this new vehicle.

Dawn was breaking as they transitioned from Massachusetts and onto the New York Thruway. It wasn't long until they circled around Albany to Latham and then did a straight run up I-87 N better known as the Northway to Bolton on Lake George. He had just traversed onto the Northway when the sun rose fully. Traces of snow peeked out from under the trees on either side of the highway left over from the surprise blizzard last week. Harry turned his mind away from that thought. If Kate hadn't come to rescue him from a hired killer, he would have frozen to death in that blizzard, buried in the snow.

Once onto the Northway, he watched as the trees on each side of the highway changed from the deciduous, which mere weeks ago had people flocking from the city to view their colorful leaves, to the evergreens majestic on either side of the highway. It was a smooth stretch of road with little traffic so he relaxed. When he was about twenty minutes from Bolton, the car phone rang. He'd forgotten it was linked to his cell. Without thinking, he started to fish his cell out of his pocket, only to remember he didn't need to. A screen on the dashboard lit up telling him he had a call coming in from Otto. Harry pushed the button on the steering wheel and tentatively said, "Hello?"

"Harry, it's Otto. Are you on your way?"

"Yes, we're almost in Bolton and Camp is only about fifteen minutes beyond that."

"Good. We have a problem here that I can guarantee is the very last thing you need on your honeymoon, and I am sorry."

"What kind of problem?"

"The dead body kind of problem."

"Was it a man?"

"A man."

"How did he die?"

"They won't know until the autopsy."

"When did it happen?"

"Well, the coroner estimates about sixty years ago since I think that's the last time the basement floor was dug up to work on the drainage pipes. I wouldn't even know that if the inspector you had in for the house hadn't left such a thorough report."

"So I don't have to worry about our getting shot at by bad guys. What do the police say? How did they find it?"

"Yeah. The guy from the coroner's office said it was an early middle age Caucasian man. That was the best he could do without a complete examination. Oh, and they found a bullet under him which he said could have contributed to his cause of death, but he still needed the exam. On the positive side, my nephew managed to fix the drains before the body was found."

"Glad to hear your 'cup-half-full' take on this. Is Helen okay?"

"She's fine. She fed the police coffee and cinnamon buns which put everyone in a more relaxed frame of mind."

"Thank her for me. Tell her to save me a cinnamon bun. I'll be there soon." He pushed another button on the steering wheel ending the call when a voice came from the bundle of blankets next to him.

"I remember that voice. I heard it when we'd visit The Castle. I haven't heard it in several years because Gramps was too sick to do the week-long show circuits. Why were you talking with Otto?"

"Because we're going to have our honeymoon at the same place where your parents had theirs."

"Oh, Harry, that's wonderful."

"Well, it may be wonderful. Otto was calling because there is a slight unplanned event."

"What kind of unplanned event?

"The dead body kind."

"Anyone I know?"

"I doubt it since they think he's been dead since before your father was born."

"Where did they find him?"

"Buried in the basement. They came across him when they were fixing the drains."

"Did they get the drains fixed?"

"Yes. You're pretty cool about the whole thing."

"Well, I'm a country girl. Working drains are important. Plus, I figure who ever shot him is old or dead, so I don't think I'll be dodging bullets. The bar for what upsets me has been radically adjusted in the last few months. I look at it this way. I get to spend my honeymoon with the man I love and three of my dogs in my childhood dream house and I might get home without needing my bulletproof vest—life is good."

-2-

Sunday Midday

Harry heard Kate sigh and watched her gaze up when they drove through the gates to Camp. They passed the stone lions crouched atop pillars on either side of the entrance. The pair were a smaller version of the ones in front of the New York Public Library.

"Did you ever name them?"

"Yes, Arthur and Galahad."

The driveway, once past the gate, wound into a forest which felt at one with the unspoiled natural world of the Adirondacks. Part of Harry's modernization had been to repair and repave of the drive. It would make it much easier to plow once winter set in. Glancing at the dashboard screen for a second, he pushed the camera button and noticed both Liam and Dillon were alert and seemed to know where they were. Quinn, still a puppy, slept on.

As they emerged from the forest, they spotted four police cars and a coroner's van parked in front of the entrance. Those vehicles jarred with the beauty of the building built to blend into its natural surroundings. Harry was sure the architect intended the visitor's first response to be one of peace, contentment, and relaxation. It said, 'you have left the stress of your life behind and have now come to a place where clean air and quiet will feed your soul.' Harry chose not to add to the crowd in front so he pulled around the side of the house to stop in front of the nearest door in the carriage house. He hadn't asked Otto if the building was ready to hold cars but hoped it was.

Kate pushed open the door, crawled out from under her blankets and at the same time pulled on her parka. There was a definite nip in the air. With Thanksgiving over and Christmas close at hand, snow, as they had last week, would become more familiar here in the mountains. Harry pushed a button on his key fob and the rear door rose to reveal the crates holding two standing Samoyeds ready to rock-and-roll. He pushed another button and the side door, behind Kate's seat, slid back allowing her access to Quinn's crate. Snapping leads on the dogs, and grabbing a handful of poop bags, they closed up the car and headed toward the house.

"Katie, oh Miss Kate, you are here. What happened to your beautiful braid? All your golden hair is gone. Oh, and you are not Miss Kate anymore. You're Mrs. Harry. My sweet girl has grown up and married." Helen swept Kate into a hug leaving Quinn free to jump on both of them. Helen stepped back, careful not to fall as Quinn tangled his lead around their knees.

"Quinn, sit." Harry's command, was almost as firm as Kate's usual word that had dogs instantly complying. It had the desired effect. Quinn sat. Harry reached over and unwound the lead and then telling Quinn to heel, walked all three dogs to a new gate. A large yard, about fifty feet square, now extended out from the rear of the house. One side went off from the kitchen and the other side from the bedroom wing on the first floor. "Is the other gate shut and locked?" he asked Helen.

"Yes, Mr. Harry. You can let them run free. They will be safe."

He unhooked the leads, and the dogs took off, racing each other as they explored the freedom of the new yard. Kate, her arm still around Helen, walked to the fence.

"You even found a cable spool."

"Otto knows where to find anything and everything," Helen laughed.

"I always thought he was a miracle worker, from being able to find old wagons which still worked to being able to repair broken croquet mallets."

"He varnished that old croquet set last winter. It will be good as new when you have children."

Leaving the dogs to play, they mounted the porch steps and headed toward the front of the house. A policeman was on duty at the front door and stepped forward to halt their entrance.

"Let them by, Caleb Jones. This is Mr. Harry Foyle, who

now owns Camp. The detectives will want to talk to him and his Mrs. Harry, our own Miss Kate."

At Helen's statement, 'now owns Camp,' Kate's head snapped in his direction. He caught her eye, shook his head and mouthed the word, "Later."

They opened the massive front door. It was solid oak and carved in a bas-relief. It displayed a tree that seemed to grow from the door bottom, with its exposed roots, twisting up from the surrounding ground. Peeking out from behind the tree were a raccoon and a deer. In the branches above, a bobcat crouched. A blue-jay perched on the branch above his head. Kate's hand, on auto-pilot, patted the heads of the animals and waved to the bird.

Harry smiled as he realized that on this trip, he was meeting the young Kate Killoy. Kate had become sophisticated by the time they met. Despite the obvious drawback of a dead body, he had to agree with Ann that this was the perfect place for their honeymoon.

The entrance hall should have been dark. Its polished log walls covered massive amounts of space. But a series of windows, rising to the level of the second-floor balcony, shown light which filled the area with a warm glow. He could hear voices coming from the back of the house so he followed the sound, leaving Kate and Helen to discuss the changes.

He pushed through the door under the staircase and walked into a new modern kitchen which boasted a wall of floor to ceiling windows looking out across the dog yard to Lake George beyond. A breakfast area took advantage of that view allowing anyone a chance to sit there to watch the dogs as the room's occupants were now doing. Everyone followed the antics of three generations of Samoyeds racing the length of the yard, jumping on and off the big spool, and having the time of their lives.

Otto was holding forth to the police on the beauty and history of the breed. He had been well taught by Kate, her father, and grandfather. Harry's mind filled with a picture of Kate sitting in the nook for hours watching the dogs and their children playing together. This would be a perfect place for summer vacations. With all the bedrooms, they could even hold a Killoy family reunion without feeling crowded despite the size of her family.

"Is there any of that coffee left?" he asked as he entered.

"Ah, Mr. Harry. I see we have a new puppy in the crew."

"Yes, Dillon's son, Quinn."

"He's a fine-looking pup. Looks a little more like Liam than Dillon though. He should do well in the show ring."

"I'm in training to handle him, working hard so I won't hold him back."

"He will need your long legs to go with his speed."

A middle-aged man who'd been sitting at the table stood. "You are the new owner, I take it."

"Yes. My wife and I bought the place from Miss Durgin. My wife's grandmother is Vivian Durgin's cousin."

"I take it your wife is Killoy, not Forester?" A young cop, not in uniform said.

"My wife is Kate Killoy."

"I figured as much from seeing Dillon running around the yard. That dog has beaten me out of two Group One ribbons, so I know him well."

"What's your breed?"

"Alaskan Malamutes," Kate said from behind him. "Hi there, George. I see they have promoted you."

"Hi, Kate. I see you lost your braid."

"Agnes decided I needed to look like a grownup."

"You could give her a run for her money now. How is our favorite supermodel?"

"Believe it or not, she's a banker now."

"She still wouldn't be interested in a cop like me."

"I hate to break it to you, George, but she's engaged to a Connecticut state trooper."

"Sergeant," the older cop grumbled, "if we could get back to the case at hand rather than your social life, we have a dead body to deal with here." The man pulled out his ID and offered it to Harry, introducing himself as Detective Gil St. Amand. "Harry Foyle," Harry answered shaking his hand.

"You seem calm for a man who has just found out he's bought a house with a dead body in the basement."

"Well, to tell the truth, considering how my last week has gone, a sixty-year-old corpse doesn't even move the needle on the excitement meter."

A uniformed cop leaning against the stove asked. "Are you any relation to Sgt. Peter Foyle, the Boston cop who just blew open the Mob conspiracy?"

"He was my father."

"Wait, were you and Kate the couple who the killer tried to shoot during their wedding yesterday?" He started getting excited.

"Yes," said Kate. "This is the start of our honeymoon. But I must agree with Harry. An old corpse that won't have people shooting at us day and night is something I can handle. Do we have any idea who he is? Did he have any identification on him? Have you been able to trace him as a missing person? I realize that it hasn't been that long since they found him and that record-keeping sixty years ago was not up to today's standards, but is there any way we can know what he was doing here, and why he was killed?"

"Enough questions, Magyar. There is no we, little lady. This is a case for the authorities, not for amateurs."

Kate looked at the group in front of her. "Not a problem, so you won't need us. I'd like to look around the house with my husband and see what improvements he's installed. It was nice meeting you, Detective. We can catch up later, George."

Taking Harry's arm, she pulled and headed back through the door to the foyer. Letting go, she ran up the stairs to the second floor with him in hot pursuit. When they reached the circular bedroom in the tower, she sat on the end of the bed and looked back and forth from window to window. Harry sat next to her, silent but waiting. Kate stood and paced from one window to the next, and back again. After two more round-trips, she sat and leaned up against him. Harry gathered her into his arms and held her without talking. They remained this way for a while, and then Harry asked, "Do you want to take the dogs for a walk? You could show me how big the property is and all your favorite places are."

"What about the cops?"

"What cops?" He said standing and held out his hand. They

walked down the stairs and out the door, stopping only to grab the dog's leads off the entry table.

The next few hours were everything they could have wanted for their honeymoon. They strolled the property with Kate pointing out her favorite spots including an old oak tree. She told him that the massive bent limb before them was perfect for sitting, feet up and reading, hidden away from everyone. They walked down to the dock. This end of the property was the narrowest part since frontage on the lake was in high demand. The reinforced dock had two Adirondack chairs placed near the end so visitors could sit and watch the birds and water-life.

They sat, though it was too cool to stay long. Looking over the water, she entwined her fingers with Harry's. This seemed to bring her the peace that Detective St. Amand had taken with his condescending attitude toward her questions. As they explored the boathouse, Harry reminded her she'd gotten spoiled.

"Spoiled. How am I spoiled?"

"You've got the top people in the FBI, the NSA and many police departments around the country hanging onto your every word. So when a cop blows off your reasonable questions, it upsets you. However, let us allow for the fact he doesn't know that you are Kate Killoy, super detective, and not just Kate Killoy dog trainer and designer extraordinaire. I think you showed great restraint. I restrained myself as well since I wanted to brag about my wonderful wife, but I realized that it was the wrong time. We want this contretemps to go away and leave us in peace. The best way to achieve that is to avoid doing our thing and just be on our honeymoon.

"I don't know about you, but honeymoon or not, I'm getting hungry and I want to try out my fancy new kitchen. Wait till you see the stove Helen's nephew found me. Your brother, Mr. William Killoy, chef extraordinaire, will be in tears when he sees it. Maybe we should have the family here for New Years Day and let Will play in the kitchen. I know that Sal will be available to cover the kennel since they are going away for Christmas. It's something to think about."

"I hate saying this, but you're right. That's a perfect idea."

By the time they returned to the house, all the cars and signs of the police were gone. They found a note from Helen and Otto saying they would be in their house if Kate and Harry needed anything. Harry had updated one cabin to provide a year-round home for the couple. This left them all to themselves. So, after eating Harry's special spaghetti, with a salad Kate threw together, and freshly baked bread that Helen had left, the newlyweds wandered their new house. They explored the books in the library obviously added to by a variety of generations. They looked into the sitting room, the pool and the game room.

However, when they got to the ballroom, Harry went over to a panel in the wall, and pushed a few buttons. The room filled with the sound of a Strauss waltz. Smiling he held out his hand to his bride and she took it and smiled. They danced and danced, whirling around the entire room and Kate laughed, feeling like a true princess. Fatigue gripped her eventually and they locked up, gathered the dogs and headed into the master bedroom. It was located behind the south tower with sliding doors leading to the dog yard, giving a view of the mountains and a slight glimpse of the Lake George through the trees.

Later that evening, Kate lay cuddled in Harry's arms, her head resting on his shoulder. She smiled up at him. "Thank you for my Princess house. I loved dancing in the ballroom. You're a wonderful dancer."

"You are welcome. So why do I feel there is a 'but' coming in this conversation?"

"Can we afford this? We're building our new home and though my business is making good money now, as is the kennel and training facility, I hate to start our marriage loaded down with debt."

"Remember when you asked me about money at the National when your motor home got shot up and I paid to have it repaired? I put off giving you any detailed information about my net worth. That was because I didn't want you to think of me as some millionaire trying to impress you. But, in answer to your question, I have been earning good money since I was a kid at Caltech so, we're good. Okay?"

"Okay. But the other thing which bothers me is, though it would be fabulous to think only of enjoying two weeks of bliss here and exploring the Adirondacks, we do have 'an eight hundred pound gorilla' so to speak in our basement. I want our honeymoon, but I must face the fact that a man was murdered and buried in this house which has been in my family since it was built. The likelihood of this happening without the knowledge of my family is very slight. If you were to think like a cop, you would assume that one of my grandmother's relatives might be a murderer. There are few people alive who would remember that period of time at Camp. The chances of finding answers to the questions I asked the detective are disappearing fast. Harry, would you be mad at me if I told you I want to find out who was killed, why it happened, and even though I know in my heart it's impossible, I want to find out, if someone I love or loved, had anything to do with it?"

"I was wondering when you would try to find the answers. You know me and my love for searching to find the answers to your questions. We can start in the morning after breakfast. I think our first step will be to visit your grandmother's cousin. Vivian was determined that the house remains in the family. She said she promised. I hope that the police who have talked to her already, haven't traumatized her to where we can't get information."

"Wait." Kate added, "I just remembered that every time anyone visited, they signed the guest book. It has years of signatures. Even Teddy Roosevelt stopped for a visit and signed his name. It might help us nail down who was here around that time."

Harry smiled at her. "Excellent, we've got a plan. Do you feel better now?"

"Yes. But I've learned how I could feel even better." Harry laughed, thrilled to oblige.

-3-

Monday Morning

Kate woke early. The sound of a sliding glass door closing made her open her eyes. She stared at the beautiful man watching her dogs romp around the yard. He had pulled on sweatpants which rode low on his hips, but his upper body was bare, displaying an assortment of scars, some from surgeries and some from bullets which had created the need. He resembled a soldier, huge, with wide shoulders, narrow hips and not an ounce of fat. But he hadn't been in the service.

No, Harry had earned the worst of the scars when working undercover as an FBI agent. He wasn't supposed to be undercover at that time since his job at the agency was more that of a math geek. He'd scan a set of facts, develop probable outcomes based on algorithms he wrote then predict the safest course of action. But this time they asked him to test his theory.

What he hadn't factored in was a traitor in the agency who wanted him dead. The killer would have achieved his goal if it weren't for Chief-of-Police, Sal Mondigliani, and his very well-trained German Shepherd police dog. Sal not only saved Harry's life, but when he retired and come to work as Kate's kennel manager, he also brought the two of them together when a case of mistaken identity had someone trying to kill her. The rest, as they say, is history. The fates smiled on her when Harry Foyle walked into her life, or rather knocked her down.

She slid out from under the covers and pulled on her warm flannel robe. Walking on bare feet, she reached for him and wrapped her arms around his waist, rested her head on his arm, and watched the pups play.

"Before we leave for Vivian's, we should ask Helen where the guest book is. I checked out the foyer table's drawer before we went to bed and it wasn't there."

"I need to touch base with Otto about the spark plugs for the truck. I want to pick some up while we're out and give the truck a tuneup before the snows fly."

"How about we shower, eat breakfast, and then go visit Vivian? Do you want bacon and eggs or pancakes?"

"Pancakes. If we shower together, it should save water and time," Harry said grinning.

"You're sure about that?"

"Possibly?"

They dressed and while Kate made pancakes, Harry fed the dogs. He called Otto to check on the spark plugs and explained their plans. Helen got on the phone and said she'd just baked some banana-bread which they might take to Vivian since it was her favorite. Harry told them he'd drop by before they left.

Kate took the phone and asked if Helen knew where the guest book was. She wanted to show Harry some famous signatures. Helen told her she'd locked it up in the safe in the library while the workmen were around. She told her that Harry should have the combination among the papers he got with the purchase of the house. They finished breakfast and let the dogs back out one more time.

Kate and Harry found the safe in the library and inside was the book containing names dating back to the time the house was built. Kate slipped the album into her tote, so they could study it when they stopped for lunch after visiting Vivian. Rounding up the dogs, they loaded them into the car which had spent the night safe in the carriage house with its recently repaired roof. Harry drove by Helen's for the loaf of banana bread. She added a second one for them to have as a snack later. They then headed out.

Kate was used to massive amounts of traffic during the summer when thousands of tourists would make even running the simplest errand time-consuming. But the roads now held only year-round residents.

They reached the long-term care facility in only twenty minutes following Helen's directions. She also gave them Vivian's visiting hours which saved having to call first.

The facility was impressive looking and larger than Kate expected. The newer iterations of care for senior citizens seemed to include restaurants, lounges, swimming pools, movie theaters and more. Vivian lived in a self-contained apartment with a living room, small kitchen, bedroom and a bathroom that was fitted to make it safe for her to live independently.

Her apartment was on the first floor and easy to find. Harry asked the young man at the desk to call and let her know to expect them. Then he checked about bringing dogs to visit. Kate's well-behaved dogs wouldn't be a problem it seemed. So they went back to the car and put the dogs on the leads. Kate took the two older dogs and Harry took Quinn, giving him a quick brush-up course in heeling, sitting and staying. When they reached Vivian's apartment, the door was open, and she greeted the dogs with enthusiasm.

"Oh, my wonderful Liam and young Dillon. And who is this little one?" she asked.

"This is Quinn, Dillon's son," Kate explained.

"Oh my goodness. Dillon, you're old enough to have a son? Time flies. Well come in, come in. Katie, what did you do with your braid. I like the curls, but all that long hair—gone."

"Agnes talked me into getting my hair cut, insisting I should finally look grownup. The hair went to make wigs for children with cancer."

"What a lovely idea. I'm sure all that lovely golden hair made beautiful wigs. Now sit and we can have a family visit. Mr. Foyle, I hope you are happy with the house and got those repairs done."

"Yes, and just in time since Kate and I got married on Saturday. This is our honeymoon and the house is perfect."

"Your parents thought the same thing when they spent their honeymoons at Camp, Kate."

Kate glanced at Harry and as he nodded she began. "I've been showing Harry all over the house and the grounds and I showed him the oak tree where I'd go to read, and we visited the boathouse."

"I hope someone fixed the weak boards on the dock."

"They are fixed," Harry told her.

"While I was telling him about Camp, I remembered all the famous names whose signatures in the guest book. You've had so many interesting people visit since Camp was built. I was wondering if you'd tell him about those early years when you and grandma Ann were young? Who came to visit? Did they ever have balls in the ballroom?"

"Yes, they had wonderful balls. It was considered quite stylish to visit the Adirondacks when the city was sweltering in the heat. This was before such things as air conditioners. They would take the train which ran along the Hudson up to Lake George. And most would transfer to the huge steamers with their gigantic paddle wheels and travel Lake George to Bolton Landing. You can imagine what a sight it was watching that triple-decker steamboat pulling into the dock and all those hundreds of passengers disembarking, happy to be away from the city. Many would stay in hotels, but my grandfather and my father had made connections through their businesses with famous people so a number of such guests would come and stay overnight every year. Some even came for longer, settling into one of the dozen bedrooms. My father, who was the oldest son, inherited camp when my grandfather died.

"Ann's mother died when she was young, but my mother was still alive until we reached our teens. She taught us a lot about entertaining. When she died, since I was their only child, I took over as Camp's hostess. You might want to take a trip on the steamboat when you are here in the summer." Quinn had settled in next to Vivian with his head on her lap. She stroked him as she spoke. The other two dogs had found spots between Kate and Harry and now dozed.

Kate spoke. "Last night Harry put on some music in the ballroom, and we waltzed for almost an hour. The evening was heavenly. Just the two of us in that beautiful ballroom."

Vivian stiffened and seemed to withdraw slightly into herself. "I waltzed with a young man in the empty ballroom once. I thought the night enchanting, but the evening turned out not to be. After that, my father didn't let anybody use the ballroom except for family dinners. No more balls were held" She stopped talking and just stared into the distance for several minutes. Then all at once, she noticed them again. "But I'm happy that you are enjoying yourselves."

Harry cleared his throat. "Vivian, when we arrived yesterday, the police were at the house."

"Oh, the police came here last night. I'm afraid I wasn't at my best. I'm not clear about what they told me. A man died in the basement or something. Not one of Helen's nephew's workmen, I hope. They are such helpful men. The time was late when they came. I suppose they'll give you an explanation, eventually." Vivian yawned. She seemed suddenly sleepy. "I think I'll go lie down for a while. Please come and visit me again while you are here. Bring Mr. Quinn with you. He is such a sweet puppy. We can talk more about Camp."

They gathered the dogs and headed for the car. Once they got the dogs settled, Harry stared at her and asked, "What happened?"

"I just scared her. She knows much more than she's saying. Something happened. Something related to the ballroom and that dance. I wonder if Ann knows anything? We should call her later and see if she has any ideas."

They started back toward Camp thinking they'd eat lunch and then go through the guest book to see if it gave them any ideas. The car had barely gotten back on the highway when its phone rang with a call from Ann. Harry raised an eyebrow and pushed the button. He was about to say hello when Ann shouted, "What are you doing? You frightened my cousin. Don't you know she's old and delicate? Here you are harassing her. I'm sorry I even suggested you buying Camp. I'm on my way up to visit her later today. Tom is bringing me. I am very upset with you. I'll see you when we get there." She disconnected.

"What the hey? Who was that?" Kate stared at Harry. "That's not the grandmother I've known all my life. What's going on?"

"I guess Vivian wasn't as sleepy as she said. I think we should go back to Camp and make sure two more bedrooms are made up. Tell me, when did Ann turn into Agnes?"

"If I had to guess, I'd say about five minutes after we left Vivian's apartment."

"Interesting. It doesn't sound as though Detective St. Amand was able to get anything out of Vivian either."

"What do you mean, either? We got information. A young man came to Camp. He was very impressive, and handsome enough catch the eye of a young vulnerable girl. He romanced her and then something happened. Something bad enough that her father refused to hold a ball ever again. We need to go through that guest book, fast."

"I can't believe you got all that out of her response to our dancing?" Harry said.

"Our dancing triggered a wonderful and horrible memory

for her. Perhaps Ann will be able to get more. She already knows some of it. They were cousins, each of them only children and almost the same age. They might have shared the experience. We'll have to wait and see."

"Oh, great. I am so looking forward to spending my honeymoon with my in-laws," he growled.

After a quick stop for spark plugs, they went back to Camp, let the dogs into the yard and headed inside. Helen could be heard vacuuming somewhere on the second floor. Kate sent Harry to the kitchen to find something inspiring for lunch, while she headed upstairs to explain to Helen that their honeymoon was about to get even stranger with the addition of family. She stayed to help make up beds in the two tower-rooms. At least her visitors would get to experience the view while there. She explained that Vivian had called Ann in a panic even though she'd seemed calm and sleepy five minutes earlier. Helen said this change in personality had begun about a year ago but had become worse recently. Kate filed that information away to think about later.

Once the rooms were done, Helen headed out since today she had her weekly quilting bee and she didn't want to miss it. Kate thanked her and headed for the kitchen grabbing her tote along the way. Harry had hearty ham sandwiches waiting with a quick Waldorf salad he'd thrown together.

"Your in-laws will be occupying the tower rooms," she told him. "Tom has never been here to my knowledge since the only time we came was for the dog shows. Ann must remember it from her youth, plus she came with you when you bought it."

"It wasn't like this then. It's had some major work done."

"Yes, I remember things being old-time fancy but run

down and tattered around the edges." They ate and then made tea and sliced generous chunks of Helen's banana bread for dessert. When done, Kate pulled out the guest book and set it on the table.

"We are looking for a name or event around 1959 or 1960". They gently flipped the pages back to that period, stopping only to note Kate's young signature when she first came at age eight.

When they got back past 1960, the style of entries changed. Events were listed and people signed their names under the event and made comments on how good a time they had or their most memorable part of the stay. In 1959, there had been a Christmas Ball, and many signed the book as house guests and others as just guests. The list of names was mostly unfamiliar except for two—the names of Ann Durgin and Thomas Killoy.

-4-

Monday Afternoon

Kate had thought of Vivian as a sweet little old lady. However, the word devious now attached itself to her description and refused to let go. The time between them leaving her yawning, requesting a nap and them being reamed out by her grandmother for harassment of said delicate creature was under four minutes. Allowing time for her to call, tell a story and draw Gram in the time-frame, proved this was the work of someone with serious skills.

She and Harry decided that the best way to approach the game was to know all the players. Dividing the list of attendees in half, they got online to play 'meet the ball-guests,' They found that all of them were wealthy which that appeared to be what got you invited to the ball.

The other attendance criteria seemed to be that if you were accompanied by a wife, you stayed as a house guest. If you arrived by yourself or with a date, you came just for the day or the evening.

After an hour spent adding information to her spreadsheet, Kate stood, stretched and put on the kettle for tea. The dogs, who had been content to sleep at their feet sensed action and immediately headed to the door to the yard. Quinn squeaked as he walked. He had been given a stuffed hedgehog with a squeaker inside as a present. He loved it. Kate had only to listen for the squeak to know where he was. She prepared let them out by going to grab her parka from the front hall. The boiling kettle distracted her, and she hung the parka on the back of her chair, and decided to make tea. She let the dogs out after making Quinn leave his hedgehog inside by the door. Watching them all trying to crowd onto the top of the spool at once, It led to each being knocked off only to jump up again. it made her smile. Liam and Dillon were stronger, but Quinn's legs seemed to have built-in springs. He bounded onto the spool with no effort, barely bending his knees—levitating.

Tea consumed, she pulled on her parka and stepped out to make use of the brand new pooper-scooper. Harry came out behind her and pointed to the garbage can, which was already sporting a plastic liner. He knew better than to offer to help her since this mindless activity gave her brain a chance to relax and wander at will. It allowed her to view problems from different directions. He crossed the deck and opened a wooden seat located near the edge. He pulled out a pail and the dogs, who must have been watching him, froze. They knew this game. A second later balls went flying. The game worked better with a dozen Sammies, but the three of them took up the challenge. They raced, eager to grab a ball, return it only to go after another which was flying over their heads and raced to retrieve it. Each ball returned got another one thrown. The game only took five minutes to wear the trio out completely. Harry would point in the direction of an unreturned ball, and they'd take off to see who could retrieve it first because the final round didn't have more balls thrown, but rather treats distributed. Kate put away the pooper-scooper and sat on the bench full of dog toys. She leaned against her husband and enjoyed the quiet.

"I've been thinking. I've decided to approach the shock of finding that my husband is filthy rich by just ignoring the money and enjoying the fact that this heavenly place is ours." Kate looked around. "Can you picture our kids here, playing with the dogs, canoeing, hiking, climbing mountains, skiing in the winter?"

Harry hugged her. "I have. The first minute I caught sight of this place I pictured a crowd of kids, pitching tents to camp out, tobogganing, or learning to ski on the slope at the back of the property beyond the cabins. Camp should be a place where kids can come and play, away from structured sports or video games. Like the dogs, this is a place to run free, feel the wind in your hair, or lie on the branch of a tree, and read a book. This home should be a place to be a child, something I never knew. By the time I was ten-years-old, I was moving into the world of adults. I never really got to know that joy of childhood.

"And you grew up in the world of dog shows and competition. Neither of us got to play silly games, live in a castle for a whole summer, pretend to be a princess for more than a week. I wanted to buy this not only for our kids but for those of your brothers, and cousins. Tom loves to ski. Camp would give him a base near the mountains. Gore Mountain is just an hour from here. Of course, he needs to have his ankle heal."

"Am I silly to dream so?"

"Not when it's been...how long since somebody tried to kill us?"

"Twenty-seven hours and thirty-eight minutes."

"You know you're spooky when you do that."

"I've always been able to know the time. Maybe one of our kids will inherit the talent, and we can be twin clocks."

"I love you, so much."

"I love you more, except for the fact that the dogs and that buzzing tells me that the front gate needs to be opened," she said pulling out her phone and clicked on an app. "Hi, Tom. Are you alone?"

"Yea. Gram decided to stay with Vivian for the night."

She pushed the button opening the gate and looked at Harry. "This was a nice honeymoon, while it lasted."

He leaned in and kissed her. Then they headed for the front door to welcome the family.

To say her brother was impressed was, an understatement. He was still having to use a cane to get around following the booby trap injury set by a mob assassin a week ago. Kate couldn't believe that he had brought her grandmother up here when he was supposed to be taking it easy and resting his ankle. They gave him a quick tour, showed him his room, and had

Otto put Tom's car in the second bay of the carriage house and bring in the bags. After a short rest, the smell of food cooking drew him to the kitchen. The floor to ceiling windows had his jaw-dropping. "That's Lake George?"

"Yes. The path that runs by the dog yard leads down to the dock and boathouse."

"This place is amazing. How do I work an in with the owners? This would be a perfect place to stay when I want to ski."

"Well, you could explain how my sweet grandmother suddenly morphed into Agnes at her worst."

"I was in the kitchen when the call came in, but though I couldn't make out the words, I could hear screaming. Whatever this Vivian person was saying, you two went from being favorite grandchildren to Bonnie and Clyde, determined to destroy this poor woman's life. I tried to make Gram talk about the call on the drive up, but she refused to say a thing."

"Did you bring your laptop?" Harry asked.

"Of course. I still have a business to run."

"Well, following supper we will explain how our honeymoon varies from our courtship only by the number of people trying to shoot us."

"You're kidding. What's the body count?" he laughed.

"One, so far."

Tom stared at them then sat at the table and said, "You better begin at the beginning."

After supper, they settled in the library in wing-back leather chairs in front of a crackling fire. Kate had her tea and the men were drinking a vintage port that Harry had found in the wine cellar. Kate continued the story. "When I told her how magical the experience was to waltz around the ballroom, it seemed to set her off."

"Wait for a second, there's a ballroom."

"Yes, but that's not the point. It was then that she seemed to turn in on herself. She whispered that she had waltzed with a man in the empty ballroom and it was wonderful until it wasn't. That's also when she told us she was tired, complete with a yawn, and needed a nap. We left but less than five minutes later a grandmother I have never met, is screaming at us over the phone."

"Let me understand this. Ann arranged for you to spend your honeymoon here and her cousin who owns the place went into a nursing home?"

"Not quite. Vivian needed money to go live in that extremely fancy senior care facility. She sold Camp to Harry since we were getting married. Harry got a crew to come in and modernize the place while keeping its beauty. He tricked me into putting my name on the deed when I was in Agnes distraction mode. Then he made this place which I've loved for years into our vacation home. I figure with the size of the family, there would be someone here all year. We were thinking of having the family here for New Year's Eve. The house has twelve guest rooms, and we thought we'd turn Will lose in the kitchen."

"He'll fall in love with that kitchen and never return to Connecticut. So my next question is how you could afford to buy this and build your home. Is your business doing that well?"

"Foyle Security is doing well, very, but I had money saved from investments. I've been investing, successfully, since I was eleven-years-old. I began when I was taking a course in the stock market and I had a Christmas check from my dad. So rather than pretending to buy the stocks I chose, I bought them. I made a lot of money, so I saved some and invested the rest. Investing turned into a relaxing hobby."

Kate added, "This part of Bolton is called the 'Millionaire's Mile.' Harry is just fitting into the neighborhood."

"When did you find out he was loaded?"

"Yesterday. When we arrived, and he was introduced to the police detective in charge of the murder as the owner."

"Murder?"

"Ann didn't mention the murder?"

"No. Not a word."

She looked at Harry. "Do you think Vivian is trying to hide the murder? Maybe she didn't tell Ann even though she and Gramps were there when it happened. We've got to figure this out."

"They were there when it happened? You mean when a murder happened?"

"As near as we can figure based on what Vivian said. I think she panicked when she realized what she told us. That was probably why she called Ann."

"Okay," Tom said, "Walk me through this again."

Kate stood and said she'd let Harry fill him in. She was going to let the dogs out and go to bed. She was tired.

Kate headed for the kitchen. The discussion would be easier for Tom and Harry to talk without her interference. Anyway, she still needed to catch up on sleep. As she crossed the kitchen, she noticed the security lights were on in the yard. The dogs sat quietly at the back window watching something. Kate reached for the door, but then stopped. She always hated movies where the girl senses danger in a story and then walks right into the threat. Instead she pulled out her phone and buzzed Harry.

"Kate?"

"The security lights are on even though the dogs are still inside."

"We're coming."

She heard Harry run through the house and then appear at the kitchen door carrying his gun. "Tom is working his way around from the front. Keep the dogs here. I'm going around on the bedroom side. Keep the kitchen lights off." Then he was gone.

Dillon moved to her side, though he didn't take his eyes off the window. Kate saw both men come into the yard and move to the far end where there was a dark shape. She watched as the men together managed to lift whatever was out there and put it over the fence. Next, they moved down the path toward the lake. She held Dillon tightly trying not to panic. Quinn whined eagerly to be outside and be with Harry and Tom. Whatever they were doing seemed to take forever until she spotted them returning up the path. Harry broke off and headed toward the carriage house. A few minutes later, he returned with what looked like a tarp, and he and Tom wrapped that around the shape. Harry then walked around, checking the yard to be sure it was clear as Tom, moving slowly came toward the house. Harry waved to her to let the dogs out. She clipped leads on the dogs and walked them out to where the men were standing. "What was out there? What did you wrap in a tarp."

"A venison carcass. I need to have it checked out, but I'm sorry Kate, I think the meat has been poisoned. I need to call Detective St. Amand. Since nobody here knows us, and since we haven't done anything, we shouldn't have any enemies. This must be something to do with the body in the basement. Someone wants us out of here and is willing to kill the dogs to do it."

-5-

Monday Evening

Detective St.Amand strode into the kitchen wearing an annoyed expression. He was followed by Kate's friend George, his sergeant. "What's this I hear about poison?"

Harry stepped forward, extending his hand. "It was good of you to come so quickly. This evening, while we were in the library following supper, someone got access to the dog yard and planted the carcass of a deer at the far end of the yard. There is white powder covering most of the meat. Luckily, when my wife went to let the dogs out, she spotted that the security lights were on even though the dogs were still inside. When Tom and I checked the path to the dock after we removed the dead deer from the yard, we found traces of blood on some rocks and on the dock itself. Whoever did this must have discovered that the front gate has security. When I set that up, I didn't realize that we were in danger from the water. That was my mistake. I don't know who did this, but it takes a lot of hate to try to kill three dogs. Since nobody knows us here, all I could think was that it was related to the finding of the body."

George stepped forward. "Are the dogs okay? Is Dillon safe?"

Kate stepped forward, Dillon at her side. "Yes, George, they are all fine. However, tell me, do things like this happen often. Why would someone want to kill these Sammies. They aren't a threat to anyone."

"No, Kate. Believe me. I've never heard of this happening before and if I get my hands on whoever did this it will never happen again. It could have been Meika, if I'd brought him over to play as I was thinking of doing. He and Dillon always got along at the shows."

"It's probably a local who could figure out which dock was attached to this property. When I stood on the dock and looked in this direction, the house couldn't be seen, only a narrow path through some woods." Tom added.

St. Amand turned and looked at Tom. "And you'd be?"

"Thomas Killoy, Kate's brother."

"Isn't it unusual to visit a couple on their honeymoon who are your in-laws?"

"Yes, but my grandmother wanted to visit her cousin Vivian

Durgin and needed someone to drive her."

George shook his hand. "I knew your grandfather for many years. There wasn't much about dogs he didn't know, or Kate's father either. Were you the one who took over K&K when they died?"

"As a matter of fact yes. My brother William will be joining me in the firm beginning in June."

"So you just upped and left your firm to play chauffeur to your grandmother?"

"You've never met my grandmother. Refusal was not an option."

St. Amand held up his hand. "This is all very interesting. Since your grandmother is visiting Miss Durgin, we might try to speak to the lady again. She was pretty out of it when we tried yesterday."

Harry smiled. "That's a great idea. They were very close when they were younger, I'm told."

Kate looked at him frowning.

"Detective St. Amand, is it possible to get that meat checked to see if it is poisoned. I will worry about letting my dogs run unsupervised until the person responsible is caught. I'm wondering, since this attack on us didn't work, what they will try next. I've found that criminals tend to get annoyed when their plans are thwarted and tend to attack again more fiercely. I'd rather not be shot when I walk out my back door. I left my bullet-proof vest at home since I didn't expect to need it on my honeymoon."

The detective and George stared at Kate, their mouths open. Her sweet conversational tone totally belied what she was saying.

George cracked up laughing. "A bullet-proof vest, Kate? Really?"

"Actually, George, I'm on my second one. The first still has the imprint of a bullet and is very uncomfortable to wear now."

He spun around to look at Harry and Tom, but neither was smiling.

"So all that stuff that Joe Maygar was spouting yesterday of someone trying to kill you during your wedding was true?"

Tom nodded as Harry said, "I'm afraid so. We can thank Dillon and Quinn for saving our lives. Dillon ripped the gun from the shooter's hand as Quinn knocked him to the floor and stood over him until the FBI agents took over."

"FBI agents?"

"They were wedding guests. I used to work for the FBI prior to starting my own business," Harry told them. "So as I told you, a sixty year old corpse didn't worry us. However, if the fact that this corpse has been found poses a threat to us now, that changes everything."

Tom had been making coffee, and had heated water for Kate's tea. He poured cups for the men and invited them to sit. St. Amand had pulled out his phone and dialed someone. "Jack, Gil. Tell me does the name Harry Foyle mean anything to you? It does. Her too. Yeah. Thanks, talk to you later."

A knock came to the back window. Everyone looked up and Harry stood to let Otto and Helen in.

"Kate, Harry, what is going on. We just got back from dinner with our daughter. There are police cars out in front again. What has happened? And who is this. He looks like a

Killoy."

"This is my brother Tom. He's visiting."

"Visiting during your honeymoon?"

"Any resemblance between this and a normal honeymoon disappeared with the appearance of the dead body," Harry said. "The reason we called, Detective St. Amand, is that someone slipped onto the property this evening using the lake and dock and placed a deer carcass, poisoned, in the dog yard. Luckily, Kate spotted the security lights were on and didn't let the dogs out. However, it is becoming clear that someone is really upset by us buying Camp and the discovery of the body in the basement. Whoever it is, they are frightened and our presence poses a threat to them. Not to criticize the police, which I respect, but both Tom and I own companies that do this kind of investigating all the time. They've threatened our dogs. I don't intend to let anything happen to them or more importantly to my wife."

Kate stood and grabbed the coffee pot to refill the coffee cups. Helen reached into the freezer and pulled out a coffee cake and popped it into the microwave.

Harry looked at Kate. Kate nodded and began to explain. She began by telling them about their visit to Vivian. When she got to the story about dancing with Harry in the ballroom, she said it seemed to set off Vivian's memory of an event. Kate told them how Vivian talked about doing the same thing which ended badly and mentioned that they hadn't used the ballroom since.

"Harry and I have been looking into the history of Camp and what has come up is that the last event at Camp was a

Christmas ball in 1959."

Detective St. Amand looked around the table and then back at Kate. "Sixty years ago? Our friend lying on a slab down at the coroner's lab, supposedly died sixty years ago. So, you're telling me that our John Doe was probably on a guest list for this party."

"Yes. There were two groups of guests invited that weekend. Those who came with their wives, who stayed in the guest rooms at Camp, and a second group who came on that evening. They all had wealth which earned them invitations. Some of the single men came with dates but a few came alone."

"I have a feeling, Mrs. Foyle, that there is one more shoe you have to drop. I am beginning to follow your reasoning and I wonder if what I am thinking could be what you are going to tell me." St. Amand looked at her and waited.

Kate glanced at Harry who nodded and then turned back to St. Amand and smiled. "As you have already surmised, Vivian was the young unmarried daughter of the house and from some of the descriptions in the guest list, it looked as though it looks as though her father invited a few possible husband candidates to vie for his daughter's hand.

Now Harry, Tom and I are researching the guests at that ball and as we uncover information, we will share it with you. However, I will tell you right now that there is no way we are going to sit on our hands and be targets for whoever tried to murder my dogs. There is someone out there who didn't want that body found and now that it has been, doesn't want any more information about the man to come out. They are willing to kill to achieve that end."

The kitchen fell silent. None of them wanted to be the one to speak first. But the choice was taken from them when both Kate and Harry's phone pinged announcing they had company at the front gate. They both stared at their phone screens then at each other. Finally Harry pushed the button. "Hello Ann. I thought you were staying with Vivian tonight."

"Harry, don't make me wait. This man doesn't believe that I belong here. You just open this gate and let us in, now."

Harry leaned over and kissed Kate on the top of her head, wrapping his arms around her as his thumb moved to the phone and then pushed the button. No one spoke. Helen stood and patted both Harry and Kate on their shoulders and headed for the front door. After a moment, voices were heard moving toward the kitchen. Harry took hold of Kate's hand and held it tight as Ann burst into the room.

"That woman is insane. She's crazy I tell you. There was no way I was going to spend the night listening to a lunatic screaming at the top of her lungs about waltzes and bodies and so many men. Around and round she went making no sense whatsoever."

"Hello, Gram. Would you like a cup of tea or cocoa and a small piece of Helen's home made coffee cake before you go to your room? You are in the south tower room. I'm sure you'll be comfortable there. Tom is in the north tower and I think as soon as people finish eating, we should all think about calling it a night. Tomorrow, I suspect, will be a busy day. Helen, can you show George and Mr. St. Amand out, I should really see to the dogs."

"Of course, Kate."

The men stood, shook Harry's hand and followed Helen. Otto began talking to Gram about the beautiful windows that had been installed in the kitchen while Kate and Harry picked up leads and headed out the back door. As the security lights flooded the back with light, they saw George and the detective loading the dead deer into the trunk of their cruiser. They walked around checking the yard before Kate let the dogs run loose.

Harry wrapped his arms around her and she leaned back against his chest. They didn't speak for a while but just watched the dogs chase each other and work the kinks out of their legs. Finally Kate asked, "Do you regret marrying me? Thanks to my family, both present and in former times, we have probably had the worst honeymoon on record. There are times when I think that crime follows us."

"I don't think it follows us, I think that we are more aware than most and notice irregularities. Often they lead to uncovering crimes which might have defeated either of us separately, but since we have been a team, we have defeated them all. We will again, Kate, I promise. You are my wife, the person I love more than anyone on earth and there is no way I am going to let this threat hurt you or destroy our honeymoon. The sooner this is solved, the sooner I can make love to my wife in every single room of this house with absolutely no interruptions."

"You mean the honeymoon we're taking which includes criminals, cops, my crazy great cousin, my grandmother and my big brother?"

"Yea, that one."

Kate was quiet for a moment and then, flashing him a small smile, asked, "Every single room?"

-6-

Tuesday Morning

Kate slowly became aware of where she was, the hint of dawn outside the window, and the wonderful warm body beside her. Her gaze rose to meet a pair of beautiful green eyes staring back at her. She smiled. Yesterday may have been awful, but last night had been delightful. Harry looked down at her and reached for a blond curl which lay just above her eyebrow, playing with it for a minute, he then lifted it to join the golden curls above. "It's early, but I wonder if you'd like to dress and take a walk with me. It might be the only time we get alone today."

"Sounds wonderful. I'll dress and be ready in just a few minutes."

The dogs thought this was a great idea. They followed the path the men had taken toward the dock. Kate was careful to keep the dogs away from the tempting smells emitted by the reddish brown smears which covered the rocks and some of the deck boards. She didn't want to take a chance of them encountering poison, though she suspected, that it had been added once the body of the deer was placed in the yard. They sat on the chairs at the end of the dock and stared out at the sunrise over the lake. A crane rose slowly skimming the water which gave them a reflected image of the flight. Kate was just beginning to notice the chill and think about getting back to the house, and about how a hot cup of tea would be an excellent idea, when their phones beeped. Harry quickly pulled his from his pocket, pushed a button and said, "Mr. Jenkins. Thank you for being so prompt. If you drive between the house and carriage house and follow the gravel toward the lake, you can get your truck close to the path. We'll see you there."

"Mr. Jenkins?"

"He's a security camera installer. I got a recommendation from your people in Connecticut. And I called him right after we found the deer. He's the one who put the security on the front gate."

"So he's putting in security system with cameras similar to what I have at home?"

"The same program so you won't need to learn anything new."

"He's installing it in here?"

"I figured we didn't want to put a locked fence between the house and the dock, so this seemed the next best thing. At least when we have visitors, we'll know they're coming and have a way to see who they are."

"Is the proximity to the mountains a problem for the signal?"

"It would have been, but this will be a closed circuit system, using the server I installed in the house. If I am going to spend extensive time here, I needed a server for my business. It will also make it harder to tamper with since there will be limited access to the internet."

"Thank you. I'll feel much safer knowing who is sneaking onto the property."

They heard the truck stop and, stood, taking the dogs, headed up to meet Mr. Jenkins. It didn't take long to decide where the cameras should be located, and how the system would be added to the wiring for the boathouse. Jenkins said it would take less than an hour for the job and he'd bill them. He and his assistant, began pulling cameras from the truck as Harry and Kate headed back to the house. Mist covered the path but would probably burn off soon with so few clouds in the sky.

Once back inside, Dillon and Quinn settled onto a spot on the floor bathed in early sunshine, Quinn's head resting on his hedgehog. They were soon asleep. Liam disappeared as soon as he was off lead. Harry began pulling together breakfast so Kate went to look for her dog. She heard a noise from the south hall which lead by the sitting room to the game room, the pool, and finally to their bedroom.. Harry told her that the pool would require work since it had been neglected for years, so it was locked for safety reasons. That left the game room.

She couldn't think why Liam would go there until she heard the click of two billiard balls hitting. Pushing open the door, she saw her brother land a shot and then stand up in satisfaction.

"Having fun?" she asked.

"I've been exploring. I found your ballroom and was suitably impressed. What a great place to have family dinners with everybody. Dinner and dancing in one place. But this room takes the cake. This table must have cost a fortune even back when the house was built. It's teak with mahogany inlays. Thank goodness someone has looked after both the wood and the table's felt over the years so it is good as new. Have you seen the game table? You shift the table parts around to get whatever board you need from chess to Parcheesi. And there's another table just for poker with places to hold your chips. I even found a table which has fold back triangular glass panels. It took me an minute to figure what it was for until I saw a jigsaw box tucked underneath. The glass folds over to keep the pieces in place if you have to stop before you finish. All the kids and adults are going to love this room."

"Wait till Tim sees it. He loves board games. I'm here to tell you that Harry is making breakfast and we'd better get going or your eggs will be cold. You haven't seen Liam have you?"

"No, but he may be up with Gram. When Sal comes to visit, he often brings Liam. The old guy is found of Gram, or should I say old guys." He chuckled and Kate had to admit that her kennel manager and her grandmother were spending a lot of time together.

When they reached the kitchen they found both Gram and Liam. She noticed her grandmother was still attractive especially wearing a light green turtleneck under an Aran sweater with dark green wool slacks. She and Harry were chatting peacefully so Kate hoped the upset Vivian had caused was a thing of the past. As she and Tom sat, Mr. Jenkin's truck drove by and Harry pushed the button to open the front gate.

"Who was that?" Gram asked.

"My electrician finishing up some of the work on the boathouse. I wanted to be sure that anyone walking down to the dock after dark would be able to see where they were going. While he did that I had him add a few more lights around the boathouse."

"Excellent idea. I remember strolling with your grandfather down to the dock years ago. You really had to watch where you put your feet. I must say, Harry, you've done a remarkable job fixing up the place. I was shocked at how rundown it had become when we came here last month. Vivian had really let it go. You and Kate will have a lovely second home now."

"Thank you, Ann. Kate and I were thinking about having a New Years party for the family here this year to show the place off, provided the snow cooperates."

"That's an excellent idea. I'm sure Maeve and Padraig would love to come and Sybil and Agnes. If Sean's not working he should come too."

"I shall talk to Will about the menu when I see him next week. He'll be home early for Christmas this year since he's not taking any extra classes. I'll bet that Agnes and Sean will want to spend their honeymoon here. It will be perfect with the wedding next summer," Ann said.

Kate looked at her watch and nodded to Harry.

"Ann," Harry said, "There is something which has happened, and Kate and I need your help to solve the problem. When we got here on Sunday, we were met by the police."

"The police?"

"Let me tell you the whole thing first. The police were here because when one of the workmen was replacing a drain pipe in the cellar, he discovered a dead body in the cement floor. According to the coroner, the man has been dead for about sixty years. The other thing the coroner found was that he had been shot. Murdered. The two men who were here last night are policemen working on the case. They tried to talk to Vivian, but she pretended that she was gaga and didn't remember anything. You and I both know that she is sharp as a tack. When Kate and I visited her yesterday, she let something slip in the conversation. When she realized she'd done it, she pretended to be tired. We left but had barely cleared the end of the driveway at the senior care facility when you called all upset."

"Stop there. I need to apologize about that. Vivian has been a great manipulator all her life. I got suckered into believing her, though I should have known better. I am so sorry for what I said to you."

"We sort of figured that Vivian wasn't as sleepy as she said."

Kate took her hand and said, "Do you remember the Christmas ball that was held here in 1959? Both your name and Gramps' are on the guest list."

"Yes I remember the ball. It was a fairy tale setting. The house was decorated throughout. The massive tree stood in the entry hall. There were great shire horses brought in to pull the sleighs which moved around the property and then went for a mile along the road only to turn and come back to the house again. It felt enchanted, especially with Tom at my side. The dinners that weekend were like feasts out of Charles Dickens' Christmas Carol. Musicians played at lunch and dinner and several led us caroling. We seemed to be living in an enchanted Christmas world.

"But there was something going on. Several young men came without escorts and though dressed for the weekend they spent a lot of time with my uncle. They were all from wealthy families, I was told. Someone suggested that Uncle Nelson was trying to marry Vivian off to one of them.

"However, Vivian had other ideas. One of the young men, who had come with a friend that my uncle had invited, met Vivian and they clicked. From the moment they set eyes on each other, they were inseparable. I was happy for her. The young man's friend who had a Greek name, spent most of his time with Uncle Nelson, another young man had an accent, maybe Russian and they were with a woman I was told was my aunt Evangeline. I hadn't met her previously as my father made it clear to me he wanted me to have nothing to do with her. According to him, she was evil.

"The night before Christmas Eve, Nelson, Evangeline and the two men went somewhere. It left Vivian forced to play hostess on no notice and she was scrambling. Since Vivian and I were sharing a room on the front of the house. I noticed it was well into the wee hours of the morning when I heard the group return.

"The next day, something happened that upset me but the

bottom line was that your grandfather and I left the party early and didn't stay for the ball. I assume that she broke up with her young man since she never married."

"Gram, do you know the man's name?"

"I think is was Dervin or Devin or something like that. I never really knew his last name. I insisted on leaving and we got a ride to the train by the chauffeur of one of the couples and arrived back in the city in the wee hours of the morning."

"So what happened at the ball?"

"I don't know. I wrote to Vivian, making up a lie that Tom had gotten a telegram from his sister saying she needed him and we had to go. She never answered that letter or the others I sent over the years telling her about my children and about Tom bringing your father into the business and about each of my grandchildren as they came along. When Kate began showing dogs with Tom and John, Tom went out of his way to make peace with Vivian. They stayed at this house when they were on the Adirondack circuit. But Vivian never contacted or made any mention of me. I knew she was getting my letters because I called the post office here. In fact, I personally hadn't heard from her until a few weeks before I had you come to dinner, Harry, and we arranged for you to buy the house."

Harry and Kate's phones buzzed. Harry looked at the screen and then pushed the button opening the gate. "The police have arrived. They would like to talk to you about that weekend as a witness. They would also like it if you could accompany them when they try to talk to Vivian. I know it's asking a lot, but it's important."

Ann sat, not answering, and waited with them as Kate went

to the door.

Detective St. Amand came in followed by Kate and George. Harry shook his hand and the detective said, "I talked to my friend in the Bureau's New York office. You two have quite a reputation with them. Your dog, Dillon too. Why don't you call me Gil and I can call you Harry and Kate. It will make it easier. Kate already is an old friend with George."

"It's a pleasure, Gil. Kate and I have been talking with her grandmother and catching her up on what happened. I explained about the time line for the the death. She may have some information to share with you." Harry turned to Ann leaving it up to her whether to help the police or not. Silence continued for almost a minute when suddenly Kate spoke up.

"Harry, we were right about the dead deer. George said the powder which was sprinkled over the carcasses was arsenic. Rat poison. It would have killed all three dogs. Whoever it is who doesn't want us looking into this crime, barely missed killing the dogs. I hope we aren't his next targets."

Ann gasped and looked down at Liam's head resting in her lap. Her gaze then moved from Harry, to Kate and to where the other two dogs lay sleeping.

"Detective," she said turning to the man standing in the middle of the kitchen. "My name is Ann Killoy and I think you and I need to talk."

-8-

Tuesday Afternoon

Harry had suggested Kate talk to Ann and learn more about the family members at the time of the murder and maybe come up with any ideas of who the victim might be. Ann had lit the fireplace of the lovely room. Kate paused to look out the windows which overlooked the front of the property.

"I remember my grandmother, whose name was Virginia, using a hassock made like this but upholstered to match these chairs for sewing projects," Ann said. "Perhaps it was damaged. I suspect this one came from the library. This was her favorite room and I think it is mine too. The colors are restful and the windows over-look the whole front of the house. She could relax here and at the same time, keep track of everyone's comings and goings, and even those sitting on the porch. I would sit here with her in the afternoon and knit. Vivian used to tease me. She said, I was practicing for my dotage but I found it restful. My grandmother occasionally would pull out her family album. Wait. I wonder if it's still there?" Ann sprang up and went to a built-in bookcase with shelves on the top and a cupboard below. She reached up to the top shelf and after running her hand over the books, pulled out one larger than the others and bound differently. She carried the album back to the chairs.Then she pulled the table forward, and opened the photo album, so they could both check it out.

"Here is a photo of Virginia, who would be your great-great-grandmother, as a baby in a beautiful wicker baby carriage and wearing a lace bonnet and dress. Considering how much mess a baby makes, one of the washerwomen employed within the household, must have been hired to work just to keep the baby clothes clean. Her parents are standing behind her. Her mother is almost like a Gibson Girl with the long dress, leg-a-mutton sleeves and her hair piled atop her head. She was very pretty."

"That is quite a mustache her father sported. Harry would love seeing his outfit. My husband is a fan of mens clothing from earlier generations."

"Speaking of clothing from earlier generations, if you are planning to have the family here for New Years, we might plan our version of a ball. As I recall, there are ball gowns stored in the attic that would look beautiful on you and your cousins."

Kate grinned. "I know what we're doing tomorrow."

Ann turned a few more pages and stopped. "Here is your great grandfather, Timothy Durgin, my father, when he graduated from MIT. And here is a photo of him when he returned from the war, still in uniform. The nurse, Sarah Ann Connors, beside him is my mother. I think this is the only photo of her in the album because when they married, my grandfather refused to have anything to do with our family."

"But he invited you to join the family here."

"Yes, since Vivian was an only child, they invited me to keep her company. Evangeline is only three years older than Vivian and believe me, if Vivian had her way, I would've been cooling my heels in Manhattan. Evangeline was banned and I came in to fill the 'family' ranks. Luckily, I got along with my grandmother and though she wasn't a strong woman when it came to standing up to her husband, she insisted I come for two weeks every summer. If it's still here, I'll show you." Ann flipped through the pages and then stopped. "Yes, here is a photo I gave Grandma. It was taken when Tom and I got engaged. It shows my father, Tom and me, Tom's sister Sybil and Mr. Forester with Agnes who was only a toddler and was staying with her grandparents that weekend, and on the left of the group, Maeve with Padraig. Maeve looked just like you do now. After I gave her the picture, she was so happy she cried and hugged me." Ann stared at the photo. Her finger moving from face to face. Kate was sure the memory of that day was still fresh in her mind.

Kate decided then and there to scan the photo and share it with the family.

"Wait, I just thought of something, Kate. Grab me that

blue album on the top shelf." Kate handed her the blue album and put the precious first album back on the shelf until she had time to make copies of the photos.

"Ah," Ann grinned. "I'm a genius. This album holds the photos the photographer put out on the table at the side of the ballroom that weekend. He had been taking pictures of those attending during the long weekend. He printed the photos and put them in the album for people to comment on their experiences from the weekend."

She glanced at Kate and said, "I don't know about you, but I need a cup of tea. Let's take this into the kitchen and show the boys photos of the men they are researching."

When they arrived in the kitchen leading a parade of dogs, and as the squeaks told them, a noisy hedgehog, they saw the two policemen had arrived. Harry poured coffee for everyone. Kate walked to the counter and turned on the kettle and then pulled out her teapot.

Ann settled at the table and explained to them what she had found. They now had black and white eight by ten photos of all the attendees at the Christmas Ball on the year in question. Ann began flipping the pages and identifying the people in the photos who she knew. Even those she didn't recognize could be identified by discrete gold-lettered names at the bottom of each picture. It didn't take them long to find the three men who had gone missing. However, they were all of a size and nothing stood out about them to give clues as to which was their corpse.

"Mrs. Killoy, tell us again about that weekend. I see there were sleigh rides. What else happened?"

Using the photos to illustrate the different activities, she began to relate all that she could remember. The pictures seemed to help.

"Here is Vivian coming down the stair and here Tom and I are arriving. The photographer was positioned to use the carvings on the door as a backdrop to the photos. My uncle had arranged for the photographer to send copies to the attendees. He hoped they would insert the shots into the society pages of the newspapers in their area to add fame for him and his home on millionaire's row. Uncle never turned away from praise of any kind. Here is Evangeline arriving. The label reads Mr. and Mrs. Jansen DeBeer. Though I don't remember the name of the actor who enticed her to run away, I know that wasn't the name. This man is more a banker than a thespian."

"Close, Gram." Tom put in. "He is the president and CEO of an investment firm with offices in New York, Chicago, and San Francisco."

Kate who was looking over her grandmother's shoulder as she drank her tea said, "It couldn't have been an accident, it must have been planned."

"What was planned?" The men asked almost in unison.

Kate pointed, "The fact that Vivian and her aunt, who I would mention were only three years apart in age and who looked remarkably alike, would purchase identical Christian Dior ball gowns. These dresses cost a fortune and even then were usually one of a kind. Gowns such as these are not off the rack. Notice also, in this photo the way Vivian's hair is swept back with a single white rose decorated bisque comb holding it. Now, look at Evangeline. I didn't see at the time because my focus was entirely on Tom and making sure that he was treated with respect. However, either this is the height of insult, or she was up to something."

Gil flipped the pages back and forth. "Beats me."

"Yes." Harry pulled his tablet out from under a pile of papers. "At least if she's still Mrs. DeBeer. Mrs. E. DeBeer was one of the names listed in attendance at the opening of an exhibit at the Metropolitan Museum of Art. It seems she is a patron."

Gil pulled out his notebook. "Do you have an address?"

"No, but I could find it."

"Check with Sibowitz," Kate said. "If she likes fashion and publicity, he must have sent her photos at some time."

"Good idea." Harry said then turned to Gil and George, "Andy Sibowitz is the top fashion photographer in New York, maybe even the world. He just finished photographing our wedding as a favor for Kate and Agnes, both of whom are his good friends. Now that he's not proposing to my wife every time they meet, he and I get along too." Harry quickly sent off a text requesting the information, saying details to follow.

They continued leafing through the album studying each photo. Tom would read the up to date bio of each man pictured. When they found the first of the missing men, Divon Hader, Ann said, "Oh, my. I remember him because Vivian was instantly enamored. I thought he was shy. His friend was the type who was sure that women would come his way with just the crook of his finger. Vivian preferred the shy one."

"I've never found that crooking my finger got many women chasing me." George studied his hand. "Dead batteries, I imagine."

Everyone laughed and continued studying the photos.

"Hader's family has a townhouse in Manhattan, an estate in the Hampton's and a condo in Palm Beach. We are talking about old money, which came from railroads, steel, etc. I'm surprised there wasn't a fuss when he went missing. It should have been a bigger deal," Harry said. "He just seemed to stop being."

Missing man number two, Stavros Castellanos, was found pages later after Ann pointed out more family members in some candids. Tom said, "He is definitely Greek with that profile. His likeness could be carved into the side of a temple. I don't see charm here, but rather power. Mr. Castellanos knows who he is and, from his expression, doesn't care what others think of him. He's not as young as Hader, I'd say mid-thirties. If we look at the information on him that was available, his money was family money made through shipping. He had risen to be second in command on the board of directors of Castellanos Shipping. I am researching the company history, such as years. Grigori's mother liked to buy Paris originals, so her trips to France did not create suspicion, and he and his sister tended to keep much of their money in British banks. Following the war, murmurs of the Communist Soviet Union taking power grew, so they left and their fortune was waiting for them. They became active in an association of Russian nobility in New York. His family was involved in the practice of holding dinner dances, concerts, and other fund-raising projects to help the Russian Orthodox Church get established here and to build seminaries. The association is still active, donating money to various charities and still raising funds with formal dances. So attending a ball here would be right up Grigori's alley."

Kate glanced around the table. "The problem, as I see it, is that we only found one body."

Gil scowled at her and objected. "You want three corpses?"

"No, I want the logic to work. Three men are missing but one body was found. All of these men would be considered public figures and yet, following that night, they ceased to exist. There was no fuss that I can find. Ann, was there anything in the news at the time that these men went missing?"

"Nothing."

"People, especially rich people with very visible lifestyles, don't disappear. Why didn't the families come looking for them? Stavros Castellanos was in a position of power on the board of his family's company. Who took over for him? Was any mention made in the financial papers? What is the status of the company today? And what the hell is his connection with a Christmas Ball in the Adirondacks?"

"Tom, could you follow the money behind these men? We both know that's where most of the answers will be. If anything can be found, you'll find it."

"I'll get onto it. My contacts specialize in that sort of information. Do we know which one of the men is the dead body?"

Kate was about to answer when her phone and Harry's both buzzed. Harry pushed the button and saw a young woman with spiky multicolored hair astride a motorcycle at the gate.

"May I help you?" he asked her.

"I'm told that you're hiding a couple of ignoramuses with

badges inside these gates. I need you to open this gate, so I can murder them." Harry glanced at the men in question and said, "No problem." Then he pushed the button.

-9-

Wednesday Evening

Kate dashed to the front door eager to meet the future murderess. She swung it open and her eyes went wide, recognizing the person before her, though she hadn't seen her in at least five years. The woman, dressed in jeans, a beat-up leather jacket, and heavy black boots, dismounted the motorcycle and dashed up onto the porch coming to a stop before Kate.

"Your hair is purple," Kate said.

"You cut off your braid."

"Agnes made me."

"How is the supermodel these days? Still, disgustingly

beautiful?"

"Of course, but she's given up modeling and is running a bank now."

"Hum, less fame but more fortune."

"Would you expect anything less?"

"Are you visiting the crazy lady who owns this place?"

"Worse, my husband and I just bought it."

"You got married?"

"Last Saturday."

"Interesting honeymoon."

"Tell me about it."

"Well, let me at the Keystone Cops and then I need to see your basement."

They headed into the kitchen arm and arm. Kate walked up to Harry and Ann who were now sitting at the table. But before she could say anything, there was a sharp bark and a flash of white as a Samoyed threw himself onto the woman.

"Liam. Oh, my love, it is so good to see you. How is my bear? You look wonderful." The woman dropped to the floor wrestling the dog who continued barking wildly, with his tail wagging non-stop.

"Maybe I should do the introductions in the correct order. You remember Liam, and he remembers you, but let me introduce his son Dillon and Dillon's son Quinn. Boys, this is Gwyn." The woman, now part of a three dog hug fest, grinned. "Not too shabby, Killoy. They're as handsome as my favorite Sam, Liam."

"And while I'm doing introductions, Harry, Gram, This is Gwyn Braxton, Georges' cousin, who has perfect taste in dogs.

Gwyn, this is my husband, Harry Foyle and my grandmother Ann Killoy. Oh, and the man leaning on the cane by the stove with his mouth hanging open, is my big brother, Tom."

With grace and little effort, Gwyn stood, patted the dogs on their heads and quietly said to them, "Go lie down." Liam gave Quinn a shove and lead them back to their spot in the sun by the window. Her height of five foot four including her boots left her shorter than everyone in the room, but her attitude gave her stature. She whirled around and faced the two cops. "Were you two trying to be funny or something? What is this, delude the forensic pathologist week? What were you playing at? As if I don't have enough to do in this part of God's little acre, you clowns get to play scramble the body parts. We are going to get this fixed now or I'm going to drag you back to headquarters behind my bike."

"Gwyn," George spoke up. "You know we'd never do anything like that. We wouldn't dare, the chief would fry us. You got what we found, every bone the guy had plus the bullet."

"You gave me bones alright, but that was the problem. They were from more than one body."

The silence which followed her statement went on and on. Finally, Tom asked, "Anyone want coffee?"

"Thank God, I think I love you. It was a four-hour ride to get here from my last case and it's getting cold outside." She crossed the kitchen and eagerly took the cup he handed her adding the milk and sugar he offered. "You look like a younger version of your grandfather. Hopefully, you take after him because he was one of the most wonderful men in the world. I cried when I heard he died. He and I would talk for hours, and he never made me feel like a kid."

Tom blinked and smiled. "He did that with all of us. He listened to what we said and gave real advice when we needed it. I miss him more than I can say."

"So your father is running the business now?" she asked.

Startled, it took Tom a minute to answer. "My dad died two months after my grandfather. It was sudden, an aneurysm."

"No. How awful. We used to talk about searching for answers. I knew then what I wanted to be, and he felt that a forensic approach to every aspect of a crime was valuable. But then, who's running K&K? I loved hearing about that business."

"I am."

Kate looked at Harry who lifted one eyebrow then tilted his head in Tom's direction with a half-smile.

Tom had shown zero interest in women since the deaths of his father and grandfathers. Kate began to fear he'd end up a stuffy bachelor pushing papers and buried in work for the rest of his life. His reaction to Gwyn, made her silently cheer.

Gil said, "Not to question your skills, Little One, but how can you tell it's more than one person. We're talking bones here."

Gwyn whirled around to blast him, then glanced back at Tom and seemed to rethink the waspish comment she was about to let loose. Instead, she took a breath and asked, "Have you put together jigsaw puzzles, Gil?"

"Of course I have."

"Well, picture yourself trying to put together a puzzle

when the pieces from several puzzles are all in one pile on the table. The bones should all go together if they are from the same body. They don't. These are bones from skeletons that in life were different-sized people. The one thing they did get right appears to be the length of time they've been deceased since the coroner placed death about 1960. I need to see this basement, Kate."

Kate nodded and started toward the basement door. Harry stood and took her hand. Kate hadn't been down there and though he knew she was tough, the concept of walking into a crime scene, even one this old, might make her uncomfortable. Tom grabbed his cane and started to follow Gwyn. She stopped and reversed direction asking him about the cane. When he admitted he had a broken ankle, she suggested he avoid the cellar. He opened his mouth to object, but she rested her hand on his chest and said, "I'd rather you rest up to be in shape to take me to dinner. We've got more talking to do." Startled, he covered her hand for a few seconds, then smiled and nodded. Gwyn picked up the knapsack left by the door when she entered the kitchen and bounded down the stairs.

For the most part, the scene looked like a basement. There was a big open area near a new heating system and several rooms with windowless barn-like doors along the north wall. Not far from the furnace was a trench dug into the floor with cement rubble on each side. It led to the sidewall. About halfway along, the trench suddenly widened. The ground was dry so the bones had been well-preserved.

Gwyn approached the hole, circling to the side away from the trench. Then lowering herself to the floor, she reached into her bag and pulled out a small trowel only slightly larger than a dentist's mirror. She asked the men to point out, as best they could, the placement of the bones they removed even though the rough shape of the body was marked in the soil, and then she got to work.

Kate moved in beside her with something that looked like an oversized makeup brush and followed behind her scraping, using the brush to loosen the soil. The men sat watching without speaking, but it was Harry who spotted a lighter area about a foot further over. He pointed it out and the two women shifted their positions. Less than a minute later, the series of bones that make up a right hand was revealed. Gwyn stopped and signaled Kate to sit. She studied the hand then calculated where the arm, shoulder, head and the rest of the body would be.

"We're going to need some equipment to remove the concrete covering the body without disturbing the soil underneath. Gil, can you call Anderson's or if they aren't available, try your cousin Ally's boss? They both have what we need. It's just a case of who can be here by eight tomorrow morning. Before you go upstairs though, I want you men to make sure that not even a mouse can get into this basement. We don't need the surprise of hidden entrances or exits messing up this case. I don't want these bones disturbed."

The men began checking the basement storage rooms as well as the central room which seemed to go on forever. The women returned to an empty kitchen and cleaned themselves up. Ann had left a note saying she'd gone to take a nap since there was nothing she could do to help now. Kate knew Tom must be around somewhere since all the dogs were missing, so she headed for the library. He was sitting sideways behind the desk with his cast propped on an open drawer lost in research. Gwyn cleared her throat, and he looked up, a smile spreading across his face. "Ladies, you're back quickly. What did you find?"

"Another body. Well, technically the right hand from another body. We can't excavate anything else until the concrete is removed. With luck, Gil can get the specialists here early in the morning. We left the guys making sure that there are no entrances to the basement we don't know about. I hate people messing up my bones when I'm not looking."

"Well I haven't been idle. I've been doing some digging myself. Stavros Castellanos at the time of the party was second in command at the family's shipping company. Following the party, the New Year's letter was sent to all board members, family members, and investors, saying that Stavros had stepped down from his position on the board and was traveling to Greece to work with an archaeologist to uncover some ruins which had recently been discovered on family land."

"Did he return to Greece?"

"His name was on the manifest of the Olympia, though whether he boarded or not, I also can't tell you. When or where he disembarked I can't tell you yet because it made numerous stops in Greece as well as ports in other countries. But at least we now know the company's story of what happened to the budding corporate scion. However, once he got to Greece he didn't seem to be worth a mention in the Annual reports. So, if he is one of the bodies in the basement, his family has some explaining to do.

The door to the library opened and Ann stepped in. Gwyn went to her. "I was so sorry to learn about the deaths of both your husband and son. When I was young, they would bring Kate to the north country to show her dogs. I would follow them around and pester them with questions about forensics. They both knew so much about methods to seek answers to questions, no matter if the problem is financial or physical. They inspired me and I owe them so much."

Ann reached out and hugged the girl. "Thank you. You brought Tom and John back to me for a few minutes and for that I thank you. I had heard of you from them years ago. I think the terms 'smart as a whip' and 'marches to her own drum,' came into the conversation. I'm so glad I've now met you."

"This is great. Tom is taking me to dinner and you're going to come with us. There are so many questions I have to ask you. Would you please come with us?"

"Tom?"

"Gram, definitely come. Let's get our coats."

As they headed out the door, they were joined by the two policemen promising to return in the morning. A few minutes later, as Kate stood at the window of the library watching the cars go through the gate at the end of the driveway she felt arm circle her waist. She leaned back against the strong chest and rested her head against his shoulder,

"Do you realize that this is the first we've been alone since we arrived?" He lifted her into his arms and walked by the kitchen and down the hall to their bedroom. The dogs followed but Harry just told them to go lie down in the kitchen and shut the door. He lowered her feet to the ground and slowly began to explain the honeymoon he had planned. Then he began to show her exactly what that would be like.

Kate was lying draped across Harry's chest as he stroked her back an hour later when his phone rang. Neither of them moved for a minute, but then he reached out to look at the caller ID.

"It's Des."

"What could he want. Did Maurio escape?" The man who'd just tried to murder them was still fresh in their minds.

"Yes, Des?" he answered the phone. He listened, his expression getting darker by the minute. Then he sighed. "We'll see you tomorrow."

He sighed and then explained, "No Maurio Corsetti is still locked up."

"Is it just Des or is he bringing other feds with him?"

"Let's just say that the number of guests at the Honeymoon has not yet reached the number at the wedding—but it's early days yet.

-10-

Wednesday Night

Kate woke but didn't know why. She looked across her sleeping husband seeing his usually chiseled features were softened with sleep and noticed that barely an hour had gone by. It was too early for Tom and Gram to have returned from dinner. Then she heard it again and stiffened. The soft warning growl she identified as coming from Liam. Liam was her careful Sam who didn't have a hair-trigger. Mostly laid back, it took something serious to get this reaction.

Putting her hand over Harry's mouth, she woke him. "Liam's growling," she whispered.

His eyes grew large. They both slid from the bed and pulled

on sweat pants and shirts, sliding on shoes without making a sound. Kate pointed her finger, with her thumb up, and he nodded and eased open the nightstand drawer, removing his gun. Then crossing to the bedroom door, they eased it open and saw the dogs lined up staring at one of the oak paneled wall of the hallway. None of the dogs turned as they approached. After what seemed like an hour but was only a minute, they heard the footsteps quietly descending stairs. Stairs that seemed to be inside the wall.

Harry moved down the hall and disappeared into the kitchen. Kate reached for Dillon and Quinn and sent Liam to follow Harry. She kept her ear pressed to the wall trying to hear more of the stranger walking about in the walls of their home. This was not a ghost. This person had somehow gained access to their very secure home and was probably up to no good.

While waiting to see what Harry found, she ran her hand over the carved panel. Each panel in this short hall was carved to depict a different tree. Letting her hand slide up the panel, she reached the branch with leaves. Her fingers followed the leaf's shape, identifying the tree as a maple. The smooth surface of the carving was highly polished and cool under her hand. As she slid her hand down the limb of the tree toward the trunk, she hit a tiny bump where they connected. She started to follow the trunk down but stopped. Returning to the spot where the carved limb and trunk met, she felt for the bump again. It was small and could have been just an irregularity in the bark of the tree, but it felt different. It felt cold, metallic, foreign to the surrounding wood. Her finger pressed it down, but nothing happened. Using her thumb and forefinger, she tried moving it from side to side. Still, nothing. Finally, she pushed up and heard a click. Smoothly, the panel swung outward away from the wall. Its hinges smelled of recent oiling.

Flicking on the hallway lights, Kate saw a small landing about three foot square within the wall with stairs going up to the right and down to the left. Giving Dillon and Quinn the hand signal to lie down and stay, she slipped into the bedroom and grabbed a flashlight from her bureau. With the light flicked on as she stepped onto the landing. Resting her free hand against the wall, she began descending the stairs, not knowing what she would find. She had gone only eight steps when she reached another landing. The stairs continued both down from the landing, and to the left, toward what would be the pool. Here there was a small door. Kate paused to listen for any trace of movement. Nothing. All she could detect was the slight panting from the dogs above her. Realizing that Harry had gone to the basement and would intercept anyone who ventured into that area, she reached for the door latch.

A smell of chlorine met her as she stepped onto a second landing. The stairs continued for about six steps, ending at a small hall with three blank walls. Stairs to nowhere didn't make sense. Her flashlight reflected the smoothness of the panels, not revealing any hidden latches. She noticed that the joining, on the sides of the end wall, left tiny cracks rather than being smoothed over with Spackle.

Reasoning that a crack could mean a door, she ran her hand all around the edge of the end panel. Nothing. She was about to retreat up the stairs when she heard a movement on the other side of the wall. Someone was there. She softly called the dogs and as they raced down the stairs to reach her, she pushed hard against the panel. It shifted forward and slid to the side revealing the moonlight shining on the water in the pool.

She stepped through the opening and walked forward as she heard the dogs rounding the corner to descend the final flight of stairs. Her attention was on the dogs when she heard a small movement and felt herself being shoved forward into the pool.

The water was ice-cold and shock gripped her for a few seconds. Then instinct took over and she fought her way to the surface. The sound of Dillon's frustrated barks and banging on glass were interrupted by the force of a paw pushing her back under the water. Turning, to grab Quinn before kicking her way to the surface, she positioned herself behind him and away from his flailing paws. Holding him tightly, she kicked toward what she hoped was the shallow end. As soon as her feet touched the bottom, she shoved the puppy toward the stairs and grabbed the handrail to pull herself out. The spray of water from Quinn's shake had her spitting and wiping her face. A quick glance around told her that they were alone or the dogs would be seeking out new prey. She sank to the top step, allowing Dillon and Quinn to lick her face and fuss over her. She slid her arm over Dillon's back to steady herself as she reached for the railing to stand.

"Kate, Kate, where are you?"

"We're down here. Just follow the stairs."

Liam burst through the doorway just before Harry. He ran to her and started licking her face. Her husband reached her side and slid his hands under her arms, lifting her to her feet.

"Did you fall into the pool in the dark?" he asked.

"No, I was shoved into the pool by someone who hid in the dark and fled through the door to outside two seconds before Dillon got to them. I should have waited until they were with me before I opened the door. I heard a sound and without thinking, pushed open the panel and rushed out onto what was the side of the pool. Thank goodness there was water in the pool, cold though it was. If not, I'd be dead." She began shaking, whether, from the cold or shock, she didn't know or care.

Harry steadied her against the wall to the open stair-door and said, "Wait." He then dashed across to the outside door and finding it unlocked, locked it and then pushed a table in front of the handle. Then racing back to Kate, he told the dogs to go up the stairs and gently guided her up to the opening in the hall wall. Turning toward the bedroom, he hurried her into the bathroom, stripped off her sweats, and helped her into the shower. After a few minutes, he turned off the water and wrapped her in an oversized towel and began rubbing her dry from her head to her toes. Once she was dry, he grabbed a fleece top and pants and helped her put them on, then tucked her into their bed.

Her phone on the nightstand buzzed. Harry pushed the button and seeing Tom at the gate, released the latch. "You rest here. I'm going to talk to your brother and then get Quinn dry."

"He needs the chlorine washed out of his coat first."

"Don't worry about it. I'm sending Ann in with tea. Don't move, and that's an order."

Kate smiled. “Yes, sir.”

Kate wondered about a person sneaking around the house. It had to be someone who knew the house inside out. Her vote was for Vivian. She was missing from her nursing home and ducking police questioning. She was the best person to know the secrets of this house being someone who’d lived here most of her life.

Two to one, she drove the servants crazy as a child. She’d read historical mysteries a lot of growing up and old manor houses had hidden staircases inside the walls so that the servants could move about without having to be seen by the lord of the manor or his guests. She wondered if Vivian had been hiding in the attic since she bailed from the nursing home. But how did she get on the property?

Did she come before they’d put in the warning camera system by the dock? If so, where was her boat? She knew that Harry had changed the locking system on the front gate. And, though Vivian was in relatively good health, she doubted that a woman of eighty could scale eight-foot-high chain link fencing without being noticed. Tomorrow, she would take the dogs and see if whoever pushed her into the pool could be tracked.

It could be that Vivian wasn’t their only problem. Kate had forgotten for a minute that Des was on his way. For the last year she’d been playing hostess to the FBI, NSA, and various other members of what she called the ‘long arm of the law club.’ It seemed that going on their honeymoon would not serve as an excuse to keep them at bay.

A knock sounded on the door and Ann walked in carrying a pair of tea mugs. “I was going to get out the tea cart and do it up right," she said, "but I figured it was overkill, so I just brought a mug of tea the way you like it."

"Wonderful. It's just what I need. Did Harry tell you that I earned the first leg on my title of a member in the Polar Bear club tonight."

"He said someone got into the house, was walking up and down staircases hidden in the walls. They snuck up and shoved you into the pool when you followed. How did they manage that? Where were the dogs?"

"I had them on a down in the hallway not knowing what I'd encounter. I'd just called them when I felt hands on my back shoving me into that cold water. Thank goodness there was water in the pool. Harry was going to drain it to do some repairs."

"Well, Tom and Gwyn are washing Quinn to get the chlorine out of his coat. Gwyn loves the bathing set up you've got. She said it was fancier than some motels she had to stay at when she was traveling around the north country with work. I think she's the only forensic pathologist for miles around."

"I should warn you that Harry and I are building a cop book, sort of like a bird spotting book, only this would be filled with all the members of law enforcement who came along on our honeymoon."

"Oh, who else is coming?"

"Des. I didn't hear the whole conversation, but he seemed to be ranting about the old Soviet Union and spies. I assume it has something to do with Count Grigori Baturin who is the only Russian in the group of missing men. However, there weren't many aristocrats active in Russia once the Communists took over. How he figures into the mix I don't know, but I'm sure Des will have quite a story to tell when he arrives tomorrow. At this rate, we may fill all the guest rooms and have to open the cabin."

"Do you want me to go?"

"Heavens no. You're our buffer between your crazy cousin and the police. Please, stay. I'd rather not deal with that woman."

"Not a problem. I doubt I could get your brother to leave at the minute anyway."

Kate smiled. "I guess he's not the dried-up old stick I was worried he was becoming."

Ann grinned. "After listening to them spar at dinner, I have hope. But you know your brother, it won't happen fast."

"Well, two members of my wedding party are already scheduled to be married next summer with both Agnes and Cathy getting engaged, I could stand to have some weekends to do non-wedding things. Plus, he would have to get Will up to speed before he takes off on a honeymoon. Speaking of Will. Do you think he'd be up for doing New Year's Day here for the family plus whoever? I think he'd enjoy the kitchen."

"I know he'd love the kitchen. I love the kitchen. Why don't you rest and I'll check on your husband. He took both Dillon and Liam with him when he went to check for your assailant. Oh, and he was on the phone to Gil when I brought the tea, so brace yourself for an interview first thing in the morning." Ann reached over and took her cup and pulled the extra pillow from behind Kate's head, so she could lie flat. She turned off the light as she left the room but left the door slightly open.

In spite of the adrenalin which had been flowing through her body earlier, Kate felt herself slipping into sleep, and though she wanted to wait until Harry came back, it was a losing the battle. She was roused just as she was dropping off by a thump on the bed and snuggling against her cheek was a damp puppy who smelled of dog shampoo rather than chlorine. After a few pants, Quinn sighed and settled into sleep with his head resting against her shoulder. Kate smiled and thought, 'Her hero.'

-11-

Thursday Morning

Harry had climbed into bed, displacing the puppy sometime during the night. Kate snuggled against him and then realizing that he was chilled, rolled onto him to warm him up. Harry had better ideas about warming up which ended up with her draped over his warm body as they both dropped off to sleep. It was barely light when she woke, her back against his warm chest and his heavy arm wrapped around her. For a few seconds she felt as if she really was on a honeymoon, but a glance at the nightstand clock reminded her that the three ring circus was due to continue in several hours and her job was as ringmaster. Des was due to arrive around breakfast time bringing another layer to the problem.

Gwyn and Tom were already in the kitchen drinking coffee when Kate emerged from the bedroom. She took one look at them and decided not to ask any questions. She pulled a dozen eggs from the refrigerator and grabbed a big bowl to prepare pancake batter. Harry began defrosting a pound of bacon in the microwave and pulled out the toaster and got some bread from the fridge. Kate broke the silence by asking, "Did you find any trace of how our visitor got onto the property last night? I'm quickly using up my quota of surprises for the week."

"I think you're going to have to expand your capacity for surprises for this honeymoon, sweetheart. With Des on his way and ranting about the Soviet Union, the KGB and GRU, who knows where this is going to take us. Apparently the research we did into our Russian Count Baturin, set off a powder keg in the DC bureau office."

"Well, pardon me, but after the idiocy they pulled at the wedding, Saturday, they'll be lucky if I don't put ground glass in their pancakes."

"These are the guys who brought a murderer to your wedding?" Gwyn asked.

"The very same." Harry told her. "Dillon and Quinn saved their bacon and our lives."

"I agree, Kate. They're idiots." She said.

Kate poured the first batch of pancakes onto the griddle to start cooking and looked at Harry. "You didn't say what you found last night."

"You didn't tell her?" Tom asked.

"No, I got distracted by other matters."

Kate's face turned red as both her brother and Gwyn

laughed.

"So, last night the boys and I tracked your assailant around to the side of the house, across the lawn and into the woods. The trail ended abruptly about eight feet from the fence in a densely wooded area. I'd like to go back to that spot in daylight to check."

"Fine. I'll go with you. And while we're on the subject of things I don't know, why was Des so upset when he called? I heard him screaming about the Soviet Union."

"I wouldn't exactly say scre..."

"He screeched like an eight-year-old girl. So why was he so upset?"

Tom, Gwyn and Harry all laughed. "Apparently, our dear Count Baturin, was a KGB agent who had been doing a bit of spying here in the late fifties. His cover allowed him to become part of the Russian Nobility Association in New York City which raised money to help the Russian Orthodox Church in the US. His cover was good and gave him entry into the social life of some of the wealthy industrialists. He was able to plant others to do industrial espionage which he would make sure got back to the growing industrial power structure in Russia."

"Pardon me, but Des wasn't even alive when all this happened. Why the fuss?"

"He should be here in an hour. You might as well ask him yourself." Breakfast was dished up just as Ann joined them. Gwyn's phone buzzed and she told them the cement cutting crew would arrive in thirty minutes. Kate sat and ate quickly then grabbed dog dishes and made their breakfasts. They had only finished eating when Quinn barked and raced toward the front of the house and Harry's phone dinged announcing that Gil and George had arrived. Harry pushed the button letting them in and then walked over to wrap his arms around Kate. "Happy honeymoon, Darling."

An hour later, Kate decided to take the dogs and walk around the property line. Gwyn was in the basement with Gil and George and men with fancy saws working to remove the floor but leave the bodies untouched. Des had arrived bringing an older agent with him and they'd disappeared into the library with Harry and Tom. Kate hadn't even bothered being part of the introductions. Then Ann had decided that she was going to go through the attic trunks looking for gowns that people could wear if we decided to have a New Year's Eve ball—an idea that she and Gwyn had come up with at dinner. So taking a walk out in the crisp air with her dogs was an excellent choice. Just the quiet was appreciated.

Dillon and Liam were off lead, but Kate kept Quinn on six feet of leather control. There was no telling what they would come across and she didn't need to take any chances. At the moment, she felt like the young Kate Killoy exploring the world surrounding her castle. This was the first time she'd been here when it wasn't summer. Looking up at the sky, she noticed the clouds building and the air felt as though snow were on the way. Well, they were in the mountains. Winter tended to check in earlier here than at her home in Connecticut which was only a thirty minute drive from Long Island Sound.

As she walked, Kate noticed things that hadn't been important to Kate the child. The view from the front gate gave a peek at the top story of the house and the towers then took it away as the drive curved first right and then left in an S shape. The drive passed through a huge stand of ancient pines which muffled the sound of the outside world. It then swung left, completing the first semi-circle and came out of the forest to a spot where the house was presented in all its grandeur. The landscaping gave the place the appearance of having been there for hundreds of years—a settled state of permanence and peace. The final sweep to the left circled the fountain, now turned off, and ended in a wide parking area under the portico leading to the front door. Kate walked to the scenic spot in the drive and turned to look at her new summer home. In spite of all the madness and chaos, she couldn't think of a better wedding gift Harry could have given her. Just by standing here, her mind filled with memories of racing after their dogs with Agnes to the gate and back just for the joy of running after a long drive. She could almost hear their yells. But today, silence filled the air.

Walking back toward the house, she turned left and headed for the spot where the fence bordering the broad lawn disappeared into a wooded area made up of rhododendrons and azaleas, junipers, holly and yews as well as pines and bushes she couldn't name since they weren't in bloom.

Liam lead the way along the narrow path through the bushes only to emerge into a knot garden. Even though dormant, the design was beautiful. Glancing to her right, she saw that in summer this garden would be visible from the game room's French doors and small patio in front of it. She could imagine adults playing pool or cards inside on summer days and kids on the patio or the lawn around the knot garden, playing board games. She felt a sudden grip in her chest and caught her breath as the thought of her children playing there.

A noise from Dillon pulled her out of her daydreams. Something had upset him. Both he and Liam were out of sight but she could hear them moving along a path on the other side of the garden that ran parallel to the fence, toward the back of the house. She and Quinn broke into a trot to catch up with the others to find out what had caused their upset. A break in the bushes led to a smaller foot path along the fence as it circled around a large fir tree. The dogs had not continued down the main path but had disappeared somewhere behind the fir tree. Kate circled the tree slowly until she could see two white coats with their tails not wagging and their bodies held stiff, and pressed against the fence.

It was only when she got right up behind them that she saw the gate. A small gate, about a yard wide, reminding her of the gates in her kennel runs. It led to what looked like a good sized mulch pile. This must be where Otto would bring all the yard clippings. The mulch created here would enrich the gardens without costing anything but a little labor would be worth its weight in garden gold. The gate was completely invisible to anyone in or around the house. That was when she noticed that the gate also wasn't locked. With all the security that Harry had worked so hard on so that they would be safe, he must not have known about this. This, she was sure, was also how her attacker had gotten into the house and then escaped.

She pulled out her phone and texted Harry. I've found how the attacker got in and escaped. Come out through the French doors in the game room. It only took a few seconds for her phone to beep. Coming.

When she heard the sound of the French doors opening, she called, "Over here."

Harry ran down the path but then stopped. "Where are you?"

"Circle around behind the tree."

Harry, followed by Gil, George and Des came into sight much to Quinn's delight. He bounded over to Des wagging his tail with joy at the sight of his friend. Kate stood to one side so that the men could see the gate. "This is how my attacker got in and out last night. There is no lock. They didn't need to climb the fence or do anything fancy. They just strolled in."

"I had no idea this was here. Otto never mentioned it when I had the security people in."

"He probably didn't think about it as an entrance since it only leads to the mulch pile. But whoever came in last night knew. They understood that the gate was an unguarded entrance and they knew how to access it. Gil, do you know where those woods lead?"

"To a place that is closed up for the winter. The owner does a seasonal B and B from May through October. The other side of the woods is a driveway right out to the roadway."

Harry had been texting while Gil spoke and now his phone beeped. Glancing at it he nodded. "Kate, I'm going to stay here with Liam and Quinn and wait for the security crew to bring a lock to secure this gate. Why don't you take Dillon and go talk to Gil and George about last night while we wait."

She handed him Quinn's lead and signaled Dillon to come and the others to stay with Harry. They headed back toward the French Doors and cut through the game room. Des moved until he was beside her. "Kate, let me tell you again how sorry I am for what happened at the wedding."

She stopped and looked at him. "Don't worry, Des. You guys were a bunch of dumb-asses but I forgive you. You're lucky that Dillon and Quinn aren't as easily taken in by a smooth talking bastard." Gil and George gawked at her as she reamed out the agent, but Des sighed in relief.

"Thanks. You are right on all points."

"Just don't let it happen again. I'm a Kate not a cat and I don't know how many lives I have left."

Des smiled and looped his arm over her shoulder as they went back inside. "I'll want to introduce you to the agent who came with me and discuss why we came, but maybe it can wait until you finish describing your latest attack with these gentlemen."

"Good idea."

"Latest attack?" Gil asked.

Des laughed. "She's on her second bullet proof vest. I hope Agnes packed it for you."

She scowled at him as he ducked back into the library and she and the men headed to the kitchen. She'd talk to them but she needed another cup of tea first. She made her tea and toasted an English muffin. After finishing both she took the men on a tour of her adventure. She began in the hall, showing them how she'd discovered the secret entrance to the hidden staircase. She'd brought her heavy-duty flashlight from the kitchen to light the way. This time when she stepped onto the landing, she noticed sconces placed about eight feet apart along the stair. She assumed that this staircase had never been electrified. She described how they'd heard the person descending the stairs and how Harry and Liam had gone to the basement to head them off. When she'd found the latch, she followed the person down the stairs. They followed her to the place where the stairs branched off. She explained that if the person continued straight he'd have encountered Harry, so she took the stairs to the left. Matching her description with action, she headed down and showed how it ended with the wall which opened to the pool. "I had left the dogs in the hall, but when I got here, I called them. I'd just turned toward the pool when I became aware of movement and suddenly hands were hitting my back with enough force to propel me into the pool. Thank goodness it had water in it, though I can attest it is very cold water. Otherwise, I'd be dead. Even so, my attacker didn't know I could swim or thought the cold water would cause shock. Clearly, the intent was to kill me.

The dogs burst through the doorway as I surfaced and Dillon chased my attacker to the door. They made it in time and he was frustrated by the shut door. Quinn jumped into the pool to save me, forgetting that Samoyeds are not water rescue dogs. I ended up having to pull him from the pool since his coat could only be dead weight. He would have figured out swimming but I felt safer when his flailing paws were planted on solid ground."

George checked the door, which Harry had blocked with a table and then they returned to the stairs where the landing had split. George turned left and headed down to see where it exited in the basement. Kate and Gil turned right and followed the stairs up past the hall entrance and continued on to where it reached the second floor. There they found another door which opened to the second floor hall. It took Kate only a minute to locate the latch in the molding on the hall wall. She'd only just closed the door when they heard a scream.

-12-

Thursday Midday

Dillon streaked past Kate, shoving her against the wall and dashing up the stairs. Kate started after him, when another scream was heard followed by the sound of running feet passing them on the other side of the wall.

"Gil, go down. Stop whoever it is. George block the basement." The men took off down the stairs as Kate and Des followed Dillon. When they reached the frantic dog, he was scratching at a door, trying to find a way through. Kate spotted the catch and hit it sending the door flying open and the dog swinging left and down the hall. A faint sound of whimpering came from the area in front of them, and they saw Dillon throw himself against another closed door. Des was faster than she was and threw open the door. The room was small with a narrow bed which was covered with a pile of ball gowns. Kate saw Dillon dash behind the bed and whine. Pushing by Des, Kate saw her grandmother lying on the floor, her head bleeding. Jewelry was scattered over the floor next to her.

"Gram! Gram you're hurt." She bent over the older woman and felt for a pulse. It was there and strong.

"I'm alive." Ann's voice sounding more angry than hurt. "That bitch was hiding in wait. I barely had time to duck before she clipped me. If I get my hands on her, she's going to find out that I can be a bitch too."

"Who hit you? Did you see them?"

"See, no. But I smelled her. It was Vivian. She's worn that signature perfume since she had it designed for her when she turned sixteen. Here, help me up and be sure the blood doesn't get on the dresses. It's murder to get blood out of silk. Des, can you gather up the jewelry for me. I had just opened the box when she hit me. She must have been hiding behind the door."

Kate looked around the room and spotted a stack of towels. She pulled a clean one from the middle of the stack and pressed it hard against the cut on her grandmother's head. Using her other hand, she pulled her phone from her pocket and speed dialed Harry. "Harry, Gram was attacked. We're in one of the maids rooms on the third floor. Gil and George went after the attacker whom she claims was Vivian. She needs a doctor for a head wound."

Seconds later, the pounding steps announced Harry's

arrival followed by Otto who had been helping install the lock on the gate. Harry lifted Ann into his arms and with Des and Otto opening doors and steadying him as he descended the stairs, he carried her to her tower room on the second floor. At the bottom of the stairs, Kate raced around him into the tower room and turned back the covers. She slipped a second pillow under Ann's head and removed her shoes. Then dashing into the bathroom she returned seconds later with a first aid kit. She no sooner had the kit open than Gwyn raced into the room and skidded to a stop beside the bed.

"Rats. Head wounds bleed like the devil. Kate, grab some towels to put under her. These sheets are too old and pretty to be bleached to get blood out. Well, Ann. I'd ask how you're feeling, but with all these gentlemen surrounding you, you're too polite to say."

Tom came into the room carrying what looked like a medical bag. "Thanks. Now sit. Straining your ankle won't speed the healing. Your grandmother is going to be fine."

They all stood while Gwyn worked, questioning Ann as she checked her vital signs and then patched up the cut on her head. "This won't even need stitches," she said as she applied a butterfly bandage to the wound. "I doubt it will even leave a scar. Now, can you tell us who you think did this?"

"The one thing that tipped me off that I wasn't alone was the smell of perfume. I had been in and out of that room since early this morning and the smell hadn't been there. I had just come down from the attic with a box of what looked like costume jewelry. When I walked into the room and smelled Vivian, I turned and screamed, ducking away as her hand, holding something long and black, managed to hit my head. I heard myself scream again as I fell, then heard Dillon barking. She was leaning over me but turned and ran from the room when he barked. If I hadn't been so groggy, I'd have chased her and shown her what it feels like to get hit."

Gil pushed into the room. "She got away. Apparently she strolled out of the game room and down the path to where the workman was fitting the backup lock. She said hello and then shoved the guy down, pulled open the gate, and high tailed it into the woods. By the time he got to his feet, she had disappeared."

"Did you get a description from the guy?"

"Better. He said the video should have been on. He notified his boss to save it and send a copy to the department. I don't know your code for download."

Harry was keying numbers into his phone. It beeped, and he opened the video which showed the back of a woman wearing a stylish dress and Cuban-heeled shoes strolling toward the tree. You can see the struggle and for a second, her face is caught looking back toward the house before she disappears. Through the branches of the tree, the top of the gate was visible opening and then the recording stops.

Des had been watching over Harry's shoulder. "Download it onto my laptop and I'll see if I can enhance the face a little."

"Thanks." Harry turned back to Ann. "Are you really okay?"

"Harry, don't ask her just to make yourself feel better." Gwyn said. "Right now she feels like an elephant sat on her head, and she might want to barf. So I'd advise all you gentlemen to clear the room so Ann doesn't feel it's necessary to play the role of sweet grandmother, and she can swear her head off. Out, doctor's orders."

Kate heard Harry ask Tom, "Is she was really a doctor."

"Yup. She just prefers working on patients who don't complain or talk back."

Gwyn turned to Kate. "She shows no sign of concussion and the cut on her head is not deep. I recommend she take a couple of aspirin and get some rest. We can check on her in an hour." She and Kate pulled the curtains closed, and then she placed a glass of water on the nightstand next to her cell phone. "Ann, if you wake and feel sick, just call Kate or Tom. I'll be staying here tonight. So, get some rest now. In about ninety minutes, like in a hospital, I'll be back to wake you and annoy you just to make sure you're okay."

Gwyn followed Kate from the room hearing a slight chuckle from the bed. Dillon, looked at Kate and then turned in a circle next to Ann's bed and lay down. Kate looked back. "Good boy, Dillon. You keep her safe." She pulled the door almost closed, and they headed down the stairs to see what Des had been able to pull from the video.

Kate looked at the clock and was startled it was five-thirty. She was tired. She walked into the library only to have a man, to whom she had yet to be introduced, immediately go silent. The man glanced her way with a look which was all to familiar and brought out the snide in her. "Oh, so sorry to interrupt you gentlemen who are doing your super secret investigating. I just wanted to let you know that dinner will be served in half an hour. Now I'll just take my little self into the kitchen and get to work doing the women's work which I do best." She turned and closed the door.

As she started toward the kitchen she heard her brother say, "Oh boy, we're in trouble now. Harry, I think you just blew your honeymoon to hell and Des, you're back on her shit list. It's a good thing I'm her brother. She can't get rid of me."

Harry stood. "Excuse me, gentlemen. I have some charcoal bridges to repair."

"You can't leave, Foyle. We need you to analyze this data," the man said.

"Sorry. I'll leave my brother-in-law and Agent Xiang to explain how you just insulted one of the top operatives the Bureau has used this year. That lady solved multiple murders, the theft of millions, and saved the country—twice and that's just in the last ten months. Plus, as of last Saturday, she's my bride. Now if you don't want a meal of ground glass, I would suggest you start working on your apology. Pardon me, I've got to go grovel."

Kate sat, the house phone in her hand. "So, suddenly there are eight for supper plus I'm making a tray to take up to Ann. She was assaulted and is recovering from a head wound." She paused to listen to a string of excited questions. "Well, she said she recognized the perfume as being what Vivian always wore. She said Vivian had it created when she was a girl and had worn it ever since." Helen must have responded and said she was coming because Kate hung up the phone. Movement caught her eye as a white handkerchief waved through the barely-open door. Harry stuck his head into the room and judging her expression, was across the room and lifting her into his lap in seconds.

"I am an absolute thoughtless bastard, and I am so sorry. I got caught up in the Bureau mystique and behaved like an ass. Can I help you grind the glass to go into dinner?"

"Don't tempt me. Des had better have nine lives because he's going to need them at the rate he's going."

"I left the insulting agent being instructed by your brother and Des as to the contents of your résumé and your qualifications for working with us."

She snuggled closer. "I'm over-qualified."

"I know you are. Two to one you've got a vague idea about what's happening and why but knowing you, you won't admit it until it's nailed down. We've got to begin ratcheting up the security here."

"Well we weren't planning on a secret staircase. It's so Nancy Drew."

"Didn't she have a sidekick with a weird name."

"Yea, a girl named George. She was Nancy Drew's 'Watson'."

A knock came to the back door and Helen came in. "Well, this looks more like a honeymoon. What's this about dinner for eight and Ann being hurt?"

The next half hour was spent filling Helen in about what was happening. She had a hard time accepting that Vivian had broken into the house and hit Ann over the head but admitted that she had been getting strange and she'd heard she had left the nursing home.

"How had she been getting strange?" Kate asked.

"It is almost Dr. Jekyll and Mr. Hyde. I'd come over in the morning to clean up the dishes and give a once over of the rooms which weren't under dust covers, and we'd chat. Then

I see her out in the yard and I'd ask her about something we'd been discussing only that morning, and she'd snap my head off saying that she didn't know what I was talking about and I must be losing it. It's happened twice in the last month. Even though it was hurtful, I chalked it up to her age and her mind going."

"According to Ann, Vivian is sharp as a tack and only acts dotty when she is trying to cover something up."

"Well, I'll give you that. She'd gotten very secretive lately. I will admit I was happy when you bought the place, Harry. The thought of a new young family with future children and nieces and nephews racing around the place sounds wonderful."

"Well, I'm all in favor of that. Unfortunately, we have to do something about the two bodies in the basement first."

"Two!"

"Oh, hadn't you heard. Gwyn found a second body next to the first." Harry told her. "In fact, I'd better ask Gwyn if we need to add any more to the dinner crowd."

Kate took out a plastic bag from the freezer filled with her brother Will's homemade spaghetti sauce and began thawing it. She pulled a couple of boxes of spaghetti from the cupboard, dropped the pasta into boiling water on the stove, and set it to cooking. She grabbed the thawed loves of Italian bread from the microwave and after splitting them and covering them with garlic butter, set them on a cookie sheet and stuck them in a medium oven for the tops to brown. She removed the thawed meatballs from the microwave and dropped them into the sauce to simmer. Kate looked back at the clock. Dinner was ready with two minutes to spare.

Tom led the group into the kitchen and stopped. Des stepped forward and asked, "May I introduce your guest, Kate?"

"Of course."

"Agent Oliver Bailey, FBI New York field office. Oliver, this is Kate Killoy Foyle who has saved the bureau, NSA and State Department multiple times in the last ten months. Her work has for the most part been kept under wraps for her own safety. Most recently, she undid the plot by organized crime to infiltrate and take over law enforcement in this country. The work was attributed to others, but believe me we never could have done it without her. And then to thank her, we unknowingly brought the main assassin to the wedding disguised as an agent. If it hadn't been for Dillon and Quinn, he'd have succeeded. We owe her big time. So show the lady respect. She can think circles around all of us plus she cooks."

The man shook Kate's hand. "I sincerely hope to stay on your good side, ma'am. Your brother tells me you have a dozen of these dogs in all, and they're all trained to obey your commands. Of course, some of them must be bitches so that should make it a little easier."

"Agent Bailey, have you never heard the saying, 'The female of the species is more deadly than the male'? I guarantee you, my bitches are much tougher than my males. They'll just look sweeter as they tear your throat out." Kate indicated the table which like her table at home, was made to seat crowds.

"Spaghetti for dinner. Enjoy," she smiled and Harry held her chair, as she sat at the end of the table. Tom held Gwyn's chair on her right and took the one beside her. Once the women were seated, Helen placed the platters with garlic bread on the table and served spaghetti to everyone. She ladled out the sauce, instructing everyone to help themselves to bread and salad. Then with thanks from Kate for the help, she left.

"So," Kate asked, "what shall we talk about first? The dead bodies? The missing Russian double agent? The KGB or GRU? Your choice. Oh, please go ahead and eat."

-13-

THURSDAY EVENING

Silence filled the room following her list of topics. Kate smiled blandly and looked around the table. Picking up the salad bowl, she served herself and then asked, "Salad anyone?" as she passed it on. Gwyn began to chuckle and then laugh. Harry broke next followed by Tom. Soon everyone at the table was laughing and conversation resumed.

"Okay Kate, how did you figure he was a double agent?" Des asked.

"I didn't have to figure it out, you told me. Why else would you come flying up here when Harry and I were vainly trying to have a honeymoon unless there was a Russia/US connection.

My suspicions were doubly reinforced with the appearance of an agent who was working when this crime happened and the USSR was still active."

"But I was just introduced to you," Bailey said.

"I know you didn't know Harry from his days working for the Bureau in both Washington and New York because I heard you being introduced to him. You aren't NSA because you're armed, and the CIA doesn't work inside the country. Interest flared with the discovery that our third missing man was a Russian Count. Someone, I believe it was you, knew who our Russian was, and threw up a red flag. I surmised he was posing as a millionaire to get inside the Russian Nobility Association and hide among those who worked to help the Russian Orthodox Church in America. Connections made there got his contacts to information. That information he sent back to the Kremlin. At the same time, he supposedly worked for the Bureau as a double agent. I have three questions. Is he the killer or the victim? Was he on our side or theirs? If he's still hanging around our house, what does he want that's still here?"

"Is she always like this?"

"Yes." Des, Tom, and Harry answered in unison.

"So, Gwyn, why don't we see if this gentleman might have information which would help identify your bones. They should have an accurate physical description giving height and maybe some physical identifiers which could either confirm or eliminate the count as being one of the …

Liam and Quinn's heads shot up and both dogs scrambled to their feet, racing out of the kitchen toward the front stairs. Kate, Harry, Des, and Gwyn went racing after them a second later. As she rounded the newel post and raced behind the dogs up the stairs. Kate could now hear Dillon's low growl. Something was wrong and that something he viewed as a threat to Gram.

Harry raced past her, his long legs taking the stairs two at a time. He reached Ann's room only to hear a door slam above them. "Ann, are you okay?"

"I'm fine, Harry. I woke when Dillon growled and then I heard someone move away from the door."

"I'll check," he said and raced up the stairs to the next floor.

Kate had her phone at her ear telling Des that there was someone in the house and to make sure they didn't get out. Gwyn grabbed her bag from the chest under the window where she'd left it and slipped a blood pressure cuff over Ann's arm.

Kate pulled up an app on her phone while muttering to herself that all these cameras had better be good for something. She sat on the edge of the bed, pressing a series of keys to bring up different screens. "No. No. No. No. Where are you, damn it. No. No. Wait back, is that... Yes! There you are." She called Harry on speed dial. "He's heading for the dock, trying to keep out of sight in the trees. Hang on I'm putting you on hold." She punched in another code and checked the screen. Pulling off hold she said, "He's half-way to the dock and there is a boat coming across the lake in this direction."

"Let us see," Gwyn said. Kate slid toward the head of the bed and held the phone, so they all could see the screen. They watched as he ran out of sight. Kate hit another number and a new screen appeared showing the man moving quickly, though still trying to stay hidden. The camera didn't have sound, but she could tell when he realized that Harry was coming up behind him. He turned. Looking over his shoulder. Kate hit another code and a box appeared asking if she wanted to save the photo, she clicked yes and the screen went back to the video. They could see the man reach the dock and race toward the water. Harry and Des came into view when he was about halfway to the end. That's when Kate saw that the boat she'd seen was almost to the dock and swinging around so that it could ease in broadside. Harry and Des were closing on him when the man reached the end of the dock and threw himself into the back of the boat. Kate pulled the phone back and hit some more buttons, paused, and went back to watching the broadcast. The person piloting the boat gunned it. It flew away from the dock sending a huge plume of water splashing onto the boards. The men had to slow their chase, skidding to a stop on the wet surface, barely keeping their footing.

"It's a good thing there is no audio," Gwyn said.

Kate opened her mouth to say what she thought when she heard, "Kate!"

"Sorry, Gram." She muttered.

"Well, if you need more sleep, Ann, we'll leave Dillon," Gwyn told her. "But you seem to be doing well and I don't see any reason for you staying up here when all the action is going to be downstairs."

Ann threw off the covers, slipped on her shoes and pulled a sweater on to fight a sudden chill. Then the three of them went down to join the returning men.

Gil was hanging up the phone as they entered the kitchen. Ann went to sit at the table while Tom placed a cup of tea at her place and a plate of food. Ann looked at him and smiled. "You can save that worried look for someone who hasn't been declared to be in tip-top order by her doctor. Is this your sauce or Will's?"

"Will's."

"Then I'll take an extra slice of bread. His sauce is delicious, but it's not as easy on my stomach as yours." Tom reached for the bread, a smile flashing onto his face. Then everyone got serious. As everyone settled at the table, Harry noticed his bride was missing.

"Where's Kate?"

Ann looked back the way they'd come. "She was right behind me."

He stood. "She probably remembered something. I'll go get her. There is apple pie in the refrigerator which just needs warming and you have a choice between ice cream and cheddar cheese to go with it." He walked back into the entry and then stopped, listening. It only took a few seconds until he heard the sound of a computer printer in action. He strolled into the library and spotted Kate gathering a stack of papers together.

She looked up and smiled. "I needed to take a detour to print this out." She came up to him and then put her arms behind her keeping the papers out of sight. "There's a toll."

Harry wrapped her in his arms, her body leaning back against the desk. She let the papers drop on the desktop and wrapped her arms around him. After a few very satisfying moments, Kate rested her head against Harry's chest. "Happy Honeymoon," she murmured. Harry kissed her on the top of her head, then lifted her chin so that he could look her in the eye.

"Was that payment of the toll enough?"

"For now. I suppose you want to see what I have. I made copies for each of you." She felt behind herself and picked up the papers. Harry recognized the printouts as the kind that Kate's security cameras produce. "Let's show them to the guys."

They went into the kitchen and Kate, feeling like a school teacher returning students' exams, passed out the papers, with two different sheets for each. Gil was on his phone talking to the powers that be in Bolton when she gave him the printouts. He yelped and then read the hull number to the person on the other end of the conversation. He informed him he also had a photo of the assailant. Ending the call, he looked at Kate. "How did you get these?"

"The security system here is the same as I have at my home and kennel. I've had a lot of practice in the last few months, capturing the faces of people who wanted me dead. I am very fast at typing in the code to have the camera capture and save strings of photos. I simply printed the best. Once I got his face as he glanced back to see how far behind you two were," she nodded at Des and Harry. "The next challenge was to capture the boat. Luckily the hull number was on the side, not the back."

"The name is usually on the rear, but I saw, when it sent up that plume of water, that a tarp had been draped over the name." George put in.

There was a minute of silence while everyone stared at the printouts of the man's face and the boat. Then Ann spoke.

"I think I've seen him before, but I don't remember where."

Oliver smiled at her. "You have, but not for a very long time. Sixty years in fact. I can confidently state that neither of the bodies in the basement is Count Grigori Baturin. The man in the photo moved very well for his age, though I noticed he double-stepped down the steps to the ramp which means he either needs or recently has had knee surgery. That dive into the boat is going to cost him dearly. He's going to be wincing for days provided he didn't sprain or break something."

Gwyn brightened. "That means that the two bodies are probably Divon Hader and Stavros Castellanos."

Oliver Bailey smiled brightly at her, getting him a scowl from Tom. "According to the records I got on Hader right before the excitement broke out, he fell from a horse at the age of ten and broke his arm and collarbone. There might be traces of the breaks even if they healed completely."

"Well, now I have names to go with the dead bodies. The second corpse that we unearthed today had an older healed break in his arm and shoulder so it is Mr. Hader who still rests in the basement and Stavros Castellanos who is a guest of the morgue."

Kate looked around the table. "We've managed to get well along into this investigation. However, there are some big problems which still need solutions. One is the fact that the count is still running around and might be a murderer, but we don't have proof. It would be nice to know where he's been all this time. Secondly, why have neither Hader nor Castellanos been missed since they disappeared, and last but not least, where is Vivian Durgin?"

-14-

Thursday Night and Friday Early Morning

Ann retired to her bedroom for the night following supper. The police team left and Des and Oliver headed to the game room to work out the bugs of their theories over the pool table. "Speaking of bugs," Kate said as they headed down the hall. "Sweep the room for bugs before you start talking about what you are going to do."

"Good idea," said Harry as he went to grab the equipment needed, then joined them. Tom and Gwyn went to explore the ballroom as Kate grabbed her coat and signaled the dogs to follow her out to the yard.

Kate sniffed the air. The snow was coming. She'd have to check the weather forecast, but she had no doubt, they would be getting snow. If the smell and feel of the air didn't tell her, the fact that her three Samoyeds were going wild sniffing the air and racing around. Samoyed weather was coming and there were three very happy Sammies who couldn't wait.

A surprise snowstorm had come through Connecticut a little over a week ago. But it had, for the most part, hugged the coast. These mountains hadn't seen a flake. According to Otto, they'd had a dusting, a couple of weeks ago but nothing you could call real snow at this level, although there had been snow in the high peaks.

Kate figured that snow would be here by late tomorrow or the next day. She should give Helen a shopping list, so she had food for their growing guest list.

The bucket of tennis balls had all three dogs frozen in place. She started hurling balls out into the yard and the game was on. Five minutes later when Quinn, acting very proud of himself, returned the final ball to the bucket, she put on the lid and put the bucket away. Then all three dogs sat as her right hand slipped into her pocket and returned with a beef jerky treat. None of them moved as they watched her break the long strip into three parts. She stepped back and said, "Stack." Three show dogs were instantly stacked, feet four-square, necks arched, muzzles level with the ground, and focused on the treat with total absorption. Telling them how good they were, they each got a treat and she headed toward the door. A sound, off on the driveway side of the yard, halted her. She held her breath and then slowly let it out when she heard the distinct thud of a cane and saw Tom and Gwyn, bundled against the cold, walking hand-in-hand toward the lake. She smiled, delighted her big brother had found someone to make him happy. Gwyn was as driven as Tom in her way, and had been so ever since they met as kids. Watching them together this week, she'd come to the conclusion they made a great team.

The sound of laughter came from the game room as she opened the kitchen door. She was glad that everyone was having a good time, but if she were honest with herself, this honeymoon stank. Sending Liam up to Ann's room, she headed for the bedroom with the other two dogs. Being shot at and threatened meant she had seen very little sleep last week, or since the wedding. Plus, she remembered with a smile, she'd had other distractions that had kept her from sleeping. The thought of an early night held a certain appeal. The dogs settled quickly after all their running around and Kate, dressed in comfortable pajamas fell asleep almost immediately. Sometime during the night, she came half-awake as Harry climbed into the bed, but the pull of sleep took her back under again.

Harry searched for Kate. He realized his five-minute check-in with the agents had turned into an hour and a half. He didn't find her in the library where he thought she and the dogs would be and checked the kitchen only to find the door locked and the lights out. He headed for the bedroom, his guilt growing with every step. When he opened the door, two dogs looked at him, but then went back to sleep. On the bed, his wife was sound asleep, not wearing one of her new nightgowns, but pajamas.

Self-condemnation swept over him. This honeymoon was

his big surprise. His bright idea. He was so sure that it would be perfect and Kate would think him wonderful. What an idiot he was. Instead, it was the world's worst. They arrived to find dead bodies and cops, followed by her family, and his old work buddies.

What was she getting out of this? Nothing.

She was working as a hostess, cooking for a crowd. Then she was being treated with dismissal by agents and forced to prove her deductive talents. To top it off, she gets pushed into a pool of freezing water. This was worse than last week when was there with a murderer after her.

Kate had been a virgin up until their marriage. She followed the teachings of her traditional Catholic family and had been taught that her virginity was a gift she should bring to her bridegroom.

He had been eager to teach her about sex and romance following the wedding. This house which she loved as a child as a backdrop for a romantic honeymoon seemed flawless.

Well, he was just going to have to do something. If they couldn't be alone and romantic here in the middle of this three-ring-circus, then they would leave. Kate had told him that though she came to the Adirondacks each year to show dogs, she didn't get to play tourist. From what he gathered, this house and the nearby dog show rings were the extent of her experience in these ancient mountains.

Making sure not to wake her, he sat in the overstuffed chair near the window and opened his laptop. Twenty minutes later he put the laptop back on top of the bureau and plugged in its charger. Then changing into sweat pants, he climbed in next to Kate. She seemed to come half-awake but then settled in to sleep again, her back to him. He lay there listening to her breathing.

When he got the call about the bodies, he should have turned around and headed to the nearest airport and flown somewhere—anywhere away from this mess.

Without waking her, he eased her up against him, his arm wrapped around her waist. It dawned on him that he'd grown to need her safe at his side to fall sleep. The warmth of her body soon seeped into his and his eyes closed.

The next morning, when Harry opened his eyes, he saw that during the night, Kate had rolled over and now was sleeping draped across him with her head on his shoulder.

He heard the dogs scratch at the sliding door to the yard. He slipped out from under her, he slid off the bed, let the dogs out. After glancing back to make sure she was still sleeping, he pulled out his go bag and a smaller suitcase from her closet in which he packed what Agnes had told him would be appropriate for what he now planned.

He put on his clothes and slipped out of the bedroom door. Liam was at the back door waiting so he added him to the party.

Toting a suitcase for each of them, he slipped out the front door and into the carriage house stowing the suitcases in the car.

Once back in the house, he headed for the kitchen, letting in the dogs. Dog food was next. He fed them, and then grabbed a tote and put dog food for a day or two inside. This he set by the front door. He had just made the batter for pancakes when

Tom, followed by Gwyn wandered in. Harry handed them coffee and told Gwyn that he had something to discuss with Tom and asked her to keep an eye on breakfast. He told her the warming oven was going, so she could move each batch there to stay warm as she poured a new batch. He left the kitchen and Tom followed.

"What's up," Tom asked.

"Your sister is having the world's worst honeymoon. She hasn't complained, but I know she's disappointed. I had planned to make her princess dream come true and instead she got a nightmare."

"I know. Gwyn said that Kate always wanted to own this as her vacation home. She said she called it her castle. I never knew a thing about that dream, but Gwyn knew," Tom grumbled.

"Little girls share their dreams. Anyway, I'm going to do something about this. Kate and I are going away overnight. We're taking Dillon and Quinn, but leaving Liam for protection. Make sure he stays close to your grandmother since this Count seems to see her as a target. Continue checking things out, but hold off letting people know we're gone until we're well away. I'll just say we're going shopping. You've got my private number but I'd like it to remain private. Right now, I'm just planning overnight. This phone," he told Tom handing him a phone from the desk drawer, "is programmed with the security codes so you can be the gatekeeper. Okay?"

"You mean is it okay for you to make my sister happy? Definitely!"

"Good, let's go eat."

When they returned to the kitchen, everyone was up and

plates were being filled with pancakes.

"I have got to get a stove like this," Gwyn told them. "Imagine all the food still hot when everything is done. That doesn't happen with the hotplate in my room above my lab."

"I can't wait until my brother Will sees it. Or better yet, cooks on it." Kate told her.

"Your brother is a good cook?" Oliver asked.

"He is as good as any five-star chef, or maybe better," she told him.

"Better." Des put in. "He catered Kate and Harry's wedding and the food was outstanding."

"You've married into a talented family, Foyle," Oliver said.

"You better believe it. And I got the best." He leaned over and kissed Kate's cheek.

As soon as breakfast was over, Harry said that he was going shopping with Kate. "There is something I want to get for her. So you guys carry on. Tom is the temporary gatekeeper while we're out."

Kate was about to ask where, when Harry looked over at her and lifted one eyebrow.

"We'll be back," she told her grandmother and pulling on her down jacket, stuffed mittens into the pockets and headed for the door. The dogs were behind them in a flash. Kate signaled Liam to guard her grandmother. Then they left, walked in silence to the garage. They got into the car and were on their way. Kate watched her surroundings change as they left Bolton. "I thought we were going shopping."

"We are," he told her, "just not here."

"Where?"

"Lake Placid." He told her as he kept an eye on his rear view mirror. No cars seemed to be following him, but it paid to be careful.

Kate watched him carefully, then switched her attention to the passenger side mirror. They had barely left Bolton when a green Ford SUV slipped into traffic about three cars back. She felt Harry slow until he was going exactly the speed limit. Over the next few minutes, all of the three cars between them and the Ford passed them. This meant the Ford was in clear view and Kate was able to see the license and memorize its number. The car sped up when they did and slowed when they did. This was going to be a problem. Their exit was coming up in a mile. Harry didn't signal but instead moved to the left lane. Not using the brakes, he took his foot off the gas and his engine began to slow the car. The Ford now was next to them in the right-hand lane and Kate noticed that the man at the wheel wore a hood pulled so far forward on his head that his face was blocked. Kate watched the exit approach fast. Just when she thought they would miss it, Harry hit his brakes and veered across the right lane, almost on the back bumper of the Ford and flew down the ramp. When he reached the bottom of the ramp, he turned right, away from Lake Placid, and forty feet down the road, which was luckily empty, did a spinning U-turn and pulled onto the shoulder and waited.

-15-

Friday Mid Morning

They arrived at Lake Placid without any more signs of the Ford. Harry pulled up under the portico of a hotel and asked the doorman if he could just leave the car while they checked in since they had an appointment in town. This being the off-season, it wasn't a problem. Kate climbed out of the car and went to the back to get the dogs. She was told where the dog exercise area was and headed in that direction while Harry checked them in. Quinn decided that this was a great place since it had tons of kids racing around. He bounced and tugged on his lead until Dillon gave one bark which translated into, "game over." Kate was just putting the dogs back into their crates when Harry returned, closed up the back and held the door for her to climb in. Then he stepped over to the doorman and showed him a piece of paper.

Kate watched the man wave his arms in different directions, pointing left and right with his hands. His final gesture seemed that their goal was next to the ski jump. Harry climbed in and pulled out of the driveway. Kate studied his face. He wasn't giving any hints, but there was an eagerness about his expression that had her anticipating whatever was coming. After several lefts then right turn, Kate looked up to see the top of the ski jump. Harry stopped, and she pulled her gaze away from the tall structure and toward a small log building wearing a sign with a carving of a dog sled. Her head snapped around to see her husband wearing a big grin.

"Let's go in. The dogs can wait here for a while."

The sign over the door read Brant Sled Hut and Sledding Training, Hiawatha Brant, owner. Harry pushed open the door setting a bell ringing. Kate stopped the minute she came in and stared. The man who emerged from the back room was huge. Though Harry surpassed him by an inch in height, in all other respect he was half again larger. Even his voice was a base so low it seemed to vibrate the logs in the floor.

"You must be Harry Foyle," he said extending his hand.

Kate was lost. She smelled the forest as they came through the door. Then suddenly, she was in a world of trees. She held her hand out as she stepped forward feeling her way into a forest but these trees surrounding her were all living second lives as sleds.

Her fingers reached out to stroke the smooth surfaces of

the runners over her head, smoothed to the point where they would fly over the snow with nothing to hold them back.

She walked deeper into this enchanted world breathing in the scent of pine and feeling the warmth of the wood. Off to the right, she saw a child's sized sled and a memory jolted her. She'd been here before. She was young, so young that she wasn't even showing dogs, maybe five or six. Her father and grandfather had been visiting someone who lived here.

They had been somewhere with lots of people but stopped at this place on the way home. She remembered wandering through the sleds the same as now, but they'd all seemed so much bigger. Then she'd seen the child's sled. She had touched it and felt it's magic. Gramps and Dad hadn't noticed her since they were talking to a man who had the information they needed.

When Gramps called her, she'd run to join them in the car and hadn't told them about the sled. It was her memory.

But now that memory came flooding back. Her fingers reached again for the child's sled, but there was no magic. It was lovely, but not special. She continued to wander until she felt herself being dragged from the main aisle toward the back, into a part of the store where there was a jumble of many sleds. A tug pulled her to the left and that was when she saw it.

Without conscious thought, she reached out and placed her hands on the sled's driving bar. Here was magic. The grip of her fingers tightened, and she closed her eyes. She felt the wind moving against her skin, her curls bouncing against her face and into her eyes. The rush of motion through the cold stung her skin as they flew over the snow. She could hear the sounds of dogs panting, dragging her sled as they raced forward, as well as the sound of children laughing—her children. A feeling of pure joy swept through her bringing tears, happy tears.

She opened her eyes and reality pushed the magic down, she lowered her head. That was when she saw it. A small Kelly-green scroll design was worked into the bed of the sled that appeared to be two S's intertwined. She felt a pull and knew she had to have this. This was the sled for her dogs. She could see it all. The children speeding over the snow, bundled against the cold as they giggled as they shouted with excitement. Kate grinned ruefully at her wild imagination, but that didn't stop her from wanting this sled.

Finally, as though emerging from a trance, she saw the big man approach with Harry.

Hiawatha said, "I must say this is a first for me. Dog sleds aren't usually bridal presents."

Harry chuckled. "Let me explain." They walked to the door and Harry stepped outside for a minute returning with Dillon and Quinn. Both dogs approached the man without any hesitation. "These are two of my wife's dozen Samoyeds."

"Now I understand." He squatted and greeted each dog individually, his hands exploring their structure. "They will both do very well though this puppy should not be put to wheel until he has grown to adult size in breadth and height. He could run on a three-dog team if you had another wheel dog like this one. He is solid muscle."

Harry saw that Kate was wandering about lost in the wonder of the more than twenty sleds on display in the place.

"And you are his bride who he wants to impress with a

special wedding gift," Hiawatha said.

"These are incredible. What a joy it would be to fly down a trail listening only to the breathing of the dogs, the swish of the runners and the beating of your heart as you speed across the surface of the snow," she said.

"It's a pleasure to meet you, Mrs. Foyle. You seem to understand my darlings here." His massive hand gently caressing the runner of the sled hanging by his shoulder. "Your husband thought you might be interested in the sled with the green design. It's for sale complete with all the harnessing and other equipment. They are highly polished with five layers of polyurethane to make the wood this smooth. The wood has been steam bent into shape before it was polished. The joining has been done with dowels rather than screws since metal reacts differently from wood at extremely low temperatures. This one is a perfect weight and shape for your Samoyeds, though the puppy must wait until he grows more before being set to wheel position. He can learn to be lead though. His enthusiasm would be perfect there."

She felt Harry's arm come around her. "This must be the one for you? I saw that you were pulled toward it."

"Oh, yes, and Harry, I remembered being here before when I was a small child. I was with Gramps and Dad. They had to ask this man questions and I wandered through the sleds."

Hiawatha asked, "Who were your father and grandfather?"

"John and Tom Killoy."

He stood silent staring at her and then nodded. "It was a dark time for our tribe. They were helping track down the theft of a great deal of money that had been stolen and which the tribe needed. They were friends with my uncle which was the only reason I spoke to them. I was so angry over the attack on my people. Winter was here and the tribe would not make it without that money."

"Did they find it?" Harry asked.

A huge smile broke out across his face. "Yes, they did and what's more, they didn't charge the tribe anything. They just said they wanted to see justice done."

An hour later, they headed away from the shop back toward the center of Lake Placid. Kate's sled was tightly attached to the luggage rack on the top of the car and the middle seat was piled with several boxes of equipment. Kate sat back and smiled at Harry. "This is perfect," she told him. She was about to say something else when her stomach rumbled.

Harry laughed. "I agree with your stomach. I'm starved. Let's go park the car at the hotel and wander the town. We can find a place to eat and see the sights. I wonder how your grandfather met Hiawatha's uncle. I doubt it was through dog shows."

"No, Gramps told me that he had a friend who was a Mohawk Indian at Winter School when he was there. Though they led very different lives, they stayed in touch."

"Winter School where he learned to climb mountains in the snow and sleep outdoors in sub-freezing temperatures."

"That's the one."

"I admire him for it, but I think I've lost any desire for sleeping out in the world of snow and ice since if it hadn't been for you, I'd have died, frozen in the snow."

"I couldn't let you die," she told him. "We had a wedding

coming up at the end of the week and I had no intention of being stood up at the altar by a frozen groom."

When they arrived back at the hotel, Harry cruised the parking lot until he found what he wanted. The car slipped into a space behind a van also sporting a dog sled. Releasing the dogs from the back, he and Kate started toward the center of town. Lake Placid was dressed for Christmas. From every light, post there hung a wreath and most of the storefronts wore garlands and other decorations. Kate noticed that most store entrances had their awnings open to keep snow from building up in front of their doorways. The sidewalks were brick in a herringbone design giving the place an old fashion and festive atmosphere everywhere. The book store and shops with clothing were crowded.

They found a place to grab lunch with tables set outside for those who wanted to watch the mountains. Since they had the dogs with them, Kate sat at one of the tables while Harry went inside to get their food. The dogs loved the attention they drew from everyone walking by. She had been there only a few minutes when she spotted a familiar green SUV turn the corner and watched as it moved slowly in her direction. She shot to her feet and quickly stepped toward a store next to the restaurant. By the shop's front doors were small Christmas trees in planters on the sidewalk. Kate told both dogs to heel and stepped up close to the tree nearest her. Positioning herself as though she were looking in the shop window, she nudged the dogs a few steps forward until they were hidden from the street by her body and the tree. Kate pulled up the hood on her parka and watched the progress of the green Ford reflected in the store's window. It crawled down the street, annoying the drivers behind it but did not seem to take notice of a woman window-shopping. Turning her head slightly she watched as it passed by, and hoped that Harry wouldn't step out of the restaurant until the SUV was gone. She watched the car turn at the corner then heard Harry's voice behind her saying, "Let's go and hurry."

Five minutes later, they were crossing the lobby of the hotel. Kate gazed at a table featuring hot cider and cookies as they headed for the bank of elevators, but they didn't slow. Harry opened the door of the room and placed the bags of food out of reach of the puppy. Then he shed his coat, pulled off Kate's and wrapped his arms around her. "You are the smartest woman in the world. The trick with the Christmas tree was brilliant. I had just reached the restaurant door when I spotted the car and noticed you were no longer sitting at the table."

"What if he finds out that we're staying here?"

"We're not. I used one of my other identities to register. And I listed the dogs as Finnish Boazovazzi."

Kate laughed. "So you told them they were Finnish reindeer herding dogs."

"Well, they are sort of. Let's eat." Harry laid out the food on the table by the windows which overlooked the mountains, the Olympic venue and even the swimming pool below. They relaxed and ate, unwinding from their scare. When the burgers and sweet potato fries were polished off, Harry pulled out a second bag which contained slices of still-warm apple pie and a thermos of hot cocoa.

"You're pushing all the right buttons with this lunch, Foyle," Kate said as she grinned at him. Then the grin slipped. "How are we going to keep this guy from spotting us?"

"Simple. I've already arranged for a romantic dinner for two in our room for my bride and me tonight and tomorrow, we will be heading back. Now I don't know about you, but I could use a hot shower and a nap after all this excitement."

Kate put tension on hold. Harry had saved their honeymoon, and she was ready for a little relaxation. "What a wonderful idea. You're a genius, Mr. Foyle."

"And you, Mrs. Foyle, are beautiful in what you are wearing, but I know you're more beautiful out of it. Let me help you with all those buttons."

-16-

Friday Night and Saturday Early Morning

The next few hours allowed Harry to teach Kate what a honeymoon should be. Their romantic dinner arrived but generated more laughter than wistful sighs.

When they settled for the night, Kate decided she wanted to talk to Harry about what happened in Hiawatha's shop.

"Harry, I'm going to tell you something. Please don't think I'm crazy."

"You are the sanest person I know and the smartest."

Kate took a breath and watched his face as she began to tell him what happened. When she got to describing the feeling the wind blowing, hearing the dogs panting and the giggles of children, Harry's face split into a grin, and he swept her into a hug, kissing her.

"Sweetheart, that's wonderful."

"But, I felt that I was there. It was real."

"I know. It's wonderful."

"Wonderful?"

"It could mean you are pregnant with our first child."

"You don't think I'm nuts?"

"No. Kate, but I do know you are more sensitive to things than the average person. When we first met, last February, you told me that you could feel your father and grandfather's hands on your shoulders when you needed them. You are tuned into those two men far more than anyone. They died, but I don't think they left you. In some way, they are still looking over you, like guardian angels. I might have questioned today, if I didn't think that it was a place where those two had been before while doing good. They brought you there. I think their connection is still with you and I think they were allowing you a peek at what is going to happen in your life."

"You are unbelievable.

"When is your next period?"

"Next Tuesday."

"Then we'll wait until next week. But from all that you've told me about those two men, I have every confidence in them."

"You're the one who is nuts."

"You said the giggles of children. Children. Not child, children. Twins run in your family."

"Harry, we have been married for less than a week and you have me pregnant with twins? Let's change the subject."

"Okay, what shall we talk about?" he asked snuggling her closer and kissing the top of her head.

"Christmas. What are we going to do about Christmas? It's less than three weeks from now. I don't know about you, but I am feeling very 'Bah Humbug' at the moment. Christmas is my favorite holiday and I haven't been able to do anything about it because of these dead bodies and our killer Count. Not to be whiny, but I want my holiday back. Even if it's just decorating the house, I don't care. But I don't want to let a murderer stop me from celebrating. We're getting snow tomorrow and I want to go back to the house, decorate it and take people out for dog sled rides on my Christmas present if they are still hanging around. Maybe they will have figured it out while we were away."

"Tom has this number. He'd have called, if they had."

"Rats. Okay, I vote we take the dogs out, and pack tonight. We can get a good night sleep, since you are so good at making me sleepy, and head out early tomorrow. We might even be able to avoid the green Ford."

"Sounds like a plan."

They went down to the back entrance and Harry checked before they took the dogs outside. Both Dillon and Quinn took care of business right away. Kate had trained Dillon to do this as soon as they got to a show, and he apparently had passed the word to his son. Kate watched them sniff the air. They were definitely excited. "Harry, we're going to get snow tonight and the way these two are behaving, it will be a lot of snow. How early can we check out?"

"Well, we can leave at any time. The bill has been paid."

"I vote we get some sleep and get up at five o'clock, so we could be home by breakfast."

"Perfect. Maybe the man with the green Ford will still be asleep."

There was already about three inches of snow on the ground when they left. Luckily the roads were well plowed, so they had no trouble making good time back to Bolton. In addition, they were the only car on the road. They rolled up to the gates and Kate opened them and closed them once they were through. It was good to see that Otto had plowed the driveway. Harry pulled into the carriage house, leaving the sled on the car roof. He grabbed the suitcases and Kate got the dogs and their food bag, and they headed inside. When they unlocked the door, Liam was waiting for them and as Kate unclipped leads the dogs set off to romp together. The light was on in the kitchen but nobody was there. Quinn came flying into the kitchen with his squeaky hedgehog. They'd left it behind on their trip, and he missed it.

Kate immediately put on the kettle for tea and took out eggs, milk and flour for pancakes. Then she pulled out bacon and sausage.

Harry found a couple of Helen's coffee cakes in the freezer and put them into the microwave to thaw. Once everything was cooking, he wrapped his arms around Kate and whispered, "I can't wait until next Tuesday."

Her face turned red, and she swatted him, though a smile crept onto her face. "Behave yourself. I need tea."

"I could use some tea as well," a voice from the kitchen doorway. Kate swirled around. Vivian Durgin stood there, snow still on her boots.

"Vivian, where have you been?"

"Oh, here and there. I thought that I'd drop by and see how you two are getting on. This is a big house to be alone in," she told them.

"Well, speaking of being in this house, Vivian, how did you get in?" Harry asked.

"I live here. Why shouldn't I get in? It's where those I care about are."

Kate watched her face and said, "That would be Divon and Stavros."

"They couldn't be left unguarded. I had to keep watch over them."

"Did Grigori ask you to guard them?"

"Don't call him Grigori. His name is Count Grigori Baturin. You must show him respect. He is royalty. He is a great man." As she said this, she reached into her pocket and pulled out a small very shiny gun.

Harry stiffened, but Kate reached for his hand a squeezed it halting his move. Her eyes watched Vivian but also noticed the dogs now silently moving up behind her. Kate smiled at her. "Could you please put that gun away? I don't like guns."

"No, I don't think so. You see, I have to come back and guard. I have to keep you from telling anyone. Grigori wouldn't like me to tell anyone." She lifted the gun just as Kate said, "Stick."

Vivian screamed in pain as the dog ripped the gun from her

hand and at the same time, Des appeared behind her grabbing her furious and struggling body. Two seconds later, a hand slapped her across her face hard, twice.

"You filthy bitch. You selfish worthless spoiled bitch. You crazy, warped, idiot. I hope they lock you up and throw the key away. If you get anywhere near my granddaughter again, I will kill you myself. Gwyn, patch up her hand and call Gil. I want her out of here." Ann pushed past her and walked over to Kate wrapping her in a hug. "I am so sorry I brought you anywhere near my corrupt family."

"Gram, what we need to know is how did she get in. She walked in with snow on her boots without a blink. We've had all the locks changed. How did she manage it? If she can get in, the Count can as well. See if you can find out while Gwyn patches up her hand."

"She won't tell me. She knows I hate her."

"Give it a try. You might want to take one of the dogs with you," Kate told her with a slight smile.

Ann looked at her and she flashed a malicious grin. "You are as sneaky as your grandfather. I always loved that about him. Come on boys. We have someone to intimidate."

Harry watched Kate turn back to the stove. She picked up the bowl holding the pancake batter and stirred. After testing the heat of the griddle, she poured out neat circles of batter.

Kate had been shot at and threatened with a gun multiple times. She had been shot and hit, though thankfully that time she had been wearing a bullet proof vest. But he knew that these threats took a toll on her. So he waited and watched. He knew what would come.

She moved around the kitchen with ease, putting breakfast together, and had just finished cutting the bread and putting it into the toaster when he saw it. She stopped. Not stopping what she was doing but stopped all movement. He knew she was still breathing because of the keening sound which came from her as she stared straight ahead. He was out of his chair in an instant whipping the spatula out of her hand and passing it to Tom. "Finish breakfast. Excuse us." With that he swept her up into his arms and quickly headed for their bedroom. He slammed the door behind him and placed her on the bed, pulling off her boots and kicking off his own.

Crawling onto the bed next to her, he pulled the heavy quilt from the bottom of the bed up over her and wrapped his arms around her. He rocked her gently, waiting it out. After about five minutes, he began muttering what he hoped were consoling words. "Kate, darling. Come back to me. We have much to do. You've got to create Christmas here. We'll get the tree up and decorate it. And we'll get the sled off the top of the car and hitch up the dogs. It may take a while to get Quinn settled enough so we don't go flying across the lawn at eighty miles an hour, but he'll settle. I've never done Christmas, Kate. Christmas was always a time when people went away to their homes and I had extra time to study or work on research. I need you to teach me. And Kate, next Tuesday is coming. I can barely wait until Tuesday. I love you so much."

Harry heard the door open and looked up to see Ann staring at him, her face gray with shock. Tom, Gwyn and Des were behind her.

Des was saying to Ann, "She's been through this before.

She'll come out of it. When she was shot, it took longer, but just wait, and she'll be fine."

Ann turned to him. "She was shot? When was she shot?"

Des seemed to realize he'd said more than he should have. He hadn't realized that Kate and Harry had hidden the horrors they'd been through from her family. Shifting his feet, he muttered, "She wasn't hurt more that bruising. She was wearing the bulletproof-vest Sadie had sent her under her clothes, so when the bastard pulled the trigger, his bullet bruised her ribs, but that was that. Harry says that in spite of saying she wouldn't, Sadie sent her a new vest as a wedding present."

They all turned to stare at the bed when they heard Kate mutter, "You're really hung up on Tuesday."

Harry grinned at her. "You bet I am. Are you feeling better?"

"Yes, I'm back. How long was I gone this time?"

"A little over ten minutes. Not too bad. I hope you're hungry. Tom took over making the pancakes."

"I'm starving. I hope I didn't scare anybody."

Harry looked at the crowd standing in the doorway. "You just startled the ones who have not heard your keening song. I think you may need to have a talk with your grandmother. She didn't know about your history with people wanting you dead. It's been a shock for her."

Kate followed Harry's line of sight to the crowd in the doorway. Feeling embarrassed, she said, "I'm sorry if I scared you folks. It turns out I have an allergy to guns. I flake out when they are pointed at me. There is nothing I can take for it so as with poison ivy, I try to avoid all contact with people who like to use them. I feel fine, except that I'm starving. All I've had to eat since we got up in the wee small hours was a cup of tea. We wanted to beat the storm back and avoid the guy who trailed us to Lake Placid."

"Someone followed you to Lake Placid?" Des asked.

"A green Ford SUV. The driver wearing a hoodie with the hood pulled so far forward you couldn't see his face. However, Harry, with some of the flashiest driving I've ever seen outside of the movies, and lost him on the way to Lake Placid. Later we spotted him in town, but managed to hide. Since we left before dawn, we didn't see him on the way back."

" Kate will give Gil the license plate number and see what he can find." Harry helped Kate get up and everyone headed to the kitchen. The house was quiet. "Where is everyone?" he asked.

"Gil and George took Miss Durgin to the courthouse. She will be seen by a judge and then either put in jail or a hospital, under guard." Des told him. "The guys ate and are in the game room, working. It seems that our Count may still be in the game."

"Working for...?"

"Russia."

"Interesting."

"Fascinating, I'm sure but spies can wait, I need food," Kate said. Everyone laughed as Kate linked her arm with her grandmother, and headed for the kitchen.

-17-

Saturday Morning

Kate dug into a big stack of pancakes plus home fries and sausage with applesauce. Harry joined her after he got them each a cup of tea. As they were finishing, Gill and George returned and everyone drifted back into the kitchen until the table was full. "Well, they've put Miss Durgin into a psych ward under twenty-four-hour observation since she did try to murder you two. There is still no trace of Baturin. Des said that you two were followed by someone to Lake Placid."

"Yes, Gil, I wrote down the license number, color, and model for you. He may have realized by now that we're not there and be heading back, though the snow seems to be mounting up." Kate told him.

George informed them that he might have to fill in on storm duty since this one is now predicted to drop over a foot, maybe even a foot and a half. "At this rate, we won't need cars, we'll need dog sleds."

Kate and Harry laughed. When people stared at them, Harry explained that the trip to Lake Placid was to get Kate's Christmas present, a dog sled.

"You went to see Hiawatha?" George asked.

"Yes, the place is magical," Kate told him.

"It certainly is."

Harry stood and moved behind Kate. "That was the second reason for our trip. I know that it's been forgotten in all the fuss, but this is our honeymoon which so far has consisted of two dead bodies, and meaning no offense, two cops, two FBI, a forensic pathologist, a brother-in-law, and grandmother. This was not the honeymoon I planned. Plus, Kate reminded me that Christmas is right around the corner. We need to wrap this up fast. I'm putting Sadie and my people on it. Ann, I would like you to contact as many people you know who might have been at the party back then. Sadie will help you with contacts. We need to know where Baturin has been for sixty years. From what Vivian said to us, he's been able to keep her here to watch over the bodies all this time. Ann, did you have any success in finding how she got into the house?"

"None. Though, now that she realizes that Dillon is around, I suspect, she won't try that again."

Gil cleared his throat. "About that. We have ordinances here concerning dog bites. Though I'm sure it was justified, he will need to be taken and quarantined until a judgment is made."

Kate's back straightened. "Excuse me, Gil, but is that the case when one of your cops injures a criminal during an active crime takedown?"

"No, but they are police officers."

"Harry, could you hand me my purse, please?"

Harry smiled and reached for her purse on the counter behind him and pulled out her wallet, handing it to her. She reached into her wallet and pulled out a laminated card and a badge slapping them on the table in front of Gil. "Dillon holds the rank of sergeant in the state of Connecticut, but he is also a licensed police officer in New York and the rest of New England. He spends most of his time demonstrating training techniques with police officers in the Northeast, but he has seen active duty multiple times during the past year."

"Including at their wedding," Des added, now grinning. "If it hadn't been for Dillon and Quinn, these two wouldn't be here. Since the top brass of the FBI has seen the dog in action, I think there might be an objection to quarantining him."

"Fine. I'll just explain things to my boss."

"Gwyn. Did you ever find the bullet which killed the second man?" Harry asked.

"Not yet. I was going to do some sifting down there this morning."

"Good. I've got a feeling that it will be from a different gun. It's just a suspicion, but I would be interested."

"I'll get on it."

"Oh, and before you lovely ladies go, maybe you could do

something about bringing some Christmas cheer to the place this afternoon. There must be some decorations somewhere."

They all smiled. Ann said, "There were wonderful decorations for both inside and out. I think that most of them are in the attic. Come to think of it, except for my finding the gowns, which led to me being attacked, the attic hasn't been searched at all. After lunch, we can kill two birds with one stone and search both for clues and decorations."

"Great." Both Kate and Gwyn said together.

Kate fed the dogs and cleared up the dishes as Harry talked to Sadie. She was furious that their honeymoon had turned into a disaster.

He stressed that the sooner they could get this solved the more likely they'd be to have some time alone.

Kate pulled a plastic bag off the counter. With the dogs sitting in a row, she opened the bag holding a glove that Vivian had dropped when she went for her gun and let them sniff. Dillon growled in the back of his throat. "My sentiments exactly, Big Guy, but I need you to backtrace this. I know Quinn hasn't tried this at all and you two have only each tried it once, but what the hey. Let's see if we can find her trail back. BACK SEARCH." This was something she'd been planning to add to the training, but so far, it had been a hard go.

Dillon and Liam immediately went to the front door, where Vivian had been last. Quinn wandered around aimlessly, doing his puppy thing then he went wandering down the hall and pawed at the door to the hidden stair. Kate looked a Harry, cocked her head and opened the secret door. He was through it like a shot and running down the stairs.

Kate quickly headed after him while Harry called the other Sams. By the time they were through the door and heading down the stairs, Kate had reached Quinn who was standing on his hind legs, pawing at the wall. Someone had painted a mural of people in various bathing suits romping on the side of a pool with greenery behind. Kate saw hooks that had held towels running along the wall but no amount of pulling or wiggling released a door. Harry, reached up toward the ceiling and felt a slight draft. He slid his hand to the left and after a few seconds, the draft stopped. He marked that spot with his left hand and moved right. This time the draft didn't stop until his arms were about a yard apart. The fact that the draft was only coming through a horizontal crack near the ceiling puzzled him until he realized that the hooks were for pulling the door closed. Sliding his hands down to waist height, he shoved. A highly insulated door opened showing him why the draft was only on the top. The door went all the way to the ceiling where there wasn't the same room for insulation.

Quinn, Dillon, and Liam rushed through the door and down the stairs beyond the landing. Kate and Harry raced to follow. The trail leveled out into a dirt-floored hallway. Quinn was moving fast, barking for them to keep up. Harry panted as they ran, "I think we have left the house and are under the driveway. If this is heading where I think it is, I pretty sure I know where our Russian has been hiding. Just in case, let me go first." He pulled out his gun and made sure Kate was tucked in behind him. Quinn's barks suddenly changed, and they saw that the hallway had ended in a flight of stairs. "Kate, call the dogs back."

She called them, though Quinn was reluctant. Once they were all at her side, with her firm grip on Quinn's collar, Harry stepped forward and reached for a latch holding the door shut. The door swung open. The room beyond was empty except for a cast iron stove to one side. He checked for heat but found none. Quinn wiggled free from Kate's grasp and bounced over to the door.

"So, Vivian came in through here tracking snow on her boots, went through the tunnel and strolled into the house," Kate muttered to herself. She looked out the window and saw Otto and Helen's house maybe fifty yards away. If someone used this stove, they would have to have known unless...she turned and crossed to the first door off the main room, a bathroom. The second room was a closet that held an electric heater, a hot plate, a tea kettle, and an ice chest which served as a pantry holding a lot of canned and dried foods. Walking back to the windows she noticed room darkening shades and curtains. "Provided that someone didn't mind eating processed food while Vivian had company, this would be a perfect hideout. Once people left and if you knew Helen's cleaning schedule, it would be no problem staying in the main house."

"Do you think that the Count and Vivian were living together?" Harry asked.

"No. I think that the Count was giving her crumbs, to get her to stay here and keep his secret, but Vivian didn't get that dotty from getting regular sex. I think that it was a case of him telling her, "If you care about this you'd...fill in the blank with whatever request you like. I think it was a carrot and stick arrangement. Let's go back. I need to talk to Gram."

Kate called Quinn to join her and the other two dogs. With a hand signal from her, they sat. Then she lavished on the praise and presented each dog with a beef jerky treat. Walking to the tunnel door she said, "Okay, go to the house." The dogs dashed down the steps and headed back along the tunnel. She turned to see Harry padlocking the latch of the cabin. He followed her into the tunnel and padlocked that latch as well.

"That's clever to think to bring locks."

"I think there are some extra two-by-fours in the basement. I will nail the door at the pool hook end shut and that should slow them down a bit."

Kate was quiet while they walked back.

Harry watched and wanted to ask what she was thinking, but he knew she had her process. She'd disappear into her head and then as Tom calls it, she'd come up with a plan. If it wasn't the answer, she'd figure a road map to find the answer.

By the time they reached the hall by their bedroom, her feet were dragging.

I need to talk to Sadie," Harry said. "We left very early this morning. You might want to go lie down for a while. If you fall asleep, I'll wake you for lunch."

"I'd feel guilty about lying down at ten-thirty in the morning, but I am exhausted, so you don't need to ask me twice. I'll see you at lunchtime."

She went into the bedroom and Harry sent the dogs after her. With all that had been happening, he wasn't taking a chance on leaving her alone. He watched while she kicked off her boots and crawled under the covers. He turned back toward the kitchen and then went down to the cellar. Soft voices could be heard coming from the far end of the large room. As he reached the bottom of the stairs, he noticed that Gwyn had laid out an old door across two sawhorses and was using it as an impromptu table to layout her bones. He had no sooner reached the bottom of the stairs when there was a shout of "Eureka!"

"You found it," came the other voice which Harry now identified as Tom.

"Your brother-in-law is a genius."

Harry laughed as he approached. "Well, I'm glad to see somebody here likes me. How am I a genius?"

"The two bullets, when viewed through my comparison microscope are indeed different which indicates different guns and perhaps different shooters. I would like to tell you from which gun the bullets were fired, but as of now, the law requiring firing pins to be stamped with serial numbers hasn't been passed. It's all very well to find the bullet and possibly be able to lift a usable print with fuming and other methods we use now, but a system which would stamp a bullet saying it came from a specific gun during the firing process, would be much better."

"When will that happen?"

"When the gun manufacturers are required to do it. I only know that it would make my job a lot easier as well as Gil's and the judge in any trial."

"But with what you've been able to get so far, do you have any idea what kind of gun we're looking at?"

"Well, I was able to eliminate any manufactured after 1959. That still leaves a lot. I am also focusing on handguns since we are assuming that it happened during that party weekend. Those people were here for a party, not to hunt deer. So, I'm inclined to think it would be a small automatic which would fit in someone's pocket, even if that person was wearing a tux."

Harry watched his brother-in-law gaze at Gwyn with something close to awe. He suspected that their minds worked similarly. He also suspected that Tom had found his soulmate.

"Any ideas what gun would go with this bullet?"

"One that would fit the bill in the timeline, would be the Beretta 950 Jetfire. It takes a .25 ACP cartridge which this is and it was less than five inches long. It came out in the fifties, so it would have been available and it was used for police and undercover work because it could be hidden. The other bullet was a .45 caliber. Since it was standard on the Colt M1911 or 'Government' as it was called, it's a possibility. That gun is a standard-issue single-action semi-automatic recoil-operated pistol and was issued in wars since WWI and is still used now. Browning designed it and it's proved itself to be a good gun for soldiers to use as a sidearm. Since so many have been manufactured, it is readily available. Now I'm just guessing at possible guns, but these are possibilities and might give the powers-that-be an idea of hypothetical murder weapons."

"You know a lot about guns. What kind do you own?"

"Oh, I don't own a gun. I see too much damage done by them to contribute to the carnage. I just study them for fun and to help with the job."

Tom asked, "Where's Kate? Did you come down here to check on what Gwyn had found?"

"I hope Kate is sleeping. I came down looking for some

tools and a two-by-four board to blockade a secret doorway. We found how Vivian got in and probably the Count as well. Since surprise visits from them can be deadly, I'd like to cut off access to the house."

Gwyn pointed. "Boards and power tools are in the room over there, second door from the stairs. When is lunch, by the way?"

"As soon as I finish the door unless a certain Killoy male who has just been sitting around would like to volunteer."

"You go seal that door and keep my sister alive," Tom said. "I'll go cook."

-18-

Saturday Afternoon

Kate woke slowly. She hadn't planned to sleep but Harry seemed to know her better than she knew herself. She realized that the noise which woke her was Quinn at the sliding door out to the dog yard. Sitting up she walked to look out. It was light enough to see that the snow which was already about six inches deep was unbroken. There were no tracks of anyone up to no good, so Kate turned to the dogs and asked, "Who wants out?" All three dogs bounced against the door. She slid it open, and they flew out at top speed, racing in circles and plowing through the snow.

A minute later behind her, the door opened and Harry

walked in.

"I figured you were awake when I saw Quinn fly by the kitchen window. I was on my way to wake you. Tom has cooked lunch and it smells good. Did you sleep?"

"Yes. You knew I would."

He wrapped his arms around her, and they both watched the antics of the dogs. Their pure joy showed in racing flat out at high speed, throwing snow up behind them. 'Did your brain have any luck in solving the problem which was bothering you?"

"I think so. But I need food before I explain. I also need to talk to Gram."

"Let's go eat." He kissed her and then wrapping his arm around her waist, headed for the kitchen.

Food seemed to do the trick of gathering everyone together. The pups were let in, and they brought a ton of snow on their coats. They shook and had people hopping out of the way as the snow flew onto everyone. Kate grabbed towels from the grooming room and dried the dogs while Ann passed out dish towels for the rest to dry themselves.

The shepherd's pie, which Tom made was dished up, people began to eat. Gwyn told the guys about finding the other bullet and the fact that it didn't match.

"So we have to look for two killers," Oliver said.

"Maybe." Kate turned and looked at Ann. "Gram, is there anything else you wish to share about that night. I know that you and Gramps left, but you didn't say goodbye, did you? You snuck out. Made a run for it. You wanted to be as far away from what was happening as possible. When did you realize that there was something criminal going on?"

Ann looked away. Kate reached across the table and took Ann's hand. "When you are ready to tell us why you two ran, we will listen and not judge."

Oliver looked at Ann and said, "I have discovered something that might prove your decision was a wise one. I've been checking into the single men who were there that evening but were not shot. Not being shot does not mean they were unhurt. Of the nine survivors of the evening, I have so far been able to track three where I could get a detailed picture of their lives from that time. One had a severe financial hit to his businesses which effectively made him no longer considered well off. Another was injured in a car accident and is still in a wheelchair. The third married but his wife was murdered in a drive-by shooting a year later. I am still working down the list but I'm finding that these men are keeping a low profile."

Ann slumped in her chair. Her face white. Tom made her a fresh cup of tea, but Harry held him back for a second while he pulled the brandy bottle from the cupboard and added some to the cup. "Drink this, Gram. All of it."

Gwyn reached for her wrist to check her pulse and nodded to Des to get her bag.

As Kate stood to go to Ann, her phone dinged as did Harry's. He pulled his out and headed for the front door saying, "It's Gil and George. They may have been freed from storm duty for a while." He walked through the entry and pulled the door open in time to see Otto in the new truck doing a neat job clearing the entrance. The driveway was cleared as well but would need plowing again soon with this amount of snow coming down. He waved at Otto who paused his plow long enough to tell Harry how much he liked the new truck. Harry gave him a thumbs up and let the two police officers in.

Locking the door, he led the way to the kitchen.

"Mrs. Killoy, don't take offense, but your cousin is totally bat shit. The doctor is throwing around words like possible Obsessive-compulsive Disorder."

"She told us while pointing the gun at me," Kate said, "that she had to be here to take care of things. When I asked her about the bodies, she said that the Count told her she must guard them, and she was willing to kill us to accomplish that. Which brings me to a question I wanted to ask you, Gram. When Harry and I first went to visit her in the nursing home, I told her about us waltzing by ourselves in the ballroom. She got very sentimental. She said she waltzed with a young man in the empty ballroom once. Kate thought it was enchanting but it turned out not to be. After that, her father didn't let anybody use the ballroom except for big dinners. There were no more balls. You said that Vivian had fallen for Divon."

"Possibly. Let me explain why we left that night. On the day of the ball, there had been sleigh rides before luncheon. Tom and I had returned, and he went to his room to begin packing because he had to be back on campus in two days and wanted to see his sister in New York City before he headed to Boston. There was only one train on Christmas day, so he had to be up early to catch it. I had planned to stay until my father arrived for New Year's Eve and then go home with him.

"I went looking for Vivian who I hadn't seen. When I neared the library, I heard angry voices. One of them was my uncle but several other male voices were involved. I couldn't help but overhear. It took me a minute to get the drift of the disagreement. It was something about plans, locks and diamonds and the upheaval that would be caused. I didn't understand what they were talking about but then I heard one of the men tell my uncle that if anyone at this party got a whiff of what they were doing, they'd all hang. My uncle said if anyone found out, eliminate them. That was when I heard someone coming, so I dashed down the hall and ran up the hidden staircase.

"I found Tom's room and talked him into leaving then and there. We quickly packed my things, and then we waited until everyone was gathering for tea in the drawing-room and went out the back and found one of the chauffeurs. We told him we had to take a train because we'd had a call that Tom's family had a medical emergency. Tom and I just caught the train to New York. Tom had gotten a call from his roommate about meeting him in the city to take the train together back to Boston so if anyone had asked if we had really gotten a call—we had."

Ann sighed and looked around the table, returning her gaze to her granddaughter. "I should have been upfront about this before, but your grandfather and I decided that in this one case, ignorance, or the appearance of ignorance might save us from being dragged into a deadly situation. Letting the driver, the train conductor, and your great aunt all know that we weren't there that night might have kept us alive. It was a cowardly thing to do, but Tom was frightened. Just the fact that we'd been there at the beginning of the weekend might put a target on our backs. When nobody came to question us and there was no scandal, we figured we could get married and settle in Connecticut. Any contact I had with my family after that would be from a position of pure ignorance. But it seems our staying silent now threatens you. I'm so sorry, Katie."

The women spent the afternoon in the attic finding Christmas decorations, and the others sat in the library working at getting information about the other players in the Christmas Ball farce. Oliver was especially thorough in checking each man's whereabouts and activities. Tom was working on their financial status and Des was searching for possible crimes that had occurred in that time period. The sounds of laughter distracted them and Harry, who had been running his own trace on the Count was the first to investigate. When they stepped into the front hall, piles of greenery lay on the floor and more was being carried in by Ollie as the women came down the stairs carrying boxes of ornaments, ribbons, and garlands.

Harry asked Ollie about the greenery. It seemed the family used to decorate the house every year and had a supplier in town to handle the greenery. In the last few years they hadn't done it, but when Kate told Helen what she wanted to do, Helen called the nursery and the truck had just arrived.

"Stand to one side, everyone," Ollie shouted. He threw open the huge front door and the bottom of a pine tree entered being carried by one man. By the time the top of the tree passed through the doorway, six men stood gently lowering the tree to the floor. It was huge. Des doubted it would fit. The nursery owner declared it would be perfect since he had been putting this size tree in this entry for near forty years.

He looked around and then asked Kate to bring him the

blue box with the white ribbon around it. She did, and he opened the box and unwrapped the most beautiful star any of them had ever seen. He fixed it to the top of the tree, adding an extra clamp that had been in the box to hold it in place.

The men had found boxes of lights, unwound them into four long strings and with one man holding the strings at the top and four each holding one at the bottom, the owner and Otto rolled the tree across the foyer causing the strands to wind perfectly around the tree. When done, the four ends plugged into a master controller which was attached to the bottom of the tree.

The stand, which Otto had brought from the carriage house, was attached and with all hands on deck, and some handy clamps on poles, the tree was lifted into place, the branches were freed from their ropes, the tree was shaken to settle the ropes of lights and it was done.

A plug found in the entry floor was uncovered and the lights were plugged in.

Helen said, "Kate and Harry come over to the wall beside the library door." She pointed to a normal light switch which nobody had noticed. When they flipped the switch, the tree lit up including the star on top.

Ann told everyone it had been specially made by a famous craftsman, caught all the lights giving the effect that each point of the star radiated its own shimmer and seemed to be in constant motion.

Kate stood with Harry's arms wrapped around her staring up at the star. All around them, laughter filled the air while the workmen carried out the boss's directions and in less than an hour, they and all their guests got to decorate the tree. Kate and Harry pitched in and the halls were decked inside and out. Kate was fascinated with the unique ornaments. Though there were the usual glass balls, angels, and reindeer, the ornaments that seemed to have been collected from around the world fascinated Kate. Their workmanship was exquisite and with many, the sparkle picked up the lights and sent arrows of color bouncing off the walls. It was enchanting. Helen served hot cider to everyone when they finished and sent each of the workmen away with a small box wrapped and tied with ribbon containing her special Christmas fruitcake.

It was magical, everyone agreed.

Harry thanked Otto and Helen for making Kate's Christmas dream happen. After hugs all around, Ann announced she had decided to take charge of dinner with Tom and Gwyn's help.

Harry had spoken to George earlier about coming over when he went off duty for the day. He arrived to help Harry and Des unload the sled from the car and get the harnesses properly attached. Finally, with Liam and Dillon in harness and with Quinn, just running free, Kate reviewed what Hiawatha had told her with George, who had competed in races with his Malamutes.

Then, with Harry climbing on for the first ride, they were off across the lawn speeding toward the gate. When they met up with the driveway, which had several inches of snow covering it since last plowed, Kate gave the dogs a command to turn, and they neatly transitioned to follow the driveway through the trees and back to space in front of the portico. They all took turns as passengers with George and Kate trading off as driver and on the last two rounds, they even were able to take a now calmer Quinn and get him to work as lead dog.

Gwyn came to the door, as they finished the final round, to tell them that dinner was in twenty minutes so the sled was put away in the carriage house, the harnesses hung up to dry and the dogs brought inside to be dried and fed. Harry went into the bedroom to find the spare charger they'd brought since he'd depleted his phone's battery taking so many photos. When he came back he was carrying some papers.

Everyone was sitting around the table. Kate looked up and noticed they were the ones she'd thrown in the bureau drawer to be read when she had time, but she'd forgotten about them.

"Kate, are you planning to rob a bank in your spare time?" he asked.

Kate stared at him. "What are you talking about?"

"Are these your papers?"

"They're the ones I found the other day. I hadn't had time to read them. I assumed they had been in the house forever and was going to check them out."

Harry handed the papers to Oliver and asked, "Is this what I think it is?"

"My God. I've been looking for this for years. Where did you find it? Were there more?" He leaped up but Ann called "Stop. Sit. Nobody leaves the table until I say so." Tom grinned at Kate remembering the hundreds of times they'd heard those words growing up. "The papers will still be there after you have consumed this delicious dinner. Oliver sat and the conversation returned to the decorations and sledding. After dessert was consumed, Ann stood and indicated that everyone follow her.

-19-

Saturday Evening

Ann made herself comfortable in the wing-back chair facing the fireplace in the sitting room. Then as everyone gathered around, she ran her hands around the hassock until she found the latch. Pressing it, she lifted the top and revealed sacks of papers, notebooks, and after these were removed, at the very bottom lay two handguns.

"I was right," Gwyn shouted pumping her arm in the air. "Two for two." She pulled a pair of surgical gloves from her pocket and lifted out the guns. "The Beretta 950 Jetfire" she said waiving the first gun around and, "the Colt 'Government'.

I am so good." She grinned and whirled around until Tom caught her.

"You are the best," he told her.

"Damn straight I am." She kissed his cheek and headed for the kitchen to get plastic bags to hold them.

Oliver, who had also donned protective gloves as well was lifting stacks of papers and placing them on the sofa. Harry turned on the reading lamps at each end of the sofa and brought the desk chair over to put it in front of it. "There you go. You can do a rough sort here. George and I will set up some tables in the ballroom so that you have plenty of room to work. There's a lot to sort. When you take a break, perhaps you can explain why these papers are so important and what they have to do with our Russian Count and Ann's uncle."

Oliver grunted, not taking his eyes off the papers while he sorted them.

It only took half an hour, and the ballroom was converted to a crime lab. The body had been carefully transported on the door to a separate table in the ballroom. Gwyn placed the door on the table but was able to finish reconstruction thanks to the fact that the ballroom had one wall of floor-to-ceiling windows giving her much better light. Next to the body lay two plastic bags, each containing a gun and one had a bullet as well. The rest of the tables were covered with papers.

Des called a halt to their work. He agreed with Harry that Oliver needed to do some explaining.

After making sure that the ballroom was locked up tight, they all moved to the kitchen for a cup of whatever brew each wanted and some conversation. Oliver began with the story of how he got involved.

"In December 1959, I was an agent fresh from Quantico when a case came up. The word on the streets was that something big was going to happen involving the Greek embassy. As someone still wet behind the ears I considered myself lucky to be included in the investigation even though I was primarily a go-for. The agent I was shadowing got word from his source that there would be a break-in at the Greek Consulate in New York City. Since my boss was of Greek descent, he was assigned to the case and was to make the initial approach. I went along. When we got to the Consulate, we found that the shipment had arrived and the shipping company was setting up the display in the reception room. As you might guess, the company that handled shipping the artwork was owned by Stavros Castellanos family and the gentleman himself was there, making sure that nothing was damaged.

"Now this tip was not a priority at the bureau. Director J. Edgar Hoover's focus then was Russian spies and the Southern Christian Leadership Conference and Martin Luther King, Jr, who he felt were stirring up dissent. So our investigation consisted of my boss and me. When we arrived at the Greek Consulate, my boss spoke to the person in charge of the exhibit letting him know what we had heard. That person told us that they had new burglar-proof safeguarding the treasure. We were thanked for the interest of the American FBI, but the Greek government had it well in hand. The exhibit would be moved to the Metropolitan Museum of Art the next day under tight guard.

"My boss decided to check with the New York Agent in

Charge letting him know our information. There as well, we were told that they had everything in hand. When we finished there, we decided not to return to DC until the next day. We had supper and checked into a hotel. The next morning when we went to breakfast, the newspapers boys were screaming about a theft at the Greek Consulate. We contacted the New York office and were told that we were needed at the Consulate. It seemed that overnight, three burglars had broken into the Consulate, tied up the guards, opened the safe and removed all the pieces of jewelry and art which were to be put on display. Then they left, all without setting off any of the alarms which had been armed.

"The only descriptions available from the guards where that they were young, and one spoke with a Russian or Eastern European accent, and one with a Greek accent. One of the guards thought that one could have been a woman but the others didn't agree. They all wore identical outfits, tuxedos, and identical full face masks. They were gone over an hour when a guard finally got free and gave the alarm. The Bureau, the Greek's security, and the New York Police Department all worked together trying to catch the thieves, but they escaped without a trace. My boss was furious and I had to start my career with a failure. Needless to say, I have not forgotten that theft. Castellanos fell off the face of the earth. The name our contact gave us of the possible Russian, Count Grigori Baturin, completely disappeared as well. I had no name for the third man.

The date of the break-in was December twenty-second. The two men must not have left any word that they would be attending a Christmas Ball here. They were just gone. I have searched over the years with no success. I had tagged those names in our files so when Des searched for information on them, it raised a red flag with me and I had to come with him to check this out. The papers that you found, Kate, were detailed plans for the break-in and theft. What I have not found, though, is any trace of the items which were taken."

"Do you have a list of what was stolen?" Kate asked.

"Yes, with photos of each item."

"Good. It's late and this day has been very full. I suggest that we all get a good night's sleep. The ballroom is locked up tight, but if you want to sleep on a cot there, I can arrange it. Tomorrow, after breakfast, we can begin to search the house and grounds for any trace of the stolen items."

"I will take you up on the offer of a cot. I have spent too many years with this crime as a stain on my reputation to be away from what we've found. I have been less than honest with all of you. Des introduced me as an agent, but I was forced to leave the Bureau because of my age ten years ago when I turned seventy. However, I linked my home computer to that file at the bureau which is how I found out what you were searching for and Des took pity on an old man and let me come with him."

"We understand," Harry told him and the men went to the second floor where there were cots stored for overflow guests.

Kate called the dogs and went to the kitchen door. The lights in the yard were off and there was no sign of movement. She grabbed her parka and opened the door. The dogs headed out into the deep snow, less running than leaping as they sank into the powder snow up to their shoulders. Kate grabbed a shovel which was resting against the wall and shoveled a path across the deck and into the yard. By the time she reached the far end, the dogs had discovered the path and were running back and forth between her and the door. She made a ninety-degree turn and shoveled across until she was aligned with the bedroom windows. Turning again, she had just made her first scoop when strong arms reached around her and took the shovel.

Harry whispered, "I'll finish, and then we can work on warming up." Kate stepped back and let him go watching his strong arms make quick work of the path. He shoveled up the bedroom windows across that deck, then shoveled a path across to the kitchen. Kate had worked her way back to the kitchen, dodging as the dogs raced back and forth on the now cleared path.

Harry met her on the back deck and they headed back inside. Kate stopped the dogs outside the kitchen door and said, "Shake." Snow flew everywhere, and when she let the dogs into the kitchen, there was practically no snow on them. She grabbed a towel that had been left on the back of a chair following dinner and rubbed the three dogs down, including drying their feet and making sure there was no ice wedged between their toes. Harry took the towel when she finished and tossed it into the basket in the laundry room.

When he returned, he found her sitting at the breakfast nook staring out at the snow. It was still coming down, but it was much lighter now. Harry doubted that they would get another inch before it stopped. He slid onto the seat across from her and reached for her hands. "Today has been unbelievable. Who would have thought when we got up so early this morning that so much, both good and bad, would happen. I'm trying to hold the memories of the sledding and the Christmas tree in my head to block out the horrors."

"I like that idea. I'll try to do that too. If you hold me tight, you can probably keep the nightmares away."

"I'll hold you."

They turned off the kitchen lights and took one last look at the tree, sparkling in the darkened house. "I keep thinking about this being the first Christmas I've celebrated since I was a very young child," Harry murmured. "I was always at school studying when everyone went home or away for the holidays. I got to look forward to it as a quiet time when I could work uninterrupted. However, in the back of my mind, I knew I was missing out on something special."

"You didn't go home for Christmas?"

"No, my parents couldn't afford the plane fare. I could have paid my way after the first year, but that would have meant explaining why I had more money than my father. A conversation such as that, I realized even at that age, would be uncomfortable for both of us. So, instead, I worked."

"No more. You are my family and you will be a vital part of Christmas for the rest of your life, Harry Foyle."

"It will be my joy and pleasure, Kate Killoy Foyle."

After a lingering kiss that sealed their commitment, they shut off the tree lights and headed for bed. Kate stopped in the doorway of the sitting room and looked at the now-empty hassock. "I wonder where my great-great-grandmother hassock is? Ann said it was upholstered in the same fabric as the wing chairs. This one belongs to the library."

"That's a good question. I think we need to look for it in the morning. We should look for anything that seems to be out of place because we won't know what will be a clue to where the jewels from the Greek heist might be. I didn't realize that Oliver was eighty. He has been haunted by this theft for sixty years. I would like to wipe the stain of that crime from his record and give him a chance to earn the praise he deserves."

Kate accepted Harry's help in getting ready for bed. He had tucked her in and was about to join her when he stopped and went to the door to the hall, and opened it slightly. Then he climbed in next to her, his arm pulling her to him to snuggle.

-20-

Sunday Morning Very Early

Kate woke to a semi-darkened room. She felt Harry's warm body against hers and leaning forward, counted three white ghostly shapes asleep on the floor. She lay still and it was quiet. Closing her eyes, she relaxed ready for another hour or so of sleep, when a beep came. She grabbed her phone and punched in the numbers for the cameras. One-by-one she went through them, checking. It wasn't until she got to the dock area that she saw the source of the alarm. In spite of the snow which was piled deep on the dock, a small motorboat was trying to align with the dock so the single passenger could alight.

"Harry," she whispered. "Someone is trying to gain access to the property by the dock. They've got a small boat."

He was up and pulling on clothes, shoving his feet into socks and tall waterproof boots as he punched some numbers into his phone. He hit the speaker and a groan followed by a sleepy, "What?" Came from the device.

"We've got company. They are trying to get onto the snow-covered dock. I'd like some company in arranging a surprise party."

"I'm on my way."

Kate had pulled on warm clothes and the dogs were already at the sliding glass door staring out into the predawn night. Harry walked down the hall and grabbed his parka just as Des and Oliver appeared at the bottom of the stairs. The gray of predawn shining through the kitchen windows provided the only light. She looked down at her phone again. "He managed to clear enough snow from the end of the dock to pull himself up. He's got a small folding shovel and is clearing a path as he goes. I haven't been able to get a good look at his face but his size and shape could fit the Count.

"My cross-country skis are in the closet by the front door," Harry said, moving that way. "If I stay close to the trees, I might be able to get behind him. Des, you approach from the front. I suspect he is heading for the blue cabin beyond Otto's place. Move in that direction. He's going to be surprised when he finds it locked, so we will have to play it by ear but be careful. Oliver, I want you to cover the house if he gets by us. Remember, he's been around this place for years and may still know ways we haven't found. Rely on the dogs to clue you in to possible breaches."

They were gone without a sound or any sign of movement. Kate slipped into the breakfast nook, knowing that the dark house would hide her presence and followed the progress of the man on her phone. Oliver grabbed two cereal boxes off the counter and placed them between her phone and the window. "Your phone lights up. It's not much, but he'll be looking for any signs of life."

"Thanks, you're right. When he gets closer, we can move back, so we won't get caught if he shines a flashlight on the kitchen windows. He's cleared the dock and is working his way up the trail. Ah, Harry has gotten almost even with him but is off the trail and not easily visible in the trees. Baturin is slowing down. The amount of snow he's had to move is taking its toll. He has now turned the corner in the path that will take him toward the cabin. Harry has moved to the end of the deck and is untying the boat. It is drifting out into the lake. Later, we should tell Gil so that it can be picked up. Harry's coming back and moving fast. I'm going to change the angle on the corner camera for the dog yard." She closed her eyes to think and then pushed some numbers. Shaking her head, she tried again and this time she smiled. Switching her view, the camera caught both the approach of the man with the shovel and the sight of Des ducking behind the end of the cabin which he had approached from the far side of Otto's cabin to leave no tracks.

Oliver had his phone out and was speaking quietly. "Sorry to disturb you be we have a man who approached by way of the lake sneaking onto the property. He is heading for the blue cabin. Des is waiting by the cabin and Harry used his skis to get behind him and untie the boat. He's now coming up behind him. Have them approach silently and just push the button on the gate. Kate will let them in. There's only an inch of new snow since the driveway was plowed, so they won't have trouble. See you soon." He looked at Kate. "Back-up is on the way. The nearest car is only three minutes out."

The minutes seemed years long, but finally, a beep came on Kate's phone.

"Hi, Caleb. Our uninvited guest is headed for the blue cabin beyond Otto's. He's wearing a white parka with a hood," she said as she opened the gate.

She closed it as soon as he was free, not wanting anyone to enter she didn't know about. Oliver met the patrolman as he pulled up under the portico. Together, with guns drawn, they moved around the corner of the porch and approached the cabin. Kate watched them pass right below the camera where the porch and yard met. They stopped and squatted down. Kate caught the motion of the Count approaching the cabin. Any enthusiasm for digging had left him as he could barely shove the snow aside.

Lifting it was no longer an option. He reached the cabin door and lifted the latch, pushing against the door. Nothing happened. He reached into his pocket and pulled out something small. She realized that he thought it was locked, but he had a key. He inserted the key and again lifted the latch. Nothing. As he threw his body against the door trying to get in, Des stepped up behind him and said something causing him to whirl around and reach for his pocket. But Des' gun pointed at his head from less than a yard away stopped him. When Harry came up from behind and Caleb and Oliver arrived, Baturin just slid down in exhaustion collapsing onto the steps. Caleb and Oliver pulled him to his feet and secured his arms behind his back. Des reached by them and removed the gun from his pocket. Then slowly, they all headed back toward the house,

Two minutes later Kate opened the gate so that Gil and George and an additional patrol car to enter. They all gathered in front of the porch. Kate looked out and saw she wasn't needed, so she headed for the kitchen to make food. She turned on Harry's coffee machine to be ready for the men and got her tea kettle heating. Harry was the first one in. He wrapped his arms around her then reached over her shoulder to drop a pod into his coffee machine and push the button.

Holding her tightly, he smiled at the dogs and said, "Thanks, Quinn. You saved the day finding that secret tunnel. Locking the cabin and every door in between kept our Russian killer out. He's not talking but Oliver looks as though Christmas has come for him. He shocked Baturin when he told him he was being arrested for the theft at the Greek Consulate and the murders of Hader and Castellanos plus the attempted assault on Mrs. Ann Killoy. Once he's been booked, Des and Oliver are going to question him. They'll need breakfast first. Eggs would be quickest."

Kate got out the eggs and said, "They can ask him if he knows where the jewels are. But I've been thinking. I don't think he does know. I think that's the reason he's been hanging around all these years. I don't think anyone alive knows their location."

"What do you mean?"

"Well, why here? I suspect the reason that Gram heard them arguing over the crime in the library is that her uncle was involved up to his greedy neck. I think when they robbed the place they brought everything here to divide it up. Only with a house full of guests, they had to wait.

"Something happened that changed those plans. What we know is that two men died. Vivian was made to guard Camp and Baturin did not get the treasure. That leads me to believe that Nelson hid it. There were no more balls. While he lived, according to the dates and names I checked in the book, almost nobody came here. There was a large gap that ended when Gramps, Dad, Agnes and I started coming."

"Where do you think the jewels are?"

"They could be here. Nelson was able to hide them quickly if Baturin was searching here."

"However, I don't think this house is going to be the peaceful vacation home you and I dreamed of until they are found, so I vote that while the long-arm-of-the-law club is off playing with their Russian spy, we should have a treasure hunt. After breakfast, I think that we should start at the top of the house, in the attics, and explore every inch."

"An excellent idea." Ann came in with Liam at her side, followed by Tom and Gwyn. "What's this about playing with Russian spies?"

"Ah, you missed it. The Count came to visit and the guys managed to catch him. He is now a guest of the Bolton lockup. Des and Oliver are going to go question him after breakfast."

"Ah, food, good. Never question a suspect on an empty

stomach. Is there any more of that boysenberry jam left?" Oliver said as he entered the kitchen with Des right behind.

"Sit down and I'll give you some food so that you can go take that man apart," Kate laughed. "Oh, and remind Gil that Harry set Baturin's boat is floating free so the lake patrol will find it hung up on one of the islands."

"I'll remind him. I wouldn't be surprised if our Russian friend stole it from someone's boathouse." Des said.

Kate pulled out her phone and scrolled back through the various stills she collected during Baturin's take-down. When she reached the beginning, she held her phone out to Des and pointed to the number on the side of the boat which was different from the last boat they used. He grinned and wrote it in his notebook. "That should help."

"Do you mean we slept through the take down of the murderer of my two bodies?" Gwyn asked.

"Possible murderer. He could have killed them but so could your uncle, Gram, or even Vivian. They may be able to pull prints and or DNA from the guns or even the papers. So while these two are squeezing this guy for information, we're going on a treasure hunt." Kate dished up a plate of food for herself and began to eat. Harry had finished, so he fed the dogs and let them out. Then he told everyone Kate's theory that the Russian may not know where the treasure is, and that it may be the reason he didn't dump Vivian years ago. He needed to keep control of her to have access to the house so that he could search. And now he had her completely under his spell.

"I'd feel sorry for her if she weren't such a complete bitch," Gwyn said.

"She doesn't need your pity," Ann said. "She had every advantage, and she tossed it all away. She never had to struggle a day in her life, and yet she demands that everyone treat her as someone who has suffered. Sorry. I'm not buying it. But before you go I have a question for the Count. Where does he go when he's not camping out here? Something that Helen said has me wondering if more of my less than a glorious family might be involved. See if he'll tell you. I'd like to know."

"What do you suspect?" Oliver asked.

"Let's see what he has to say, then I'll tell you."

Since the only Sunday Mass in winter was at eleven o'clock, the women ate breakfast first and spent an hour organizing the magazines. The men went off to continue their research. When the time came to drive into Bolton Landing, they decided that they'd only need the one car. Harry arranged the center row of seats to hold three. He and Tom were in front and the women in the middle. Des and Oliver remained behind. Harry gave Des the extra phone which had the codes for the gate, and the warning of anyone trying to get entrance.

The church was lovely. The wall behind the altar was made of highly polished split native logs arranged in a geometric pattern. But that was only the first symbol acknowledging the area's Native American heritage. The altar itself was an upended birch bark canoe surrounded by symbols of the mountains--pines, birch logs, snowshoes, and salutes to the bear, fox, and raccoon. Kate was enthralled. It was not traditional but was truly beautiful. The workmanship in a blanket draped over the lectern caught her eye, and she guessed the symbols were Mohegan.

The Mass was familiar. When it ended, Gwyn introduced them to the priest and some of the congregation. Everyone knew about what had been going on with them. Like all other small towns, gossip was the coin of the realm and everyone had questions about the bodies and Vivian going crazy. Ann, on the other hand, was treated as returning royalty. One of the old men had been a child when Tim Durgin was driven off by his father for turning his back on the heiress his father had chosen and marrying a nurse. This made him a hero according to the town. One woman remembered Ann as a teenager. After listening to remembrances for a while, the group was able to reach the car and head back.

Once on the road, Gwyn told them, "You're now officially part of Bolton Landing. You are not summer people because you have history here. They love that you've not only bought the house, Harry, but used local men to restore it to its original glory. You shop here and spend money with local merchants. And, most of all, you're down to earth and not snooty. Yes, you are residents of Bolton Landing from now on. Welcome to Lake George."

Kate hugged Gwyn and thanked her for easing their entry into the town. It was good to know some of their neighborhoods.

When they got back from church, Harry went to fill Otto on the happenings of the morning and to warn him that they might have more cops crawling around the place before the day was over.

Kate and Ann decided to explore the attic and went to get warm sweaters, since the attic wasn't heated. Kate put on her heaviest sweaters knit of pure Irish wool and added fingerless gloves before heading upstairs, followed by the dogs.

On the way up, she grabbed flashlights and a couple of portable battery-powered lanterns to give them light. She had to admit to herself that finding the treasure would be nice.

However, finding the history of the house was far more important to her. Even if that reveals more larcenous relatives. Vivian's father sounded like the kind of person you wouldn't like to meet in a dark alley or, truly, anywhere.

-21-

Sunday Late Morning

Though the sun was out following the snow storm, the attic was dark with only a few small windows. They decided to divide up the area. Ann wanted to continue sorting the clothing and Harry found her a couple of folding tables to use. Tom and Gwyn took the north side of the attic and Kate and Harry the south. Kate took the part facing the back of the house and Harry the front. The first thing Kate noticed were the cupboard doors under the eves. She pushed a pair of floor lamps out of the way and pulled open the first set of doors. Right in front were two trunks with one word written on them, 'TIM.' She must have made a sound because

Harry was beside her in a second. He looked at the trunks and then at her. She turned toward him, a smile on her face while tears brimmed her eyes. Harry hugged her and then nodded to the others.

"Tom, Gram, come see what I've got. I found my great-grandfather's things."

Tom and Ann both rushed over with Gwyn right behind. Harry began pulling trunks out of the cupboard. Behind the trunks were three large boxes. Ann gasped. "His college trunks. He had to leave them when he went off to war and when he married my mother, he was no longer allowed to return here. I thought they had thrown them out since they didn't send them to us."

Kate waved to Tom as the oldest in her generation to do the honors of opening the first. He pulled it open and exclaimed, "The Journal of Timothy Durgin," Tom read. "He kept a journal all his life Gramps told me. Gramps said that his father-in-law got him started keeping a journal when he was his adviser for his PhD. Most of what he wrote about was family and thoughts he'd had during the day. He gave me my first journal when I was ten and helped me get started. I've kept one ever since. These will be wonderful to read. We should keep them with those that Gramps wrote."

They found more boxes of books and clothing, and trunks filled with things he needed in college, papers he had written, charts and tools.

One box was labeled 'Winter School'. It was filled with cold weather gear, crampons, belay ropes, and other things needed for safe hiking and climbing in the High Peaks during the coldest part of the year. Ann said that her father had told Tom about it when he was advising him, and that's why he attended. She looked over at her grandson who bore her husband's name and said, "You might enjoy doing that with your brothers."

Harry leaned over and kissed Kate, hugging her. Last month she had used some skills her grandfather had learned at Winter School and passed on to his grandchildren. Those had saved his life.

He'd learned in Lake Placid that the school still continued. They were still teaching people skills for survival when challenged with climbing the high peaks of the Adirondack Mountains. He could easily picture Tom, once his ankle healed, and Kate's younger brothers attending.

The next stack of boxes was roped together. It was labeled Tim's train. When they opened the top box, they found a collection of smaller boxes containing the engine and cars of a Lionel model train. Gwyn pulled open the box under it which was filled with what looked like miles of track and instructions for putting the sections together in different layouts. The third box contained miniature buildings in scale to the train along with trees, wagons, crossing signs, people, and everything to create a perfect small world. There was even a green felt cloth with roads marked on it. Harry and Tom grinned at each other.

"I know what we're doing tonight." Tom said.

"Under the Christmas tree." Harry grinned as he carefully repacked the boxes and put them next to the attic door.

Ann picked up the box with the journals and added it to the pile of things to be taken downstairs. Then they returned to work. Kate opened each box, checked the contents and then sealed it labeling it. After an hour, she came to the conclusion that her grandmother's family never threw anything away. Her stack of neatly labeled boxes was waist high when she opened the fourth cupboard and stopped. She had found her great-great-grandmother's hassock.

"Gwyn, could you come here?" she called. Gwyn dashed over followed by the others.

"Is it my imagination, or is that blood?" Kate asked as she pulled the hassock out into the open area.

"It looks like blood to me. I've got testing materials in my bag downstairs which can confirm it."

"I would say that at least one of the murders took place in the sitting room." Harry said. He lifted the heavy hassock and carried it to the attic door. "I don't know about the rest of you, but I'm starved. I think it's time for lunch. Treasure can wait. As far as I'm concerned, the train is the best treasure. I can't wait to play with it. I never had a model train when I was a kid."

They all stood and followed him down the stairs each carrying boxes. Ann gave Tom the box with the journals which he could manage one handed and still use his cane. The women divided up the train boxes.

Sunday's lunch though late was relaxed consisting of hamburgers, pasta and spinach salad and chips. Talk was about the journals. Ann had been skimming them and when she finished her food began reading them a bit from the journal which told of how her parents met. It was dated October 15, 1942, a Thursday. She began to read. The first entry spoke about his enlisting in the army. His father had been furious. Luckily, his anger was no match for the US government and

Tim quickly finished basic training and was sent to France. He spoke about the ship stopping first in England and then his lieutenant said the platoon was to be moved across the channel under cover of darkness.

Ann flipped ahead until she found the date she was seeking and began reading word-for-word. "We've been up for more than twenty-four hours and I need sleep, but I am too tired and at the same time too excited to close my eyes. The men covered a mile and a half with the litters, dodging incoming from the German nest on the hill above the farm. We arrived at the aid station just in time, since they were getting ready to move back. We offloaded Carson, Brown, Kruszewski, and Rubino. Rubino kept telling us that if something happened to him we were to go to Brooklyn and explain to his girl that he loved her. He was beside himself that he hadn't asked her to marry him before we shipped out. I felt for him at the time but the nurse said he'll be able to tell her himself. His wound is bad, but he'd live.

The nurse reassured me when I asked. And what a nurse she was. She knocked me sideways harder than if I'd been hit by a howitzer. She is beautiful even though she looks exhausted and is wearing an apron covered in blood. Her eyes are pure blue like Lake George when the sun is shining. And her smile could put that sun to shame. Her bouncing golden curls peek out from under her cap even though she'd been on duty for ten hours.

I sat on a bench next to the mess. When she came out with a mug of coffee, she smiled and sat beside me. Her name is Sarah Ann Conners.

"Sarah knew I'd been worried about my comrades. It turns out she is from Connecticut, southwest of Hartford. We talked about home. She no longer has any family since her brother died at Midway months ago. She is still getting used to being alone and feels she is lucky there is so much to do here that she doesn't have time to think.

"Sarah said that she'd like to find a job somewhere in New England or New York when this mess was over. I told her that I was studying at MIT, and planned to be a college professor at Columbia in math.

"We talked for an hour, and then she chased me off to bed and I said that we should try to stay in touch. I promised I'd write. She'd asked if I'd seen the movie 'Love Affair' which had come out a few years ago with Irene Dunne and Charles Boyer. I told her I had though didn't mention that I'd taken my little sister who'd bugged me until I did. She told me we should meet at the top of the Empire State Building if we both survive on Christmas Eve following the end of the war. We laughed at how sentimental we both were, but I know that if I survive, I'll be there."

Ann, Gwyn and Kate all wiped their eyes and sighed. Gwyn asked, "Did they meet at the Empire State Building?"

"Yes. They became engaged that evening and were married four days later. My father brought her to Lake George the day before New Year's Eve to meet the family. His father went ballistic and disowned him on the spot. They didn't even collect his things but just got the first train back to the city arriving in the middle of the New Year's Eve madness. They spent the night in Grand Central Station. But a month later he was teaching at Columbia University and she was nursing at the Medical Center. I came along nine months after they were married, and we were a family." She didn't read anymore but simply clutched the journal and stared off into space. The others didn't talk but left her with her memories.

Kate and Harry took the dogs out for a walk along the driveway. The temperatures were keeping the snow from melting and the sunshine sparkling off all that whiteness forced them to wear sunglasses.

They were nearing the front porch on their return when their phones dinged announcing the return of Des and Oliver. Kate grabbed Quinn's collar to keep him away from the approaching car. The men looked tired and grumpy. It turned out they had been booted out of questioning Baturin when the cops found out that Oliver was a retired agent and that Des was on vacation. Agents had arrived from the city when Gil had touched base with his contact at the bureau. "They said that they didn't want any court case messed up by having retired and off duty agents involved in the questioning."

Kate laughed. "Don't worry, boys. You can come and I'll heat you up some lunch and some hot coffee and pie. If you're very good, you can play with our model trains tonight."

"Model trains? Who has model trains?" Des asked.

"They belonged to my great-grandfather."

"Fun. Have you found any sign of the treasure?"

"Well, truthfully, we are searching blind since we have no idea what this treasure looks like."

"I am so sorry. I have spent so many years looking for these pieces, I forget that they are not foremost in everyone's mind.

I will print out photos of the jewels as soon as I finish this delicious food. The pieces are very distinctive. The main one is the necklace. It is quite large. It is a cascade of white gold and diamond pendants with each shaped like an animal native to Greece. The base is a large phoenix. Above that are the dolphin and goat. The top row consists of an ox, a goose, a lynx and a lizard. The bracelet is a chain with medallions of Greek gods hanging from it. There are two sets of earrings, one of dolphins and one of stars beautifully worked in gold. Since all the pieces date back to about 400 AD, they are considered priceless. The statues are all goddesses."

"They sound incredible. I'd love to see the pieces," Ann said. "As soon as we finish here, we can continue going through the attic. Now that we know what we're looking for, we should check every tiny box. If they split up the collection, each piece, except the necklace wouldn't take up much space."

As they headed upstairs, Des' phone buzzed. The rest of them continued up to the attic. Des joined them he was definitely angry. It seemed that Baturin had pull. The Russian consulate sent lawyers and consular officials and the people from the New York office who replaced them came up against it. They caved and Gil couldn't influence the judge to hold him. He's now out on bail with only an ankle bracelet to keep track of him.

Anger filled the room. The men all started talking at once. Harry asked Des of it was possible to tap into the ankle bracelet software so that they would know if he were to return here. Kate heard a door open and close and stiffened.

"Kate?" Helen's voice sounded from downstairs.

"We're up in the attic," she answered walking to the door and then looking down the stairs.

"I just wanted to let you know that I've brought the groceries, and I was able to get a nice roast for supper. I'll get it put away and I've put some desserts into the freezer. I was surprised to see Vivian had been released. I would think that trying to shoot you would mean she'd stay locked up until her trial."

"Vivian's out? How do you know?"

"I saw her. When I came out of the grocery store, I saw her getting into a car with some man."

"You're sure it was Vivian?"

"Kate, I've worked here forever. I know Vivian when I see her."

"I'll have Gil find out what's going on and let you know. If you see her again, call me right away."

Kate went to turn around and bumped into Harry. "You heard her. What does it take to keep criminals locked up in this town?"

Harry already had his phone out calling Gil. He answered and Harry yelled, "What in the world are they doing, letting Vivian out of custody? She tried to kill us."

They all turned to watch him as he listened to Gil. "Got it," he finally said and disconnected the call. He looked at them in confusion. "Gil said she hasn't been released. He and George are questioning her now since the doctors have gotten her to the point where she is somewhat coherent. He was looking straight at her as we spoke."

Silence filled the room. Ann asked what all of them were thinking. "How can she be in two places at once?"

Kate stared off into space going over everything she knew or had heard about Vivian. It took a moment but a glimmer of an idea came to her and she took off down the stairs running.

-21-

Sunday Afternoon

Kate raced into the kitchen and looked around, then raced to the sitting room and the library. Everyone crowded in after her. "Where did it go?"

"Where did what go?" Harry asked.

"The album with the photos of the Christmas ball."

"I put it in the safe. It's evidence." He walked over to the safe and opened it, pulling out the album and putting it on the desk. Kate pounced on it and began flipping pages. She found Vivian's photo, marking the page. More pages were turned until she found what she wanted. Holding the intervening pages together, she flipped back and forth between the pages, then she looked up at them. "There are two Vivians."

"What," Des asked, noticeably startled.

Kate turned the book, so they all could see it and flipped the pages back and forth.

"Evangeline," Ann said. "You're right. They could easily be twins or the same person. It would explain the personality changes that Helen mentioned. They both grew up in this house and know all its secrets. They're as close as sisters."

"Do you think that Evangeline is involved in the theft and the killings?" Tom asked staring at his grandmother.

"It wouldn't surprise me in the least. She was always someone who would break any rule if it was to her benefit."

They all stopped talking when they saw that Harry was again on the phone to Gil. He sat, leaning on the desk and looking at them. "Yes, the aunt, Evangeline. Helen saw what she was sure was Vivian in town. Right, she saw her up close getting into a car driven by a man. I don't know if she called out to her or not, she didn't say. But, Kate pointed out that according to Helen, Vivian has been exhibiting multiple-personality symptoms. It could be that Helen was talking to Vivian one minute and then Evangeline dressed exactly like Vivian, the next. No, she didn't say who the man was who drove the car. Ann thinks that Evangeline might have been involved in either the theft or the killings, or both. I'll have Des get someone to check out her place in the city and talk to her husband. See if Evangeline's name gets any reaction from Vivian. Right. Later."

Harry looked around the room at them. "He's going to drop Evangeline's name before they wrap up today's interrogation. Des, can you take care of getting someone to track down the husband and find out what's going on. In the meantime, we should continue searching. They are constantly trying to get into this house. I can only think of one reason why, which is that they didn't hide the treasure. Someone else did it. Someone who is not able to tell them where it is."

"Uncle Nelson." Ann whispered, staring at Harry as he sat at the desk. " Uncle Nelson was sitting right where you are, Harry, when I heard the argument. He died of a heart attack less than a month later. Vivian never married but continued living here with servants ever since. He too must have been part of it. He might have been behind the whole thing. I remember that my parents didn't hear about his passing until his funeral was over. A letter came from an attorney saying that the family had decided to have a service for only those close to him."

"Gram, think back to that night when you and Gramps left the ball. All the characters in this play were still alive then. Who was in the library arguing with Nelson?"

"Baturin, I recognized his accent, but there were also other male voices. I don't know whose or how many. I didn't hear any women's voices and when I peeked in the door, the only one I could see was my uncle."

Tom spoke up. "You know, we checked to see who at that party was still around after the ball. However, we never questioned them. Those who have suffered harm following the event might have something to say. Maybe they knew what happened. Oliver, have you found out anything from the paperwork you've been going through?"

"Nothing specific. However, I think you might be right about more people being involved. Stavros' family owned the ship which transported the treasure. Stavros was in charge of the security plan for the transport. Since the treasure had been delivered to the consulate in New York City, his family was not held responsible when it went missing, but Stavros did insist on double-checking all the security at the consulate before turning over the treasure."

"So the fox was shown the layout of the hen house and all the ways they would use to keep him out," Kate said.

"Essentially."

Tom looked around the group. "I'm going to do more checking on the backgrounds of those attending, especially what they are doing now. I'll talk to Seamus and Satu as well." He looked at Harry. "I know that my brother and his girlfriend work for you now, Harry, but he's my little brother, and he'll do this if I ask him. Those two are so good at finding out about people's background, we'll know everything about these men including the kind of toothbrush they use before they're done."

"They finish their exams tomorrow, so they will be able to begin after that," Harry told him. In the meantime, Sadie is also working on this so why don't you start by contacting her. Oh, and don't tell her about Vivian trying to shoot Kate. We don't need her here, armed and ready to take on all comers. Plus, she'd tell Maeve."

Tom laughed. "You do realize that the two of them would probably solve this in five minutes, don't you?"

"Yes," Harry laughed. "But I don't think my ego can take having those septuagenarians taking over the investigation. We'll keep Kate's latest adventure just among ourselves."

He was met with silence, followed by nods. Then Ann spoke. "Well, if you don't mind, I think I'll take this septuagenarian upstairs and take a nap. Liam can come with me just in case."

"Good idea," Kate told her glancing with raised eyebrows at Harry. "I'll take Dillon and Quinn up with me as I search."

"I'll come too," Gwyn said. "I'll take a break from my bones."

The afternoon was already half over, and being so late in the year, the light was fading outside. As they left the library, she walked over to the switch on the wall and flipped it. The tree lit up, sparkling with the lights and ornaments. Gwyn hugged her. "It is so beautiful. In spite of the dead bodies and killers, this puts me in the Christmas spirit. Tonight we should assemble the train and the village under the tree. After supper, we can set it up and then take turns playing engineer."

"Excellent idea." Kate looked out the window and noticed that the outside lights had come on and were reflecting color onto the snow. "I'd rather be sledding, but I guess treasure hunting is a good second choice. Let's go show the men how efficient we can be at finding the golden fleece or in this case, the diamonds and statues."

-23-

Sunday Evening

Dinner," a shout came up the stairs. Kate moved a pile of photo albums off her lap and stood, stretching. Gwyn looked at her watch in surprise. "Wow. That time went fast. I'm afraid it got away from me when I found all these National Geographic. I could spend weeks looking through these."

"I know, they're addictive. We should move them down to the game room. When the family comes for New Years, the kids will love them."

"Kids nothing. Everyone will be going through them. You should set up a bookcase just for these. I also noticed that the indexes are here as well. As far as I'm concerned, I've found the treasure in the attic."

"Before we set up the trains this evening, we can have the guys carry the boxes down to the game room. I'll see if I can consolidate some games on the shelves to make room for them. If not, I'll just have to add a bookcase, but it will take time since the wood would have to match the rest of the room."

They met Ann on the stairs heading down for dinner. "What are you two talking about?"

"A home for the world's most fantastic collection of National Geographic Magazines. They are all up in the attic. Kate decided, with a lot of pressure from me, that they should be moved to the game room. They are the perfect read for a rainy day."

"You do know that they are digitalized," Ann put in.

"It's not the same as just picking up a magazine at random and learning about places you've never even heard about. And photography. I don't care. It's not the same to pull it up on your phone." Gwyn argued.

Ann chuckled. "I know. I'm just pushing your buttons. I agree with you. You're quiet, Kate."

"I was just wondering if National Geographic ever did a story on our treasure. Those jewels and the history behind them would be just the type of story they would have covered."

Gwyn pumped her arm. "That's brilliant. Now the guys can't complain that we're wasting time having them move all the boxes down here. You know, Kate, your brain is much twistier than your brother's. He thinks in a straight line and you are all over the place. But he says that you come up with the right answer every time."

"It doesn't seem twisty to me. When I explain how I get an answer, they always agree that it's logical."

They had reached the kitchen and Tom smiled at Gwyn asking, "What's logical?"

"Kate's thinking."

"Well, that brings into question the definition for logical. The rest of us think as if we were driving the highway to our destination. Kate thinks as if she were driving all the twisty little one-lane back roads. Except she does it at the speed of a supercollider and gets there first. It just happens. We all learned to accept it years ago."

Harry came up and kissed her. "I, for one, love your twisty brain. What brought it up?"

" Gwyn found the quintessential collection of National Geographic Magazines and I wondered if they had possibly done a story on our treasure."

"They did," Oliver said. "Somewhere in my notes is the listing of which issue."

"Perfect," Ann said as they settled into their usual places at the table. "After we finish this feast that Helen was kind enough to fix for us, we can bring down the issues and put them in the game room. Then, while Oliver figures which issue has the article about our treasure, we can set up the trains under the Christmas tree."

Kate sat eating and letting the conversations float around her. She stared at her very modern kitchen. Having visited the attic and seeing photos in an album, she'd thought of an earlier time when the house was first built.

The had been hoping to come across plans or information about the early house, but so far she'd had no luck. Her eyes swept the room. With all this chaos, she hadn't had time to look at this wondrous gift Harry had given her.

She thought of their rocky courtship which still made her smile. The day she met him, they got engaged. She fell in love with him a little that day, but her love grew as she came to know him and realized how much she wanted to make her life with him.

Harry's carpenters had kept the original moldings around the ceiling as well as the ceiling medallion which was centered over the table. But modern lighting gave the room a warm companionable feel, making this kitchen the heart of their home. It would be a second home for them. However, it was Harry's vision that all the Killoys would use it and love it.

From what she'd seen of the photos of the original mansion, the place was built to be a true mansion. It was made to impress those less fortunate than its owner. Its purpose when built was formal and somewhat cold. But it wasn't cold now.

It was still impressive, but the sharp edges of ostentation had been softened and would be softened more so during the years to come. Her gaze fell on the big refrigerator and she smiled. What that appliance needed was a bunch of shopping lists, photos, and children's drawings attached to it by magnets to fit the warmth that the room now had.

"Daydreaming?" Harry whispered in her ear.

"I was visualizing the refrigerator covered with our kid's artwork. You've taken this ostentatious mansion and turned it into a warm and loving home."

She leaned into him, resting her head on his shoulder.

"I should order everyone out of here. This isn't a honeymoon, it's just another case."

"They won't go until they get answers."

"Do you want to leave?"

"No. I want this finished. The sooner we can find this treasure, the sooner we can have this place to ourselves. I'm ready to set up the trains and then go to bed. It's been a long day, and we have church to attend in the morning."

Harry's hand settled on her leg, just resting there. She glanced at him and he raised one eyebrow. He knew it drove her crazy that he could do that, and she couldn't. He leaned closer bringing a warmth that spread through her body, and then he kissed her cheek. His chair scraped the floor as he stood and cleared his throat.

"Hey, guys. Let's save dessert for later while we work on the train. If the ladies will load the dishwasher, we'll go bring down those boxes."

They stood and Gwyn told Tom that his job was to clear the shelving in the game room while the others carried boxes downstairs. They cleaned up the kitchen and moved to the entryway.

Only two hours later, Kate gazed at the floor under the tree. It had been transformed into a miniature Christmas village. The trains, one for passengers and one for freight, were moving sedately around the complex layout of track, traveling over and under each other with the bridges crossing both tracks and roads. A station stood at each end of the long green fabric which served as land. Roads were marked as well as lakes and rivers. Fabric covered hills and mountains rose close to the base of the tree. Tiny cast-iron people, realistically painted, were placed where they could do their work. The fields held cows and sheep and the children, outside the schoolhouse were accompanied by small dogs. The sounds of a whistle filled the room as one train arrived at the station while the other emerged from a tunnel that ran under the hill.

Quinn was fascinated by the train. He would chase each train squeaking his hedgehog every time a whistle blew. Dillon and Liam watched the trains but from their position next to Kate and Ann.

Kate leaned back watching her husband, who now held the controller for the passenger train, lying on his belly and announcing that the train was about to depart. "All aboard!" he shouted. Her eyes shone with tears and her throat swell making swallowing impossible. This was the life she'd always wanted. Arguments and laughter, over who was next, filled the room when Harry blew a long blast on the whistle catching everyone's attention. "It's late and time for bed. The train will be here for everyone to run to their heart's content tomorrow. Kate and I need to put the dogs out and get some sleep. We wish you all, good night."

Kate wished them good night as she rose from her comfortable seat. Looking again at Harry who was gathering up all the tiny people and animals to put back into their wooden box. The size of those pieces would make great toys for Quinn to choke on, and he wasn't taking any chances. The sparkling lights from the tree lit him and the village giving the scene an other-worldly feel. She took a step back to switch off the power to the trains when she stopped. A thought came to her but just as quickly disappeared. She waited, but it didn't come back. She knew if she left the idea alone it would return, but this felt important. The foyer was a holiday wonderland. Harry stepped closer and wrapped his arms around her, not speaking, simply enjoying the moment. Whatever it was that was playing hide-and-seek in her brain would wait.

-24-

Monday Morning

The morning had started with a quick trip to town to check in at the police station. They wanted to sign their statements from yesterday but found that Gil wasn't there. It felt good to get a chance to explore the town a little more. They had left the phone with Des so they would be free to wander around and even do some Christmas shopping.

When they got back to the house, they found there had been an another attempt to get onto the property. Des explained, "Not long after you left, a boat approached the dock. They must have seen you go out the gate. Your fancy phone dinged and I looked at the code list Kate taped to the inside of the kitchen cabinet and was able to turn on the correct camera. I didn't recognize the man getting ready to climb onto the dock, so I decided to see if we could scare him off. I opened the slider and let out all the dogs. They must have picked up his scent because they headed straight for that corner of the yard and began barking up a storm. Whoever the man was, he decided that he wanted nothing to do with ferocious dogs and climbed back onto his boat and took off. These guys make great guard dogs. It's the first time I've stopped the bad guy while just sitting at the kitchen table pushing buttons."

"What did he look like?" Harry asked.

"Well, it wasn't the Count. I don't know if I pushed the right buttons to capture his face." He handed the phone to Kate. She pressed a few buttons and a series of photos appeared on the screen. She flipped through them and finally pulled up one that was relatively clear and headed for the library. Soon she was back with a couple of printouts of the man's face.

She passed around copies of the photo saying, "I think we've got a new player. I don't recognize him. He's too young to have been part of the theft. Do we know if any of the men who might be involved have children?"

"No, we don't," Des said. "I was trying to get information on Evangeline today, but didn't have much luck."

Kate looked at the men sitting around the table and sighed. This was taking forever. They'd never get to have their dream honeymoon at this rate. She had to do something. She looked at Harry and said, "You're in charge of lunch. I've got a phone call to make."

Pulling out her phone, she hit speed dial and smiled when

her great-aunt answered. "Hi Maeve, how is Padraig? Great. I have a small favor to ask. Yes, we are technically on our honeymoon, but I'm afraid our lifestyle hasn't changed much from what's been happening since February. Only two bodies but they've been dead for sixty years. However, there is still a threat and because of that, I need your sources to track down everything about Gram's aunt Evangeline Durgin DeBeer. She's one of the 'ladies who lunch' in Manhattan from what I've heard. A patron of the MMA, et cetera. Right. Do you remember the big theft from the Greek Consulate about the time that Gram and Gramps left the Christmas Ball and came to visit you? Right. A treasure was stolen. Well to make a long story short, that crime is connected to the two bodies which were found buried in our basement when we arrived at our honeymoon.

"Is that Padraig laughing? Well, the cast of our honeymoon now consists of Gram, Tom, Des, my old friend Gwyn who's a forensic pathologist, a couple of cops and an agent named Oliver Bailey. Oh, you do. Maeve says hi, Oliver. Anyway, the sooner you could find out something about Evangeline and everyone who might have anything to do with her, the sooner we can end this game and begin our honeymoon. You will. Thanks. Oh, and if you don't have plans for New Years Day, we're planning a family get together here so save the date. I'll talk to you soon. Love, you."

She stood and began setting the table for lunch.

"Was that Maeve Donovan? MI 5 agent Maeve Donovan?" Oliver said.

"She's my great-aunt. She remembers you and sends her

regards."

Oliver sat looking stunned. "She knows who I am?"

Des laughed. "Maeve has that effect on everyone, Oliver. I met her last summer and have become one of her biggest fans."

Oliver was still in awe when lunch was served. Talk flowed around the table about the case and about the fascinating church they had attended that morning.

When lunch was cleared away, the men returned to their research. Ann headed to the sitting room with her Kindle and Liam following. Kate and Gwyn returned to the attic, after adding an extra layer to keep out the chill. Gwyn went back to space where she'd been working. She'd found a lovely mahogany drop-leaf table and a matching chair which she'd turned into her office. Kate noticed that she'd brought a notebook with her and several pens and markers. She watched as she stacked unopened boxes on her left and placed an assortment of empty boxes on her right within easy reach. In five minutes, Gwyn had created the perfect workspace. Kate walked over and hung one of the lanterns from the rafter above her head. "Remind me the next time I decide to remodel, to call you. That was the fastest office creation I've ever seen."

"Well, when you drift from town to town, working on different crimes, you learn to make do with what's available. I've made offices out of much worse than this. I would guess that this table was once in the library, but both it and the chair would be a perfect addition to the south tower bedroom. If placed on the opposite side of the tower from that mahogany trunk, it would tie the room together and give whoever stayed there a place to sit and work while enjoying the fabulous view of the mountains rising in the distance."

"Brilliant idea. Once you test the blood on my great-great-grandmother's hassock, I'd like to try to get the upholstery restored so it matches the chair in the sitting room."

"I know some people who specialize in getting blood stains out of fabrics. I'll contact them once we finish the case. Where are you going to work now?"

"I thought I'd check out the area above the south tower. Since Ann isn't sleeping, and I won't disturb her."

"Sound's like a plan."

Kate wandered the aisles trying to find a spot to settle. Ever since yesterday, she'd been working to pull the thought which kept escaping from her mind. No luck. She hoped if she found something mindless to do, it would come out of hiding. It had better because it was making her grouchy.

The first thing she spotted when she walked around a large tri-fold dressing screen covered with a heavy-weight sheet to protect the silk fabric beneath, was that someone had created an office, complete with an oak desk and matching armchair. The amount of dust lying on the surface of the desk attested to the fact that nobody had worked here in a very long time. Kate moved back into the central area and searched the piles of boxes. One was marked kitchen linens. When she opened it, she found not only table cloths, but a pile of dish towels. After closing up the box to protect the table cloths, she moved to the desk and got to work. When done, her office only lacked an Axminster carpet on the floor.

Settling in the chair which had been made for someone

about four or five inches taller than she, Kate reached for a stack of account books which held down a dozen red, legal wallets, tied with ribbons. The account books contained lists of construction supplies and tools along with the date, amount used, cost and balance. Kate realized that this was the ledger book for the construction of the house. She set it to one side and lifted the first wallet. While holding her breath, she began to untie it. Folding back the flap, she reached inside and drew out a heavy folded piece of fabric. She'd seen something like it used as a tablecloth for the picnic tables. Oilcloth, Dad had called it. Why would a piece of oilcloth be folded into a legal wallet? Moving the account book aside, she unfolded the oilcloth. It was a slightly stained off-white color, but when she turned it over, her breath caught, and she stared. The blueprints. The front of the house complete with towers and the ballroom off to the side was rendered in exact detail, every square inch of it. Kate sat for another minute gazing at the sheet before her and then reached for her phone and texted Harry, House Plans - In the attic over So. Tower.

The house details were exacting. Picking up the ledger, she noticed a column she'd ignored the first time through. It had a series of numbers and letters. What she now found was those number/letter listings matched the windows, shutters, chimney caps, and hundreds of other pieces that made up her new second home. She had been so enthralled with the details on the plan marked front elevation that she jumped when Harry's hand dropped onto her shoulder. She looked up at him and smiled. "I've found the plans to my castle."

"These must have been the builder's copies of the plans,

backed with oilcloth, so they'd hold up to a lot of rough handling. They counted eight legal wallets, each holding a plan for a distinct part of the house. Harry found a carton and loaded all the plans inside, along with the ledger. Then he looked around, studying the area. "I wondered who worked up here? This desk and chair have been here for a long time."

Kate opened the top right-hand drawer to find it loaded with journals. She reached for them only to have Harry's hand cover hers.

"We'll take these down with us and read them tonight." He scooped them into the box and added a bunch of smaller letter sized wallets to the stack."

She stood ruminating on what she had found and began to look around her for other possible finds. Harry sat at the desk slowly going through the drawers, checking each piece of paperwork he found. Kate walked over to a line of boxes that seemed to form a sidewall to the 'office' The boxes were wooden, each with a slatted front. When she pulled on the knob, the front slid down into a pocket on the bottom of the box like a roll-top desk. Reaching out, she lifted old leather-covered books with black paper pages. The covers were attached with what looked like shoelaces. Her hands came away covered in a brown powder from disintegrating leather. Resting the top book on the box, she opened it and saw men dressed formally in suits, vests and tall hats and women in long dresses in light-colored coats over them. They were all looking at men surrounded with piles of stone and logs. Kate must have gasped because Harry was next to her in an instant. Silently, she turned page after page and watched as the house grew, into their house. She felt Harry's finger wipe a tear from her cheek.

"This is wonderful. It's as though we were standing there watching as it is built." She looked over her shoulder at him.

"I agree. We need to be home soon enough to take the same kind of photos of our home being built. They'll be a record for generations to come."

"As far as I'm concerned, we've found the most important treasure.

She opened the other boxes as Harry stacked the photo albums. The final one was newer. The first page showed three women dressed in very conservative one-piece bathing suits sitting on the edge of the dock. The date was written below is July 4, 1953. She looked over at the writing on the inside cover of the album—Virginia Durgin. Could this be Ann's grandmother? She needed to take this downstairs. Quinn, who was no longer sleeping in the corner with Dillon, stuck his head under her arm sniffing the album and then began looking around for something to steal. He was becoming quite the kleptomaniac.

"Leave it!" The puppy sat and gazed at her looking as though butter wouldn't melt in his mouth. No sooner had she put the albums on the desk than both their phones rang. Harry brought up the graphic from the gate camera. Two men, both older and well-dressed sat in a car scowling at the camera on the gate post.

"Can I help you?" Harry asked after pushing the button.

"You can let us in. We need to talk to the owner." He turned to the other man who had begun yelling in a language Kate didn't understand, and yelled back at him. Harry pushed the button which opened the gate.

"Let's go. However, keep in mind the old saying... 'Beware of Greeks...'"

-25-

Monday Midday

They took their treasures down to the library and Kate ducked into their bedroom to wash some dust and dirt off and change her sweater. Her jeans just needed a little dusting. She was beside Harry when they opened the door to their uninvited guests. The man who had been yelling in Greek in the car raised his arm, waving it around and began yelling again. Harry held up his hand and replied with a curt phrase that to Kate's surprise seemed to be Greek. At least it had the desired effect of stopping the man's wrath. Harry said something else and the man switched to English.

"I beg your pardon, sir. I have been so upset since I got a call from our consulate that the body of my older brother had been found. Please understand, he has been missing for most of my life with no word. Our parents and my older sisters have all died not knowing where he was or if he were alive. My name is Mikolas Castellanos. This is Demetre Papadopoulos from the consulate."

Harry extended his hand. "I'm Harry Foyle and this is my wife Kate. This is our home. I assume that Stavros Castellanos was your older brother. I do believe that your brother was one of two skeletons which were found when the basement had to be dug up to repair pipes. Since my wife and I have been in residence for only a week today after purchasing the residence, we do not have a lot of information. The FBI has been doing an informal examination of the situation. The agents are here and will be happy to speak with you. A forensic pathologist who examined your brother's body is here as well. I am sure you are still recovering from the shock and the trip up from the city, so will you please join us in the kitchen for coffee and some refreshment. I will ask the people with more knowledge on the problem to speak to you. Kate, could you show Mr. Castellanos and Mr. Papadopoulos to the kitchen while I fetch, Des, Oliver, and Gwyn?"

"Gentlemen?" Kate waved them toward the kitchen after hanging up their hats and coats to the left of the door.

"Your husband said that you have only been in residence for a week. How long have you owned this magnificent residence?"

"Well, we were married last week and my husband purchased the house as a wedding present for me so that we could spend our honeymoon here. I had visited this place as a child multiple times and had always loved it. Unfortunately, this has not exactly been the honeymoon we planned since the bodies were found right before we arrived."

"Your wedding trip? This is horrible. It is certainly a beautiful place, but the chaos must have come with this shock. I am surprised you remained," Papadopoulos said.

"My husband is a former FBI, so not unfamiliar with chaos."

"Nor are you, Kate," Des said as he and Oliver, Tom, Gwyn, and Harry walked in. Oh, good, coffee and is that a blueberry coffee cake I smell?"

"Yes, so get your coffee and sit then I shall make the introductions," Harry told them.

Everyone settled in and Harry did the introductions. Gwyn spoke first. "I'd like to offer my condolences on the death of your brother. I am a forensic pathologist and as such handle the study of the bodies. It is only through circumstantial evidence that we were able to do the identification of your brother. There were two bodies. One we were able to identify through medical records as belonging to Divon Hader. Does that name mean anything to you?"

"That was my brother's best friend. It was assumed that they were together when they disappeared."

"He was with your brother when he finished checking the security of the pieces at the consulate," Papadopoulos told him. "Stavros introduced him, telling me that they had been at college together." He turned to the others at the table. "Stavros disappeared soon after we had a theft of an ancient Greek treasures from our consulate."

"Iolanthe's Treasure," Oliver said.

"Yes. How do you know?" The consul asked.

"My name is Oliver Bailey. "I was one of the two FBI agents who warned you that we had heard about possible theft."

"A warning we ignored because we had just spent a lot of money installing a new vault and security system."

"I have never stopped trying to recover the treasure. It was my first assignment and I have tried to locate the treasure ever since."

"And you are here because?"

"A name came up during the investigation of these bodies. It was a name that I had, in my research, felt was connected. When I began researching that person, the association with your brother, Mr. Castellanos and Mr. Hader came up."

"I don't understand."

"Perhaps I can help," a voice from the doorway said. "Good evening, gentlemen. My name is Ann Killoy. I and my fiancé were in attendance at the Christmas Ball weekend here when the agents think these deaths occurred. Your brother and Mr. Hader were attending as well. It was the weekend of Christmas Eve. They were here with another man, Count Gregori Baturin."

"I remember this Count. My father did not approve of him. He wanted my brother to stay away from him, said he was trouble."

"Was, and is. The Count is presently out on bail after breaking into this house multiple times and attempting to assault me. Luckily," she reached down and stroked the Sams who had settled between her and Kate, "My great-niece has trained her dogs to work as police dogs, and they defended me. The weekend of the ball, I accidentally overheard a discussion in the library where men were arguing about something which sounded criminal. My uncle and Baturin's voices were the only ones I recognized but there were other men. What they said and the amount of anger in their voices frightened me and I convinced my fiancé to leave, We returned to the city that night. I can not tell you for certain that your brother was in the room during this argument. All I know is that diamonds were mentioned and Mr. Bailey tells me that there was a theft which included diamonds from the Greek Consulate the prior night."

"Iolanthe's Treasure was stolen from the consulate the night before Christmas Eve. It has never been recovered."

"We have been working to find information about the possible whereabouts of the Treasure, but so far, we have had no luck in locating it," Oliver told the men. Conversation petered out as people seemed to disappear into their thoughts.

A knock came at the back door. Helen stood holding a large baking pan. Harry jumped up to let her in. "Oh my goodness, Kate, even more company. It's a good thing this is a large roast. I made a potato casserole to go with it this morning while you were a church. The rolls just need to be put in the oven and the green beans heated up and you'll be ready to go."

"Thank you, Helen. Your timing couldn't be better. We will get the table set. Gentlemen, I hope that you'll join us. As Helen says, it's a large roast so there is plenty to go around."

The two men looked at each other and agreed. Everyone pitched in setting the table while Kate fed the dogs. Gwyn took Mr. Castellanos aside to discuss arrangements for his brother's burial. She asked for contact information on the Hader family so their son could rest with his family.

Dinner was surprisingly relaxed. The men talked about taking both Greek gentlemen into the library and discussing what they had found so far about the theft in the consulate.

Kate realized that much as they had done, what they didn't have were details about the crime, knowledge of who was responsible for both the theft and the murders and where the treasure was hidden. They had spent a whole week working, they still were floundering around struggling to find answers. This problem needed to gather more facts.

She wondered what Oliver had found in the papers from the hassock. Were any of the participants named? She needed to get Gwyn to test the blood on the hassock. Maybe they could get DNA, though that seemed to take forever. Would there be fingerprints on the guns, on the bullets?

There were so many steps left. She felt movement by her leg and looked down into Dillon's beautiful face. As much as a dog could, he looked concerned. He must be feeling her frustration.

What she needed was to take the dogs for a walk and clear her mind. Once the table was cleared, she grabbed her coat and rounded up the dogs.

As she started to leave, Ann called to her to wait.

Kate and Ann put leads on the dogs and told Harry they were going to take them for a walk. They headed down the trail toward the dock. Kate thought she would show Ann how the repairs had gone. They had almost reached the end of the trail when Dillon stopped. The hair on the back of his neck began to rise and both Liam and Quinn moved in close to him, lowering their heads and bracing themselves. Kate grabbed

Ann's arm and signaling quiet, she pulled the dogs off the trail making sure there were pine needles under their feet to cushion their steps. They had no sooner slipped behind a white pine and Kate whipped Ann's bright red scarf off her neck and stuffed it inside her coat when her phone quietly buzzed. She pushed the button on the new app and tapped in a code. The face of a man she saw in the photos Dev got appeared. She hit two more buttons. The next photo showed him tying up his boat to the dock. He then reached into the boat and lifted a blanket-wrapped bundle. The next photo showed what looked like the barrel of a gun sticking out from the blanket. Kate suddenly heard a sound of feet running toward them down the trail. As the sound of running got louder, the man dropped the bundle and grabbed the gun, dropped down on one knee, lifted the rifle to his shoulder, and pointed it at the spot where the trail ends and the dock begins. Kate slipped the clasp off Dillon's lead and Liam's then passed Quinn's lead to Ann.

Quinn had other plans. He felt the lead loosen as it was passed and bolted. Before Kate could move or make a sound, he streaked from the trees and in one move sprung up hitting the man on his shoulder and head with his paws. The momentum carried the man off the deck and into the water. "Quinn!" Kate's scream brought Harry and Des racing around the trees and onto the deck. The man was trying to climb onto the dock but Dillon and Liam's growls prevented him from doing anything but holding on.

"Quinn!" Kate screamed again as she knelt trying to see under the deck. Motion to her right had her shifting as she spotted Quinn swimming toward shore. She raced back to the path and broke through the snow sliding down to the water's edge. Reaching out, she managed to snag the lead which floated beside his head. She felt hands reach around her to lift her back to the top of the bank. Then Harry took the lead from her and guided Quinn up onto solid land. The first thing Quinn did was shake, spraying everyone with icy water but the next was to pull back and grab his trophy by its strap. He backed up until the rifle was out of the water and then with two leaps, managed to get himself and the rifle up onto the bank.

"Quinn, what a brave boy," Kate told him, pulling his sopping wet body into her arms and resting her head on his. "Don't you ever scare me like that again. Oh, he's freezing. Harry, we need to get him up to the house." Des passed them leading the equally wet man whose hands were now bound behind him. Kate held Quinn who was quite ready to jump on him again.

Once they passed, she started for the trail and spotted her grandmother coming toward her, waving her phone.

"Kate, Quinn was amazing. He saved us all and I've got it all recorded on my phone."

As Des and the man walked by, she stopped and staring hard, gasped. "My God. Uncle Roger. What are you doing here? Why are you trying to kill my grandchildren? I am sorry, Kate, but I think that my entire family has turned into a bunch of homicidal maniacs. Des, lock him up and this time throw the key away so he can't get out."

"Kate, you're soaked and so is Quinn. We've got to get you back to the house." Ann switched into grandmother mode, she called Helen to get a hot bath ready in Kate's room and ask Gwyn if she could bathe Quinn since both were soaked and freezing. While walking quickly, Harry passed Quinn's lead to Ann and asked her to hold Quinn's trophy. He peeled off Kate's coat and replaced it with his own.

Gwyn and Tom met them at the back gate and took Quinn straight into the grooming room. It was a small laundry room off the kitchen which boasted a washer, dryer and a dog bath. Quinn recognized the bathtub and hopped in. He was one of Kate's dogs who loved baths as opposed to his grandmother who hated them. Gwyn soon had his coat sprayed with warm water and suds up with dog shampoo. Tom, who was an expert at washing Samoyeds from years of helping in the kennel, rinsed the coat and then poured a water/vinegar rinse over him and then rinsed again, leaving his coat clean and shiny. The shelf above the bath boasted a pile of towels, and they got most of the water out of his coat before wrapping him in a towel and lifting him onto the grooming table in the center of the room. Tom pulled the dryer off the shelf, plugged it in and began blowing the coat with warm air to dry it as Gwyn brushed it, stopping periodically to hug Quinn and tell him a super crime fighter he now was.

-26-

Monday Evening and Tuesday Morning

Kate made it to the bathroom with Harry's help, helpless with shaking, her teeth chattering and her feet so cold she couldn't feel the floor. Steam filled the room and hot water made her feel as though she were melting, not a graceful swoon, but more a puddling plop. Harry's hands were the only things keeping her upright. He closed the bathroom door and using his arm to hold her in place, the pulled off his coat and threw it on the floor, eased her sweater over her head. She was thankful it was wool and didn't cling. By the time he got to wrestling her jeans down, she was able to lift her legs to help. When done, he eased her into the tub where steamy water made her long for sleep.

"Don't fall asleep—you'll drown," He told her as he ducked into their bedroom and returned with her sweats. Then he laid the back of his hand against her forehead, as her father had done when they were sick as children. He deemed her cooked. He opened the drain, pulled her to her feet, and helped her step out. A quick rub down got her dry, and he pulled wool socks onto her feet before helping her dress.

She was tucked into their bed with a stack of pillows holding her up when Ann knocked at the door and called out. Harry opened the door widely as she came in carrying a tray loaded with a bowl of Will's homemade vegetable soup from the freezer. The smell of freshly baked bread filled the room. A mug of steaming tea was the first thing she picked up once the tray was settled on her lap. Harry nodded to Ann and told Kate that he'd be back. Her grandmother settled on the bed and reached out, as Harry had, to place the back of her hand on Kate's forehead.

"How is Quinn?" Kate asked.

"He's fine. Gwyn is delighted to work with a dog who loves taking a bath. I heard her laugh when Tom told Quinn to lie down in the tub, and she was able to wet the coat completely all at once. Everyone who has bathed that dog knows he thinks that baths are just an excuse to get super snuggled for half an hour. I was astonished when he shot toward Roger. What my idiot uncle is doing here is beyond me. I haven't seen or heard from him in forever and why he should be crawling onto your deck to try to shoot you and Harry is insane. I do hope that my mother's DNA keeps me from going gaga."

"Not going to happen, Gran. You've got nothing to worry about. Has anybody gotten any answers out of him about why? This was his second try. I remember his face from the photo that Des got on the security camera when we were at church. The dogs scared him off that time. I guess he was determined. Could it have anything to do with our treasure hunt?"

"I hope that with Gil, George, Des and Oliver threatening to lock him up and throw the key away, something will come out. I don't remember Roger as being evil like Evangeline. I think of him as the original patsy. He was a pushover for anyone who wanted to bully him into doing something as a kid. He must be eighty-ish now. A little long in the tooth for covert operations."

"Harry will find out. I'm just glad that Quinn stopped him from shooting Harry. I almost sent Dillon, but he would have grabbed the gun and fallen in the water, not taking out Roger as Quinn did. I think that I'd better begin Quinn's police dog training sooner rather than later. He's learned so much by just watching his father, he's becoming a pistol. What he needs to learn is not to go off half-cocked on his own."

Kate looked at her tray and discovered that she'd finished everything. A yawn escaped her, and she realized that her eyelids were getting heavy. Ann moved the table and took most of the pillows and put them aside. Then tucking her in, told her to sleep. When Gil and George returned from booking their prisoner and seeing his injuries taken care of by a doctor, and the lawyer from the District Attorney's office had started the paperwork, Quinn was dry and the dogs were enjoying an extra biscuit treat. After a moment Quinn left. Kate was almost asleep when the door opened and a weight hit the bottom of the bed and snuggled in beside her. The smell of a freshly bathed puppy made her smile and sleep claimed her. This was becoming a habit.

Back in the kitchen George told Harry. "Ann got the whole thing on video. I've never seen a dog go for a gun like that. It was amazing."

Harry laughed. "I think since he's seen Dillon do it twice, he just wanted to try it. I've got to admit, he's a natural."

Harry began pulling food out of the refrigerator. "I don't know about the rest of you but almost getting shot makes me hungry." Everyone laughed, but there was an air of seriousness under the laughter. Harry put sandwich meat onto a platter, noticed that Ann had warmed up soup and bread which he added to the feast. Then he pulled out a bowl of macaroni salad he'd made earlier for lunch to top it off.

"Did I hear Ann right? George asked. This guy was her uncle? He's pretty spry for a guy who must be eighty. However, he seems as bat-shit crazy as the rest of the Durgins."

" What did you get him to say about tonight?"

"He kept claiming that he thought that his family still lived here. Why he arrived at night carrying a gun, he wouldn't say. He was shocked to see Ann here talking about grandchildren. They hadn't seen each other since they were young. I can see why Agent Bailey has such a good record with the agency. He looks so forgettable, and his voice is so calm he lulls the bad guys into trusting him. He quietly moved the conversation around to ask why now and asked him who told him to come.

Before we knew it, Uncle Roger was telling us that Vivian phoned him yesterday to say that people had taken over Camp and forced her out. That her father hid a treasure in the house for his relatives to find, but now they'd never have a chance. She asked him to come to search the house and told him that if any of the bad people got in his way, just shoot them."

"And he followed her directions?"

"Well, that's not the interesting part. The interesting part is that Vivian has been under constant twenty-four-hour surveillance since she arrived. The lady has not been near a phone."

Soon after, the evening ended and Harry locked up after making sure all their guests were settled, including the Greeks. Then he headed for bed. He found Kate sleeping soundly, with Quinn stretched out beside her. He eased Quinn off the bed and watched as the puppy settled in by his father. He undressed and crawled in next to his bride, pulling her tight against him and, after telling himself that the danger was over, fell sleep.

Kate woke to feel as warm as she had been cold last night. She snuggled closer to the heat source and felt an arm tighten around her.

"How is my Kate'sicle?"

"Warm as toast. Ann says her uncle is crazy."

"I don't think he's crazy, just an old man who was told a bunch of lies and was convinced to do something about them."

"Harry, he was ready to shoot you as soon as you came around the bend to the dock."

"He was ready to challenge me. Dev checked the gun. It wasn't loaded. Roger told Oliver, who by the way is a great interrogator, that Vivian phoned him with a story about the house being taken from her so that strangers could get at the family treasure her father had hidden. She begged him to come to find it."

"But Vivian..."

"Right. She's had no access to a phone and has been on twenty-four-hour supervision since she tried to kill us."

"Evangeline?"

"Possibly—probably."

Quinn barked, bouncing up and down ready to take on the world. Harry rolled out of bed and went to the slider. After glancing around the yard, he opened the door. Quinn went speeding to the far end of the yard and back, doing figure eights and getting the others to chase him. Then he jumped onto the spool and barked. Dillon jumped up and knocked him off which sent him running again.

"I think we can safely say that Quinn is not suffering any ill effects from his swim."

"Well, I'm going to get dressed and call Maeve again. She may have found something to give us a clue into this madness. Did you take care of our Greeks last night?"

"We put them up in the guest rooms. I don't know if they are early risers, so I'll go start breakfast while you dress, then you can take over."

Harry left and Kate found something warm to wear. As she reached for the door to the hall, she saw tennis balls go flying out into the yard. Laughing, she went to see who had been suckered into the game this early. Des and Oliver, wearing warm coats and scarves and laughing hard, were tossing balls in all directions as the dogs raced to return them. When she reached the kitchen, the game had ended and Liam was racing Dillon to get the last ball. Quinn had flopped onto the deck, finally worn out. Each dog got praise for returning a ball and then once the balls were put away, they came into the kitchen.

"If we only had half that energy, it would be wonderful." Their guests had been watching the show. Kate offered them coffee or tea and asked them to relax because breakfast was being made. She was busy breaking a dozen eggs into a bowl to make scrambled eggs for everyone. Harry had returned, dressed for the day, and started cooking the bacon and warming up a bag of Helen's fresh rolls which were in the freezer. Their guests spoke about making arrangements to move Stavros' remains to the city for burial. Since the offices they needed in town wouldn't open until ten o'clock, they relaxed and ate. The discussion over breakfast avoided last night's adventure and centered on staying in touch with the men on the chance that their treasure could be located.

Since she didn't expect either Gil or George, Kate was startled when her phone and Harry's beeped telling them there was someone at the gate. Kate pushed the button on her phone since Harry was dishing up another batch of bacon, and was startled to see Maeve. Her great-aunt smiled and said they'd woken early and decided to drive up due to the seriousness of what she'd discovered. Kate pushed the button and opened the gate.

"Maeve, we just talked about this yesterday." Kate ran forward to hug her great-aunt as she came in the door. The family resemblance between Kate and her great-aunt was startling. Though in her seventies, Maeve appeared much younger and was still a very attractive woman. She also had an aura about her which seemed to command respect. Kate asked, "What are you doing here? Where is Padraig?"

"After the first twenty minutes I spent researching on the phone after your call, yesterday, I decided that we had to talk to you in person. If you're involved with this woman, you're in the middle of a nest of snakes. She's bad news and I figured it would be better to explain it face-to-face."

"Well, come have some breakfast. Ah, there you are, Padraig."

"This place is wonderful, Katie. Who owns it?" Padraig asked.

"We do. Harry bought it from Gram's cousin and remodeled it. This was the surprise honeymoon venue. I used to visit here when we did the dog shows up here. Gramps would bring us. I always felt like a princess in a castle, especially sleeping in the tower bedrooms. Unfortunately, our quiet honeymoon in our very own castle hasn't worked out the way he planned it."

"Harry, I'm sorry to burst in on your honeymoon, but it's important," her great-aunt said hugging her husband.

"Don't worry, Maeve. You and Padraig are always welcome. Anyway, you're only adding to a crowd already in residence."

"Oh, you poor dears. And, I'm bringing news to add to your concerns."

Ann came down the stairs with Liam and hugged her sister-in-law. "According to the children, this has been less a honeymoon and a more three-ring circus," Maeve said.

"You're right. I feel much of it is my fault for talking Harry into buying this place from my insane cousin."

"Is she insane?" Maeve asked laughing.

"She tried to shoot the children."

"My God! Are you okay?"

Harry smiled. "Dillon is getting to be an expert at disarming killers."

Maeve turned and scooped the dog into her lap, hugging him. "Oh, Dillon, my brave boy. I am so proud of you."

Quinn immediately jumped up, and she lowered Dillon to hug Quinn. "I'm sure you were brave too, Quinn. You are growing into a handsome puppy."

"You will hear how brave Quinn is once you get some food."

"Is someone holding a party?" Des asked from the doorway. "Hey, Maeve, welcome to the zoo."

Maeve looked up and smiled. "Des, I heard you got in trouble with your boss for moonlighting with Oliver—catching spies."

"So I've been told. Plus, my boss let the people at State influence them and Baturin is already out on bond. I would have locked the bastard up and thrown the key away."

"Well, Oliver, you should get in here too since it seems to involve your cast of characters. Kate, get your tea and sit. My phone was burning as soon as I started making calls about your aunt, Ann. Just to let you know, this is NOT a nice lady."

"That's what my father used to say and she was his little sister."

"The problem began with her marriage to DeBeers. It was a whirlwind courtship. He was flattered with her attention, slept with her, she told him two weeks later that she was pregnant, and they got married. Needless to say, she wasn't pregnant. What she was cunning. She worked her way into his company and at the same time, his health began to fail. Oh, I'll tell you the rest later after I have some of this delicious food."

-27-

Later Tuesday Morning

Following breakfast, Maeve started explaining what she'd found out about Evangeline and her husband. "It seems that the Southern District of New York has been looking into them for irregularities within the company. Since it is a publicly held company, the SEC has also gotten involved. Your call yesterday had uncanny timing. SDNY had just served a search warrant on the couple only to find the lady not at home, and when the servants opened the door, they tried to block access to the house. The police took care of that and served the warrant. They proceeded to check the place and found the door to the master bedroom locked. The pair working in the house said they didn't have a key, so the police broke the door down. Inside they found Mr. DeBeers, in bed, drugged, severely underweight and barely alive. They called an ambulance and took him to the hospital. The servants said that they had no idea that Mr. DeBeers was in such bad shape. All they knew was he was on a special diet which the misses made and brought to him. Neither of them had seen the man in close to a year. They just figured he was a crazy recluse."

The silence following Maeve's story was jaw hanging. Finally, Kate asked, "Do they have any idea where Evangeline is?"

"No, but SDNY is extremely interested in why my great-niece and her husband are interested in their case."

"We aren't. We knew nothing about this case. I called you because Evangeline has been posing as Gram's cousin Vivian. This has been going on for a long time and I think she might have been involved in a jewel theft from the Greek Consulate sixty years ago. She might also have something to do with the two dead bodies which were found in our basement. Helen, has, with her husband Otto, worked here for Vivian since she moved here permanently, soon after the death of her father. She spotted Vivian getting into a car near the grocery store in Bolton's Landing yesterday. The only problem with that is that Vivian has been locked up in a psychiatric facility since she tried to shoot Harry and me. I figured that Evangeline has been impersonating Vivian for years and is still at it. The person Helen saw climb into the car with a man, almost certainly, was Evangeline."

"She was spotted here yesterday?"

"Yes. But it gets better. Last night, we had an armed assailant sneak onto the grounds and try to shoot Harry. Luckily our 'Dillon-want-to-be' Quinn took him out, hitting him so hard they both went off the deck and into the lake. Quinn then proceeded to drag the man's rifle from the water. When we got the man out of the water, Gram identified him as her Uncle Roger. He informed us that Vivian had called him hours before to say that people had taken the house from her and driven her away to steal a treasure her father had hidden in the house. The only problem with that is that Vivian has had no access to any phone since she was locked up. So, I am guessing this could be Evangeline's work as well."

Harry volunteered to speak to her contact at any time they want. "Since the Greek Consul has just left after spending the night, he could confirm our story. Plus we do have the FBI in residence."

Padraig cleared his throat. "I could swear that you two got married a week ago and left on your honeymoon. This is NOT a honeymoon."

"I couldn't agree with you more," Harry said. "The sooner we can get this mess out of our lives, the better. Oh, and if you feel like adding another name to your New York search, Maeve, you might want to see what you can find on Count Grigori Baturin."

"Baturin—the double agent? The only time I saw him, he freaked me out. His eyes are dead."

"Well, we had him in jail for a while, but someone from the Russian Embassy pulled strings and bailed him out. We're not sure if he and Evangeline are working together on this.

However, I haven't a clue how or if what's going on in the city has anything to do with our sixty-year-old crime. I do know that I want to start my honeymoon with my beautiful wife."

Maeve stood and began to plan what they would do next. Harry smiled. He thought that she must have been something when she was a honcho at MI-5 back in the day. She was still a force to be reckoned with. Harry, Maeve, Des, Oliver, Tom, and Gil who had just arrived, moved to the library for their call. Kate and Gwyn cleared away the dishes and then let the dogs out into the yard while Padraig and Ann moved to the sitting room to talk.

"Gwyn," Kate asked, "did you pull any prints off the guns we found yet?"

"No. I should do that. I should check the cartridges as well."

"It would be good if we could just round up these criminal senior citizens and figure out who did what. I have a funny feeling that this whole mess is connected but I haven't had time to think."

"Look, since Oliver is busy in the library, I'm going to go into the ballroom and see if I can get prints off the guns. I'll also process the blood on the hassock to test for blood type and if needed we could send it off for possible DNA. I'll check to see if either of these two men had medical records with their blood types. Since both Vivian and the Count were fingerprinted when they went into lockup in Bolton Landing, I can compare any prints I find to those."

"I think I'm going to disappear into our bedroom. I found some stuff in the attic which I haven't even had a chance to look at. If anyone needs me, I'll be there."

Gwyn headed for the ballroom as Kate turned toward the bedroom. She stopped. The idea she'd had flickered back into her mind, but before she could grab and hold it, it was gone again. Maybe what she needed was to sit in a quiet room working on something else to have it pop up.

Harry had moved the boxes with Ann's grandfather's journals, the paperwork, and the photo albums into the bedroom. She pulled the boxes next to the overstuffed chair by the sliding glass window and after getting some old dog towels from under the sink, spread them over her lap and started leafing through photos.

Though black and white, and not color, the photos were wonderful and very clear. She studied the faces of her ancestors and relations and found some similarity to Gram, but none to any of the Killoys in either her father's generation or her own. When Gram had married Gramps, his genetics seem to rule. Dad's blond curly hair was seen in not only herself but all her brothers. She followed the progress of the house being built, various guest visits, and the formal photos of the family's children as they arrived.

She didn't take the time to study the photos but flipped through quickly. In the final album, she found photos of a very young Vivian standing before a Christmas tree holding a very fancy doll dressed in an outfit that matched the one she wore exactly. Kate's eyes moved from the girl to the tree. There on top was the Tiffany star. What she realized was that the decorations were almost the same as they are now. A few had been added, but not many. That must have been the year Gram's grandfather got ill and passed away, because the albums stopped.

She pulled out the journals but decided to leave them until Harry could read them with her before they passed them to Gram and Tom to read. She pulled the box with the blueprints closer and setting aside the top one which she'd seen, began opening them one at a time. The box was half empty when Harry came searching for her. Maeve had volunteered to make lunch which would be ready in fifteen minutes. She didn't hear him come into the room, with all her attention on the plans showing the passages within the walls. It seemed that there was a passage off the library on the north side of the house, which connected with both the ballroom and the north tower. Beyond that, the passage rose to the third floor, in an area beyond the servant's quarters. The stairs rose to the attic. The plans just labeled this passage as 'alt stair'. What caught her attention was a room in the attic with a 'hidden' door marked.

"Kate?"

She shrieked and dropped the plans.

"I'm sorry, Luv. I thought you heard me open the door. What had you so enthralled?"

Kate took a moment to get her heart and breathing under control and then reached down to pull up the plan. "There is another hidden staircase."

Harry squatted next to her as she pointed it out on the plan. She also showed where the hidden staircase they knew about was shown on another plan. The one she'd just found did not continue to the basement or a tunnel as the others did. "I think he installed the tunnel to the cabin so that guests could access the cabin in winter when the snow was high without having to brave the outdoor temperatures."

"Well, we can open it up again when we stop having people trying to kill us. How did you do with the SDNY and your old boss?"

"My old boss sends felicitations to my bride who is his wife's favorite designer. He informed me that marrying you was the smartest thing I ever did. The word on Evangeline's husband is that it was touch and go, but it looks as though he will live. There is a state-wide APB on the lady. I informed him that she was in disguise up here and Gil sent him a photo of Vivian telling them that this is the woman she is impersonating. We also discussed the Count. He said that he did not sign off on getting him out on bail and would check into it. The bottom line was the lawyers talked law and the Bureau talked crime and the dance went on with us not a single step forward. Let's eat." They packed everything back into the box and headed for the kitchen.

They all sat around the table enjoying the casserole that Maeve had made along with a salad that Padraig had thrown together. Maeve asked Ann, "Who else from your family might be dropping in on the kids with criminal intent."

"I don't know," she answered. "I haven't seen these people in sixty years. I only recognized Uncle Roger because, though his hair has gone white, his face is relatively the same."

"What do you know about others?"

Kate stood for a moment and went to the counter to get some papers. She told everyone that she had done research on the Durgins but hadn't been able to share much. She explained, "I didn't spend much time on Nelson since he died less than a month after the crime. I found articles about Gram's father which abounded throughout the math community online. He was quite a shining star and several of his books are still in print. Since he hadn't been at the party, I didn't spend time on him but went in search of Edmond. He married a socialite whose father had money in railroads, steel, and oil. As far as I can tell, they had no children. She died in her early forties and he married another socialite. She was from Virginia, old money, and they settled there. So far as I can tell, Edmond is still alive as is wife number two.

"Christian Durgin moved to a town west of Houston and became pastor at a small church, in spite of having no ecclesiastical education. His background was marketing and from what I can find out, he put it to good use. A mere three years after he arrived, he had grown the church from twenty parishioners to more than two thousand. He had published two books on being saved and had had a weekly radio hour when, for a certain donation, you could be guaranteed your place in heaven. It seemed that he ran afoul of the law with that one and served several years in a minimum-security prison. He got religion for real in prison and has spent the last ten years working as a missionary in Peru. There was no mention of him ever marrying.

"Roger Durgin did marry. In fact, he seemed to make a career of it. Considering he'd been raised Catholic, he managed to marry and divorce four women before settling on the present Mrs. Durgin who is thirty-five years old. This should have raised an eyebrow in his family, but apparently not. In spite of the number and apparent youth of the women, there were no children listed. Roger retired from his brokerage firm five years ago and now resides in West Palm Beach, Florida, except for his presence, at the moment, in the Bolton Landing jail.

"Evangeline had proved to be a challenge, but the information gained from the SDNY and the FBI in the city gives a picture of her not being a nice lady. Most references to her are as a socialite at some gala or the opera. The interesting thing is that the society photos of her never feature her husband. We now know why."

Kate looked around the table. "My question is if the treasure was in some way linked to the Durgins who were here at the time of the theft and murders, was it a Durgin who killed these men? Was a Durgin involved in the theft? And which Durgin is trying to kill us and why? We need answers and there is only one place where we can get them. Gil, how complicated would it be for me to visit Vivian?"

"You want to talk to that crazy bitch? Why?" he asked.

"Because she was there when it happened. She is the only witness we have who knew all the players."

-28-

Tuesday Midday

Kate, she tried to kill you," George said.

"Well, when I talk to her, I'd appreciate you making sure she's not armed."

"Right, I'll make a note of that—no guns in the interview. Kate, this is nuts. What are you hoping to get?" Gil interrupted.

"The truth. I've been thinking about the conversations I've had with Vivian. I'm beginning to think that she's just another victim here."

"Kate, what part of she tried to kill you don't you get?" Ann reached across the table to grab her hand. "It's kind of you not to hold it against her, but she's not stable. She's likely to say anything. Or she may not talk to you at all?"

"Gram, I need to do this. Gwyn, did you have any luck with the guns."

"Yes and no. I got some clear prints off the guns. That's good news. The bad news is that the prints don't match any of the suspects we have in custody."

"Ah, I thought so."

"You thought so? Do you think you know who did pull the triggers?" Gwyn asked.

"I need more information before I say anything, which is why I need to talk to Vivian."

Silence settled over the table. Its occupants looked at each other to see what the others thought.

"It will have to be in a room with an observation window," Harry cautioned.

"Of course. This will help everyone's case," Kate said. "Who wants dessert?"

Following lunch, Gil and George left to see if they could arrange for Kate to visit Vivian. Maeve and Padraig had not spent any time in this part of New York even though they'd lived in New York City for close to sixty years. So Ann offered to show them around, though many of the tourist attractions were closed until spring. Des and Oliver went into the ballroom, so they could check the plans of the theft to see if Evangeline fit as a possible participant, and to see what more they could find out about her. Gwyn and Tom just disappeared to do something together.

Kate and Harry played with the dogs for a while. Once the pups were worn out, Kate and Harry went to the library to begin a search for the other hidden staircase. They brought the plans from the bedroom. But even with the plans, it took almost twenty minutes to locate the release switch for the entrance.

The library itself was a distraction with the floor to ceiling bookcases and the elaborate carving on the woodwork. One of the books, the fourth from the end of the third shelf from the bottom of the bookcase nearest the fireplace, wasn't real. The book was The Aeneid in the original Latin. When they pulled the book as thought to remove it, it slid only partway out. When it stopped, a click sounded as a lock released, and that section of bookshelves swung open becoming a door. Harry closed the door and saw the book slide back into place as though it had never been disturbed.

He pulled the book again. Kate told the dogs to wait for them, and they both entered the stairway. When they reached the second-floor landing, they spotted a door, undid the latch and stepped into the hallway. Keeping the 'invisible' door from shutting, Harry ran his hand down the door-jam to locate the button in the carved molding which released the catch on the hallway side. He again joined Kate on the landing and closed the hallway door. Continuing up to the third floor, they were surprised when the door this time led into a small bedroom complete with curtained window, a brass bed, a Persian carpet on the floor, a small oak chest and a closet containing several suits and pairs of shoes along with a man's smoking jacket. The bed was covered with several beautifully made, though dusty quilts. Beyond the closet was a door to the hallway of what would have been the servant's floor. Behind an elaborately carved floor to ceiling mirror, Kate found the door to the attic.

Kate noticed as she looked around, that theirs were the only footprints made in the years of dust covering the floor. This answered the question as to whether this room was known by Vivian or Baturin.

Though heavy, the mirror swung easily as they opened the door to the attic and headed up. When they reached the top, the first thing they noticed was the light. Even though the attic room had only one tiny window which should have made the room dark, a section of the ceiling had been inlaid with glass block allowing light to stream down and fill the room.

Looking around, Harry couldn't find any door leading to the main attic. He checked the plans and located where the door should be, but when he found the latch, it didn't lift.

Kate found a small shiny spot in the dark wall. Reaching forward, her fingers felt a small 'S' hook that had been inserted into an equally small latch, making an effective lock. It was simple but did the trick.

Harry checked the attic beyond once the door was open. It took him a while to figure the operation of the latch on the main attic side. Kate, at the same time, began checking out the room. It seemed spartan with only a single chair, though that chair was upholstered in leather. She dusted off the chair and sat in it finding it very comfortable. As she relaxed in the chair, her gaze took in the rest of the room. What she noticed was when she sat there, she faced a semi-circular arrangement of objects all covered in dust covers. She caught her breath when she realized that the chair had been placed as an audience of one to view and appreciate something.

"Harry, come here," she called, as her hands began to sweat and her breathing came in short puffs as though she'd been running. She stood as Harry came back into the room, closing the door to the attic. Kate grabbed his arm and pulled him to the chair.

"Sit," she ordered.

"Kate, what..."

"Just sit, look around and tell me your first thought."

"That I'm about to see something?"

"Exactly. You are the audience. All you need is a show."

With that, she walked over to the cloth draped objects and one at a time, lifted the covers.

Harry gasped. "The treasure."

Six carved marble statues appeared. Each was on its plinth. They were breathtaking. The detail was so fine they seemed alive. Each of the Greek goddesses was turned so that her gaze focused on the person who occupied the chair. Harry seemed frozen in place—bewitched.

"We've found part of the treasure. Not the jewelry, but treasure nonetheless. You should call the Greek consul and let him know."

Harry slowly turned his head away from the statues and blinked, focusing on Kate. "Right. Call. Um, call the consul."

"Watch out, Foyle or I might get jealous of these marble ladies."

He stood and reached for her, taking her face in his hands and kissing her. "You needn't worry, I love only you. But, it is amazing. With the statues arranged that way, it's almost as though they can see whoever is sitting there. It's hypnotic."

"I think that's what the artist had in mind. I can see why they are considered treasures."

"I'll call the consul, and he can get in touch with Castellanos if he wants. I'll suggest they bring boxes for transporting each of them so there is no damage."

"Let's go. The dogs will wonder where we are. I think we should wait to show everyone what we've found until I know our time-line.

When they got back to the first floor and closed up the entrance to the hidden staircase, they went to the kitchen. It seemed everyone was still off on their pursuits. So, they let the dogs out and went into the bedroom to take a look at her great-great grandfather's journals. They pulled them out and Harry took the first one, but Kate decided to read the last in hope that it might give more insight into the family. He died at the age of ninety-nine in 1954.

As she got into the journal, she realized that James Durgin had some serious concerns about his family. He had been born into great wealth and had kept accumulating it. His wife Virginia brought another fortune into the family when they married, and he had raised his children to value wealth as a goal in their lives.

The only one who had rejected his teaching was Timothy, his second son. The journal spoke of his disappointment in the choices his children were making. He valued money but he had also valued hard work. That part of his philosophy seemed to be lost on all but Tim. He had read the reports that his agent in the city had been sending him about his son since he left, and realized that he had turned out quite well, without his help. The latest report stated that he was a full professor at Columbia University and had two books on mathematics published to high acclaim in his field. His wife had died the previous year leaving him a teenage daughter to raise.

The girl, Ann, was bright and beautiful and she was just a few years younger than Nelson's daughter Vivian. He'd suggest that she should be invited to visit Vivian. She should know about her family and Virginia would want to get to know this granddaughter.

His only daughter was a great disappointment to him. He admitted he spoiled her as a child, but instead of instilling a bond of love between them, she had developed an air of entitlement. He could find no sign of love or kindness in her.

Evangeline hadn't married the actor she'd run off with but instead nabbed DeBeer who had built his business from scratch to the point where he is worth several million. James felt sorry for the man. His daughter was beautiful which probably attracted the man, but DeBeer would not find in Evangeline the support he had found in his wonderful Virginia.

Kate looked up when she heard a noise coming from outside. Three black noses were pressed against the slider wanting to come in. Kate slid off the bed and crossed the room to let them in. Harry was lost in what he was reading and jumped when Quinn's icy nose nudged his hand. It seemed to take him a few seconds to recall where he was.

"These journals are incredible. Your ancestor was quite the storyteller."

"I know what you mean. I found that even though he disowned Tim, he kept track of him, getting reports from his agent quarterly. He knew about Gram and decided that she should spend time with Vivian and learn about her family especially following the death of her mother. He was delighted that her father allowed her to visit.

"The more I read, the more I feel that his other children were a great disappointment to him, and he realized that his focus on wealth without equal stress on responsibility caused them to turn out the way they did. He blamed himself for Evangeline becoming a self-centered person and pitied her husband. What are these other red wallets?"

"I haven't looked."

Harry took one and Kate another but then reached out to lay her hand on Harry's. "The call. You were going to call the Greek consul."

"You're right."

He fished out his wallet and dialed the number on the card that Papadopoulos had given him. The conversation though short had the consul explaining it would be Thursday before he could arrange for the safe transport of the statues. Hopefully, that would be okay with them. He was extremely effusive in expressing his gratitude. It seemed that even without the jewels, the statues were of such value to his country that they would bring honor to his country. He repeated that he could not thank them enough. It was arranged that he and his transport would arrive on Wednesday at noon.

Kate grinned. "He sounded like a happy camper."

"Ecstatic."

"If he's smart, and I know he is, he'll be on the phone to the MMA arranging an exhibit to go with the breaking publicity,"

"MMA?"

"You are a math nerd. Metropolitan Museum of Art."

"I know. I was just teasing."

"Remember where I went to school. I spent endless hours in those hallowed halls looking at the dog paintings of artists such as Hockney, Landseer."

"Well, I can attest that our marble goddesses will make a mesmerizing exhibit."

Their phones beeped and Harry looked down to see Padraig smiling at him. "Welcome back," he told him as he pushed the gate button. "Before they get here, which should we share, the ladies or the albums and journals?"

"The albums and journals."

Kate grabbed the stack of albums and Harry the journals as the dogs led them toward the kitchen. Tom and Gwyn were sitting at the table talking quietly, and they looked up when they came in. "Tom, go let your grandmother, Maeve, and Padraig in. They should almost be at the door."

Gwyn asked, "What have you got there?"

"Family treasures. The albums begin with the building of this house and go up to the early 1950s."

"Oh, wonderful. I love old photos. The clothes alone would do it but the hair, the way they interact, it's like an archaeological dig without the dirt. Maybe it's the change in looking at dead people as they looked in life."

"You do know that you're weird."

"Of course I do, she says to the lady with a dozen dogs."

"Touché."

Tom came in carrying a tote bag followed by Padraig with a

carton from which emanated the most wonderful smells.

Padraig set the box down and told them to set the table. They'd found the most wonderful restaurant which made take out meals. "When I told them how many we'd be feeding, I thought the guy would kiss my feet. I think my wife's charm got us the dessert for free."

Gwyn went to call the others as Harry and Kate moved the box of journals and the photo albums to the breakfast nook. Then the table began to be loaded with food, plates, glasses, cups, and saucers. Maeve opened the drawer and pulled out silverware which she and Ann set out. Dinner was a loud and cheerful meal. Des and Oliver had found more clues on who was behind the theft. They were a little hesitant to give out names but Kate interrupted and said, Nelson Durgin. Relieved, they asked how she knew. But Kate said, "I'll tell you when I've got it all."

Conversation then flowed to the sightseers. They toured the dock where the big paddle-wheel steamers land unloaded hundreds of passengers all summer long. Now it was quiet and beautiful. They saw some sailboats still out on the lake in spite of the cold. "We ran into an old-timer who had seen Ann at Mass and took over as tour guide. He took us to his home and told us stories about the early railroad being brought in to take people from the city up here in summer. Others would take the train partway and then switch to the steamer. "When I told him that there would be family staying at Camp most of the year since I had many children and grandchildren plus some great-grandchildren, he was delighted. It seems because my family built the place, I and by extension, Kate and Harry and all the family are to be considered long term residents."

Ann turned to Tom and Gwyn, "What did you kids do?"

They looked at each other and then Tom said, "We've been checking into opportunities for forensic pathologists in Connecticut. There are some openings on both the practical and teaching level."

"Well between Kate and Sal, you will have enough contacts that I'm sure you will find something you like, fast."

"Good. I've found someone to take my place here. They even have a car, so they won't freeze their buns in the middle of January when they get called out."

"Great. Harry and I have found James Durgin's journals and photo albums which begin with the building of this house. So after dinner, we can relax and go nostalgic or play with the trains."

"I claim first dibs on trains," Oliver said.

They quickly cleared away the food and loaded the dishwasher, then headed toward the hall and sitting room. Kate flicked the switch turning on the Christmas tree lights as they went by. Her eyes were again caught by the beauty and sparkle of the tree and the beams which seemed to shoot from the Tiffany star on top. As she headed for the sitting room to look at the pictures some more, her phone buzzed. It was a text from Gil.

You're on for 10 am tomorrow. I hope you know what you're doing.

-29-

Wednesday Morning

It was a little past six when she woke to the sight of all three dogs looking out at the snow which had fallen overnight. Kate eased herself off her husband and out of the bed, and slipping on her warm robe and slippers. After looking over the yard to make sure there were no threats, she opened the door wide enough to let the dogs slip out and then shut it as she watched them bound across the virgin snow making the dog version of snow angels.

Turning back toward the bed, she saw her movements were being followed by a pair of beautiful green eyes. "I'm going to take a shower and get dressed and then pull some materials

I need for my talk with Vivian. Is the photo album from the Christmas Ball in the safe?"

"Yes. I'll get it for you while you shower and then I'll start breakfast."

"You are the best husband." She said as she grabbed a warm outfit for the day.

"Ah, a wife who loves me for my breakfasts alone."

"They're on a very long list of the reasons I love you."

"Not at the top I hope."

"No, my dear spouse. I can think of several things which would be much higher on my list." With that, she laughed and ducked into the bathroom, leaving a smiling Harry gazing after her.

Dressed and ready for the day, she hurried to the kitchen to make tea and feed the dogs. Opening the sliding door only an inch, she looked down at the very happy, very snowy pups before her and commanded, "Shake." There was a blizzard of flying snow everywhere but no longer on the dogs, so she let them in. She switched on the kettle as she ducked into the laundry room to grab a couple of towels and soon had all three dogs warm and dry. Taking the bowls off the shelf, she filled them with kibble and then added the other ingredients she pulled from the refrigerator, stirred the contents while wetting it and placed the bowls on the floor. Three dogs attacked their bowls with enthusiasm. They'd finished long before she'd had time to finish making tea.

"Your album, madam."

"Thank you. Coffee or tea for breakfast?"

"Coffee, I think. Now that we figured out that your great-uncle, Nelson Durgin, was involved, I've got a lot more research to work on."

"I think that Nelson was the ring leader. He certainly ended up with all the goodies. While you're at it, keep an eye out for any clues that Evangeline was involved."

Padraig strolled into the room informing them that Maeve was still asleep, but he was happy to help get the food organized. So while Harry and Padraig cooked, Kate selected photos from the album. Then she headed to the library to scan them and make copies. Once the large portraits had been copied, she went in search of any informal shots that could have ended up in some family albums she hadn't gotten to yet. She found a manila envelope complete with photographer's name in the bookcase by the sitting room fireplace. She opened it to find snapshots that had been taken the weekend of the ball. Kate spotted a lovely shot of Gram and Gramps, looking so young, sitting in a sleigh wrapped in a blanket. She set that aside thinking an enlargement of that would make a great framed photo to give Gram for Christmas. Then, she pulled out any shots with Vivian in them. Opening the envelope, she replaced all the photos which weren't vital and then took the rest to the library. She slid the one of her grandparents into an envelope and put it in the top desk drawer for later work and spread the others in rows across the desk.

The array of photos told a story of sweet romance. Vivian with a handsome young man who only seemed to have eyes for her. Some were of them walking in the snow, others kissing under the mistletoe, and still, more of them holding hands as they snuggled on the sofa before the fire. But the photo that held her attention, was a shot the photographer caught of Vivian and Divon Hader waltzing by themselves in the ballroom. The shot had caught the motion as her dress swung out in the turn and the joy in the smiles as they stared at one another. Looking at the photo, she realized the horrible loss Vivian must have suffered. She scanned these four shots and printed them out. She was glad that Harry had stocked photo paper because it made all the copies look like the originals. Her stomach grumbled. Collecting her prints and putting them into another manila envelope, she tucked everything else into the bottom desk drawer and headed for the kitchen.

Kate hoped the viewing room was large, since the plan of her going just with Harry had grown into a parade of present and former law enforcement. Gil and George were waiting for her when the pulled up to the hospital wing. He raised an eye at her entourage but didn't say anything. Once inside, the others were taken out of sight while Kate spoke with Vivian's doctor.

"Can you tell me why you want to visit with Miss Durgin?" she asked.

"I am trying to find the truth, and she is one of the few people who would know it. I also am tired of people trying to kill me when I'm on my honeymoon, so the sooner this is over the better."

The doctor laughed for a few seconds but then said, "You're not kidding."

"No. I'm not. May I see Vivian now?"

"You will have to leave your bag and phone out here. I presume you aren't carrying any weapons."

"I just need some papers from my bag." Kate took the

manila envelope from her purse and the doctor opened first one door and then another.

Kate had been sitting at a table in the middle of the room for about two minutes when Vivian was brought in. She was seated opposite her with her left arm shackled to the table. Kate noticed that her hand only needed a regular bandage which told her that Dillon hadn't really inflicted any long-lasting damage when he took the gun. When the aide stepped back and sat in a chair by the door, Vivian lifted her head and looked at Kate.

"Hello Katie. You didn't bring that nasty dog with you did you?"

"I am alone, Vivian. However, I would argue that Dillon wasn't being nasty. He was protecting me from being shot and killed by you."

"It hurt."

"Good. Maybe you won't do anything that stupid next time. Vivian, I'm not here to talk about your trying to kill me and Harry. I'm here to talk about the last Christmas Ball." Kate watched as Vivian's eyes seemed to glaze over, and she turned pale. "I brought some photos to show you." She opened the envelope and pulled out the stack of eight by ten photos. The first was of Vivian descending the staircase wearing her gown. She had a smile on her face. Vivian looked at it and touched the edge of the photo. A similar smile flicked across her face.

"You looked beautiful in that dress. You looked happy."

"I was so happy."

"Who is this?" She placed the photo of Divon Hader entering the front door in front of her. She gasped but then reached out to caress the man's face with a gentle finger. "I love you, Divon," she whispered.

Kate then arranged three photos taken on the weekend, of the couple so obviously in love. Vivian seemed to forget Kate was there. Her focus was totally on the photos.

"Divon, do you remember what fun we had, how you held my hand, how you made me laugh?" Vivian spoke as if the dead man were in the room.

Then Kate placed the photo of them dancing together, a lone couple in the huge ballroom seeing only each other.

"That's when you asked me to love you forever as you loved me. You asked me to marry you and I said I would. I was so happy"

"You were happy, Vivian, but then something happened. When the dance finished, where did you go?"

"We went into the sitting room. There was nobody in there. I sat in my grandmother's chair. Divon knelt down on one knee next to the hassock, and asked me to become his wife. But then his friend came in, Stavros. He said that he was being used and needed Divon's help. Divon told me not to move that he'd be right back, and he leaned in and kissed me—a real kiss." Silence filled the room as Kate watched Vivian travel back to that night when she was so deeply in love.

"What happened next? Did he come right back? Was he happy? Sad? Excited?"

"He was angry. He told me that he had been used. He told me that he needed to go to the police. He said that there had been a crime, and he had to report it. He said I should come with him because it wasn't safe for me to stay here."

"What happened? Did you go?"

"I wanted to go. I loved him so much—but then I shot him."

"Tell me about shooting him. Where were you standing?"

"I was standing in the doorway, of course."

"Where did you get the gun?"

Vivian looked confused. She screwed up her face and shook her head.

"I don't remember."

The kindness left Kate's voice. She slapped the table to get her attention. "Vivian, how do you know that you shot Divon? You loved him. You said you'd marry him. How do you know you shot him?"

"I saw it."

"You saw Vivian shoot Divon?"

"Yes, Divon asked me to marry him and I said yes, and he said we had to go to the police and I looked up and I shot him. I did it. I saw myself do it."

Kate reached for her pile of photos and showed her Divon's photo. "You shot Divon."

"Yes, I shot him. I saw it."

Kate slapped two photos on the table in front of Vivian. "Did this Vivian shoot Divon or did this Vivian shoot Divon?" she asked as she slapped the space by each photo. "Show me. Show me the Vivian who pointed the gun at Divon. Show me the Vivian who pulled the trigger. Show me which Vivian shot your Divon dead. Show me. Point. Which Vivian?"

Vivian had been following Kate's hand. Watching it go from one photo to the other. Back and forth. Back and forth. She raised her hand and pointed. Then she made a fist and pounded on the photo, pounded and pounded with tears flowing down her cheeks and a keening cry filling the room.

Kate stood. She looked at the glass mirror on the wall and when the attendant stood, she shook her head and then she slowly walked around to Vivian and wrapped her arms around her, letting her cry. She whispered over and over to her, "Vivian, you loved Divon. You didn't kill him. You didn't kill him." After a minute, the doctor came in and gently took Vivian from the room. Harry, Des, Oliver, Gil and George came in and stood looking at the table where two photos of what looked like the same woman, both wearing the same dress, lay. But they weren't the same woman.

Harry picked up the slightly battered photo and stared at it. It showed a woman who looked almost the same as the woman in the other photo. What also showed in this photo, though, was the arm of a person standing next to the woman. He'd seen that woman in another photo before it had been cropped. Evangeline.

"Evangeline murdered Divon Hader."

Kate walked around the table, picked up the manila envelope and put the photos back inside. She looked at the men. "This woman had a gown created that was an exact match to Vivian's. She styled her hair the same. She knew that Hader had been roped into this crime and was a weak link. She'd come prepared to handle the problem if his honesty and character threatened their theft. She was part of the plot to steal the Greek treasure, and she was not going to let him stop them and was going to blame Vivian. But worse, Vivian's shock at seeing someone who looked exactly like herself murder the man she loved right in front of her did something to her mind. Something that Evangeline has been reinforcing, by impersonating her, apparently for years. She destroyed Vivian's life and is still trying to destroy it. Her own niece."

Taking the final photo from Harry she slipped it into the envelope, stepped out of the room, picked up her belongings and with the others, headed for the cars. She'd only gone a few steps when she found herself wrapped in an enveloping hug as Maeve stroked her head and muttered, "You did her a kindness. You really did. You've gotten her the road toward realizing that she wasn't responsible for the death of the man she loved. She may be in agony now, but you've given her a way out."

Kate's shoulders began to shake and tears began to fall. Harry handed his keys to Des who left quickly. After a few minutes, he took Kate from Maeve and lifting her in his arms, went out the door to the waiting car, slid her into the middle seat and climbed in after her, pulling her back into his lap.

They were half-way home when his phone buzzed. It was a text from Tom. "Another break-in attempt. Shots fired. Nobody hurt. I've called Gil."

-30-

Wednesday Afternoon

By the time they arrived at Camp, Kate had stopped crying. Though she'd recovered from the emotional exhaustion of forcing Vivian to see the truth, the pile of tissues in her lap was now huge as she blew her nose yet again. Gathering them up, she climbed from the car on her own, but welcomed Harry holding her, with an arm around her shoulders, as they headed in the door. The dogs came flying from the kitchen, only to circle Kate's legs, rub against her, and whine softly. She squatted, scratching their heads as her hands slid from one to another.

"I'm okay guys, just a little sad." Quinn ran to the kitchen and then sped back carrying his stuffed hedgehog. 'Squeaky, squeaky!' he circled her and then pushed the noisy toy into her lap as she sat on the floor. "Thank you, Quinn," she told him as she hugged the hedgehog and the puppy together, making the toy squeak. Quinn barked, jumped up and whirled about. Taking the toy from her, he raced happily through the house leaving a trail of squeaks.

Tom arrived right behind the dogs, squeaking less but still eager to share what happened while they were away. "I've got to hand it to these people, they are persistent. They approached the gate and said they were here to fix the security system. I told them you weren't here. They persisted but I didn't let them in. The next thing I know, your dingers are going off letting me know someone's trying to break in. I spotted them by the gate that's hidden behind the tree near the game room. Padraig and Dillon went out to check it. Padraig was carrying Maeve's Glock. As they approached the tree, Dillon barked and a shot rang out. Padraig and Dillon ducked down until they heard an engine. They ran to the gate and saw a green Ford SUV heading down the neighbor's driveway toward the street."

"I imagine they are seeing their hard work in stealing the treasure about to be a case of all for nothing"' Kate said.

"What do you mean, all for nothing." Tom asked.

"We should tell them," Harry told her. "Kate and I found part of the treasure last night. I called the Greek Consul who is coming up tomorrow with the people from the MMA to get the treasure safely back to Manhattan. I suspect someone in the city has outed us to the shooters, and they feel a time constraint in trying to grab the treasure before it is away from here and under guard. I'm afraid that it's going to get a little dicey around here for the next twenty-four hours."

"As far as how we behave for that time, we have two choices. Either we hide in the house until they come tomorrow, or we brazen it out," Kate said.

Maeve stepped up. "I vote for brazening it out, but after lunch and after a peek at the treasure."

"Sounds good to me," Des added coming through the front door, followed by Oliver who also agreed, provided that the order was reversed. "I would like to see the treasure, sooner rather than later."

"I have no problem with that," Kate said feeling stronger with a new battle to fight. "Just follow me. Dillon, Liam, Quinn—Stay." She and Harry headed to the library. Everyone watched and when she moved the book which opened the wall, they were astonished. So, it was an eager parade which climbed the stair, examining every detail of the new hidden staircase, especially how well the hidden latches blended into each wall. Then they reached the room with the bed. Des and Maeve speculated that it must have been a room where Nelson slept sometimes. Oliver disagreed. He was more inclined to cast aspersions on the man's morals based on the room. They stopped speculating when Kate pulled the door to the attic open and started up.

The goddesses, still arranged in their semicircle, gazed out at them. Their power stole voices and for Oliver, his breath. "I never saw them. I searched sixty years for something that was a mere description on a piece of paper. A fuzzy photo. I often wondered why I cared. Why anyone cared. Now I know."

Maeve whispered, "It's as if I'm the only one here, and they are all gazing at me totally focused and willing to grant me my every wish."

Harry agreed. "I think that's why Nelson had them stolen. I found a comment in one of his father's diaries talking of how, when he returned from his trip to Greece and Italy following the death of his wife, he belabored the fact that even though he was a millionaire, there were some things that even he could not buy. The diary told of his desire those things was becoming an obsession."

"There was quite an addition to his fortune following my grandfather's death," Ann added.

Harry stared at her. "You don't think..."

"No. My grandfather died of pneumonia in 1954 following a flu epidemic in this area. He was ninety-nine years old. My grandmother was still alive. She died at age seventy-eight, in nineteen fifty-six."

Maeve placed her arm around her sister-in-law. "I suspect that your Uncle Nelson didn't like being told no. A case of, if you won't sell them to me, I'll just take them."

"So, you think he was behind the whole thing?" Oliver asked.

"Don't you? Think about it. The timing. The ability to organize this. A place to hide the goods. A sister, as amoral as he, with connections to the very people who would be their victims. However, what's vital now is that we all go eat lunch because emotional roller coasters make me hungry," Kate told them.

They all descended with Harry resetting the catches on

each doorway as they went. Maeve, Ann and Padraig took over making lunch. Kate picked up her jacket from the chair where she'd dropped it as they came in, and headed for the kitchen door. Dillon, Liam and Quinn lined up. "Quinn, the hedgehog is an indoor toy. Leave him." Reluctantly, he took the toy over to a spot by the window and set it down. Then he raced back to go out with the others. He circled the yard, ran up to the window to check his toy and then went to play.

Kate was exhausted. She didn't know why, but it probably was the session with Vivian. Though not forgetting the woman tried to kill her, she felt sorry for Vivian, she was in her eighties, and for sixty of those eighty plus years, she's walked around with guilt for killing the only man she ever loved. So much life wasted. Her life essentially ended that weekend—her hopes and dreams crushed. Kate pulled the bucket of balls from the bench and began hurling them. She needed a distraction as much as the dogs.

Arms encircled her from behind and she leaned back. Harry kissed the top of her head as she waited for the last toss to be returned. "You look pooped. I think the session this morning was too much."

"Well, as usual you are right. I was standing here thinking of all those wasted years that Vivian experienced. Sixty years of having that cloud hanging over her. Sixty years of thinking she'd killed the only person she'd ever loved. And now the pain of knowing the person whom she trusted to guide her all those years was the one who did it. She's going to need a truck-load of therapy."

"The money from the house will take care of those

expenses and any others." A rap came on the window . The dogs returned the final balls and Harry put them away, then opened the door. The dogs raced inside. Dillon and Liam went to sit at the end of the table, hoping for sympathetic suckers who'd share their food. Quinn raced around asking if everyone missed him and then went to get his hedgehog and settled in a spot by his father.

"Don't dawdle over lunch, people," Maeve told everyone. "I am dying to try out this sled I've heard so much about. What do you do with Quinn while Dillon and Liam are working?"

"Last time we let him run alongside. However, he's so excited today, I think I'll keep him inside. I'm going to let Harry show you how it works and get some time as driver. I'm really wrung out after the morning and I'll keep Quinn company just relaxing in the sitting room and read some more of old James' diaries."

"Good idea." Harry said while whispering alternatives if they only didn't have a house full of people.

Kate looked down at her hands, her face warming as she smiled. Padraig laughed and ruffled her hair as he followed his wife, Harry, and the rest of the crew outside. She had just made herself comfortable in the sitting room, her feet up on the hassock, when she heard the front door open. A second later, Harry stuck his head inside.

"Mr. Papadopoulos called that he will be here in an hour. He's bringing the director from the MMA to look at the statues. They have booked rooms at a B and B in Bolton Landing. The truck which will take the statues to the museum tomorrow will be here at ten in the morning. I invited the gentlemen to supper and checked with Helen that we had enough food to feed two more mouths. You relax. Helen's cooking."

He was gone before she could say a word. Kate decided that married life with a man used to taking charge and making things run smoothly was not a bad thing. She was still smiling over the words he'd whispered in her ear before going sledding with the dogs.

As she read about Evangeline as a child and young adult, she wondered why nobody had thought to get her some psychiatric help. What had seemed rambunctious as a ten-year-old was seriously disturbing as a teenager. Even her doting father realized that the number of times he'd had to pay people because of injuries inflicted by his daughter, and the animals she killed showed he was dealing with was the classic behavior of a psychopath. The weekend he went into the city to talk to a specialist about her, Evangeline ran off with the actor. She disappeared after emptying her bank account. He immediately froze access to her trust and her stock portfolio which he could do since she was a minor. He sent out word to her friends, at least those who she said were her friends, that he was disowning her.

Kate's first thought about what Evangeline's father had done to her was that it was harsh. When she thought about it, though, it occurred to her that he was still being protective. She was seventeen-years-old, beautiful, manipulative and without a social conscience. The money she'd taken would have kept a normal person going for a year or even two, but he'd calculated that she would run through it in a month.

Evangeline's mother had made sure she had birth control

when she realized that her baby was sexually active. He'd put the detective he used to keep track of Tim onto her. The detective was good and discrete. He had to be careful, because she was beginning to influence Nelson's daughter, Vivian. That young girl was very sensitive, and he saw Vivian could easily be destroyed by the creature his own daughter was becoming.

Kate hoped that someday Vivian would be well enough to read this diary. Toward the end of this section in this diary dedicated to Evangeline, he comes up with the idea to arrange for Tim's daughter, who was just a few years younger than Vivian to spend time at Camp and bring some balance, and hopefully friendship into the girl's life.

Just as she was about to find the next journal in the box, Kate's phone buzzed. Mr. P had arrived with the MMA director. Harry texted that there were two cars, so they must have come separately.

Kate lowered her feet to the floor and put the box with the journals back into the cupboard where Harry had decided to keep them. This way they'd be safe from Quinn's new hobby of paper shredding.

Quinn jumped up when she went to leave the room and ran toward the kitchen to be first in line in case there was food coming.

Kate walked into the entry and was about to open the door when it was opened by Padraig. "Kate, this lady came with the museum director but needs to use the powder room."

"Of course. It is the door right before the kitchen on the left." As the older woman moved past her, Kate felt she'd seen her before, but she didn't know where. Maybe she'd been to

Kate's fashion show, though she doubted that a woman wearing a mink coat with a huge mink muff attached to her wrist was a dog person. When the woman left to use the facilities, Kate moved to Padraig and asked how the sledding was going.

"Our dogs are too old to do this. But Maeve loves it. So I'd say, bottom line is that you will be seeing a lot more of us this winter." Kate hugged him and laughed. He went back outside, closing the door. Kate turned to see if there was anything the woman needed and stopped. She realized why the woman looked familiar became clear when she saw a gun that pointed in her direction.

"Hello, Evangeline," Kate said.

"Well, aren't you clever."

Kate saw Quinn in the kitchen doorway and signaled him to stay.

"Not really. You look like your photo at twenty, if somewhat aged."

"Well, even a pretty girl like you will grow old and wrinkled one day...or maybe not. Maybe I'd be doing you a favor to keep your memory young and beautiful for that green-eyed hunk you married. Or, I might not. Since I'm on the board of the Metropolitan Museum of Art, I'd like to see the statues we're going to put on display."

"Oh, didn't your brother show them to you when you all stole them? Didn't he trust you?"

"My brother had one love—those statues. He could care less about his sister."

Kate watched as Quinn moved closer. His hedgehog in his mouth, but his eyes on Evangeline.

"Oh, I think Nelson did care for you. When Stavros came after you when he realized you were the one who'd murdered Divon, Nelson shot and killed Stavros. Maybe he cared, or maybe he didn't want a loose end with a conscience running to the police But he was smart enough not to worry that you would rat him out. Did you realize you dropped the gun you used to kill Divon when you ran? Because he kept it, covered with your fingerprints—just in case."

"Vivian killed Divon."

"No, she didn't. And what's more, she now knows she didn't. She knows you have been disguising yourself to look like her for sixty years in order to destroy her life. In order to keep her from finding any happiness, because you couldn't allow her to have something you never could—love."

"Enough of this. Get going."

"I should warn you before we go that there's a hedgehog right behind you."

Evangeline snorted. "A hedgehog. Do you think I'm an idiot? That I'll turn around and you'll grab the gun?"

"Squeaky, squeaky!"

Evangeline jumped, swinging around as her gun fired. The bullet buried itself in a log in the wall as Kate lunged for the gun. However, as Evangeline turned, the muff swung which was all the invitation Quinn needed. He dropped his hedgehog and grabbed the muff.

"Quinn." Kate screamed as she struggled to pull the gun from Evangeline's hand. For a woman in her eighties, Evangeline proved to be surprisingly strong. Releasing the gun she knocking Kate to the floor.

Quinn let go of his new hedgehog and ran to Kate, licking her face to make sure she was okay. She struggled to get up, while reassuring the puppy, but Evangeline was already running through the kitchen and out.

-31-

Wednesday Night and Thursday Morning

As Kate reached the kitchen, she saw Evangeline had gone through the sliders, crossed the yard and was pushing open the gate. Kate ran to the open slider only to see Quinn fly by, race across the yard, and through the gate.

By the time Kate reached the yard, she saw that Quinn was following Evangeline. The woman turned and tried to kick him, but Quinn thought it was all part of the game. His attention was focused on her arm. When she turned to run toward the dock, he struck and grabbed the swinging muff.

Kate stopped running. Quinn had Evangeline. He held the muff and was working on a squeaky that wasn't making noise but in doing so, he was dragging Evangeline back toward Kate.

"Good boy, Quinn. Tug hard. Bring it here. Good boy." Kate pitched her voice low to differentiate it from Evangeline's screeching, which made Quinn pull harder, shaking his head, and tugging the woman back and forth.

"Get that beast off her," a man shouted from off to her right. She looked over her shoulder and saw a man in a chauffeur's uniform run down the path with a gun in his hand. Behind him came the dogs and Harry driving the sled which held Maeve. As the man stopped to lift his gun and point at Quinn, a shot rang out.

Kate's yell was drowned out by the man's scream. As Harry steered the sled next to him, a leg shot out from the bed of the sled and kicked the man in the back of the knees. He collapsed like a folding chair and Harry was on him in a flash. Maeve slid off the sled and moved to hold Evangeline but laughed when she saw that Kate wasn't holding the lady, only watching Quinn play tug of war.

"How do you want to do this?" Maeve stood, her hands on her hips watching the woman writhe in the snow, her mink coat losing much of its style.

"Do you have a knife?"

Evangeline screamed, "No."

"Of course I have a knife." Maeve whipped out a small case that looked like a lipstick from her pocket, and a blade shot out from it. Two seconds later, Kate had sliced the strap and as Quinn ran in circles around them waving his new hedgehog,

Evangeline fell backward into the snow.

Maeve asked, "Should we pick her up?"

"She tried to shoot me."

"Enough said. Stay down there, Mrs. DeBeer. Oh, I have some good news for you. Your husband is in the hospital where he is working on making a complete recovery. He'll be able to testify at your trial."

Kate heard her phone buzz and saw Gil wave at the camera as she pushed the gate button. Less than a minute later, the squad car screeched to a stop. "Here to take out the garbage, Gil? We've got a double. The lady took a shot at me. Here's her gun and the bullet is in one of the log walls of the entryway."

"She's lying. I've never seen that gun."

"Yeah lady, I've heard it all before. George put the lady in the car. Joe, take the Bozo that Harry's sitting on over there and put him in your car. You might inform Count Baturin that it is illegal to try to shoot at people when you are out on bail in Bolton Landing, NY, though I'm sure that the judge will inform him of that."

Harry suddenly was there, holding her tight. "Gil, get this scum out of my sight," he yelled.

Kate felt him shaking, tears wetting her shoulder as he buried his head in her neck. She held him and looking over his shoulder nodded to Maeve. Within a minute, they were alone. Kate whispered to Dillon, "Come." A second later, the dogs were next to her with the sled. Kate pulled Harry down onto the bed of the sled as all the dogs snuggled close. Quinn climbed onto the sled and lay his head in Harry's lap, shoving a huge, snowy, mink 'hedgehog' against his chest as he pushed his head in to lick away the tears.

Harry took a shuttering breath and finally asked, "What happened?"

She tightened her grip, her arms locked around his chest and rested her forehead against his. "I was reading the journals. Evangeline's father had concluded that his daughter was a psychopath when she ran off with the actor. He froze all her money, so she had only what she had pulled from her bank account." Kate went on to describe all that she'd read, down to using Ann to protect Vivian from coming under Evangeline's influence. Then he died.

"I don't think Evangeline shot Divon because he was going to the cops. I think she saw that Vivian had found love with a decent man and couldn't stand it. I can't prove it, but that's my opinion.

"She told me she didn't want to shoot me because I wouldn't give her the statues. No, she was going to kill me so that our love would be destroyed and you'd suffer for the rest of your life.

"Quinn and his hedgehog saved my life. I warned her there was a hedgehog behind her, but she didn't believe me. When he made it go 'squeaky, squeaky,' she jumped and Quinn grabbed the dangling muff. I grabbed the gun from her hand, but she shoved me and I went down. Quinn came to check on me and she escaped. However, our hedgehog hunter went after her and brought her down."

"Are you a hedgehog hunter, Quinn? What a good boy. You are definitely Dillon's son."

They sat for a while just holding each other until Kate said,

"Well, I don't know about you, but my butt is freezing. How would you like to give a girl a ride in this shiny chariot, my knight in shining armor? I saw that takedown you and Maeve did. I knew she could shoot, but that was impressive. I'll have to have her show me the kick she used to take out Baturin's knees. It could prove useful."

"I shall happily take you home with my white steeds pulling my chariot. Before life went all to hell today, I was getting a hang of this sled."

"Padraig has warned me that Maeve is now addicted to sledding, and they will often be visiting this winter." Kate leaned back against Quinn who'd settled onto the sled behind her, and lay his head on his hedgehog. The first thing she would do when she got home to Connecticut would be to sew several squeakers into this muff and make it look more like a hedgehog. She stared ahead at Dillon and Liam pulling the sled, tails wagging. A girl could get used to this. It will make the arrival of heavy snow at home something to anticipate. They put away the sled, hung the harnesses up to dry and after a long, long kiss, went inside with the dogs at their side.

Helen had outdone herself with the perfect meal to chase away the chill, pot roast and mashed potatoes with roasted vegetables. Kate welcomed Mr. Papadopoulos back and was introduced to Normand Messier, who was to be in charge of the new launch of the collection. Everyone sat and once the meal was served, and once Helen was thanked, they began to eat. Oliver asked. "Kate would tell us what happened?"

Smiling, Kate said to Normand Messier, "You might want to remove Mrs. Evangeline DeBeer from your board. After what happened, she won't be available to attend the board meetings."

She looked around the table at the somber faces and began telling them how Quinn and his favorite toy, saved her life and caught the murderer. By the end of the meal, Quinn was drowning in head pats and snuggles.

Maeve explained that when she heard the shot since she was in the sled she simply commanded the dogs to find Kate. With their intense hearing and smell, they knew exactly where she was.

Ann informed them that since she'd learned to use Kate's codes on the alarms and cameras, she had recorded the entire thing on video. She looked over at her sister-in-law and while grinning asked, "When did you switch from playing 'M' to being 'James Bond.'"

Over a dessert of cherry pie and ice cream, Normand Messier explained how he was going to arrange the exhibit and there would be the story of how Kate and Harry and their dogs, recovered it.

Soon after, their dinner guests left saying they would see them in the morning. Tom drove Gwyn over to her place to pack. She would be staying with him and Gram while she interviewed for positions in Connecticut. Des and Oliver went to organize and pack up the evidence so that a proper case could be brought against Evangeline and Baturin. Maeve, Padraig, and Ann went to the sitting room to look through the albums which Kate had found and to read the journals.

Harry and Kate fed the dogs, loaded the dishwasher and then decided to make an early night of it. Harry let the dogs out and went to tell the others to lock up after Tom and Gwyn return. Kate went to their room and grabbed her pajamas then stopped. She went to her small suitcase where Agnes had placed makeup and all her female paraphernalia. She had included two small boxes that Kate removed and took into the bathroom, placing them in the medicine chest. Once in her pj's, she crawled into bed to wait for Harry. She snuggled under the covers, thanking God for saving her today and for giving her Harry, the dogs, and a wonderful family of friends and relatives. Snuggling deeper under the duvet, she felt herself dropping off until she couldn't fight it.

Harry entered the room, having been held up by a call from Gil that the bad guys were locked up and would not be getting bail. He told Harry that they'd be by in the morning to make sure the treasure got safely out of his jurisdiction and to get everyone's statement.

Harry saw Kate's blond curls peeking over the edge of the duvet which she'd turned into a cocoon. He went to the slider and let the dogs in. They were quicker than usual to settle, though Quinn ran to the bedroom door and barked to go out. Harry let him leave and watched as he ran to the kitchen and a few seconds later came trotting back. In his mouth, he held both his hedgehog and the cord attached to the muff. He proudly entered the bedroom, going squeaky, squeaky. Harry smiled and using the hand signals Kate had taught him, signaled all the dogs to settle down and go to sleep.

Grinning at the scene of his sleeping wife and dogs, he shed his clothes, putting them and his shoes on the shelf Kate installed to keep temptations out of the puppy's way and then crawled in under the covers. He gathered Kate to him without her even waking. Then secure with the thought that Kate was alive and in his arms, he slept.

-32-

Thursday Morning

Kate woke warm and comfortable, snuggled in Harry's arms. She lay in the secure bubble of his love and tried not to think about yesterday. At least she hadn't spaced out in the middle of dinner. But all this stress was making her weary. A month of dealing with the mob and killers prior to and at the wedding to be followed by this circus meant that there had been no recovery time. No time to just relax and think the situations through. They had less than a week here before returning home. Her business was in high gear preparing for her second annual fashion show as part of the

New York City dog show excitement. Harry had two CEOs pushing him to run around the globe doing their investigations.

What time they had left, they should lock the gates and not let anyone in, she thought. She looked around their master bedroom. The shine on the logs caught the first glimmers of sunrise. The creamy white wall behind their bed lit up what might have been a very dark room. A bank of sliders, Harry had installed, allowed them to lie in bed and catch the first sparkling glimmers of light on Lake George, winking through the trees. This house, her castle, had become something more—a home. She loved it, and she loved the thoughtful man who gave it to her.

Her body began to realize that she was awake, and nature was making its call. She lifted the arm that held her and slid out from under the covers. A sleepy grumble objected, but she just whispered, "Bathroom," and he fell back to sleep. Signaling the dogs to stay, she closed the bathroom door and went to the medicine chest, removing the boxes she'd placed there the night before. Taking a breath, she read the directions. Both products worked the same way. Saying a small prayer, she took the tests placing each on the side of the sink. She finished and then after washing her hands, her face and brushing her hair, she got the nerve to look.

She found a gift bag which Helen had left for her filled with toiletries, emptied it, placed both tests into one box, and placed the box inside the bag.

"Kate!" She heard the terrified shout. Harry was sitting bolt up in bed, breathing in panic and staring straight ahead, a look of horror on his face.

"Harry, I'm right here."

"His eyes came into focus as she dove onto the bed to touch him. He grabbed her and held on as his breathing and heart rate returned to normal. "I woke and you weren't there. Then I remembered yesterday. I couldn't tell which was real and which a nightmare."

"I'm here." She crawled forward until she was right up against him. Then taking his hand and bringing it to her cheek, she turned and kissed it.

"I've got a present for you." She reached behind her on the mattress, grabbed the small bag, and placed it in his lap.

"What's this?"

"Open it and see." She smiled and nudged the package forward.

Watching her, he reached inside and took out a box, read the label and realizing what it was, he opened the box, looked at the sticks. Then he looked up at her.

"Hi there, Daddy."

It was an hour before they got around to leaving the bed. Everyone else was already up and the smell of bacon drew them to the kitchen. "French toast with Will's homemade raisin bread. I figured you were up because the dogs are out."

"This smells so good. I'm starved," Kate said smiling.

"Good," Tom said. "The ladies in the attic will be leaving about ten o'clock, Gil and George will be here at nine, and we're all leaving after lunch."

Oliver asked, "When the trial comes up, could we hopefully use this as our home base?"

No problem." Harry told him. "We'll all be back for that."

Once the dishes were loaded, everyone went to pack. Kate fed the dogs and let them back out. Then she moved to the entryway and sat in the overstuffed chair which Harry and Otto had found in the attic. It came with a matching foot stool. She had picked up the remote control for the train and was running both engines. With care, she maneuvered them to cross paths and go over the bridges and through the tunnels. When she brought them into the station, she stretched and gazed up at the tree, appreciating the sparkle of the ornaments.

Sparkle. She stood and went to the tree. Looking up into the branches, partially closing her eyes. With her eyes almost shut, the other ornaments faded into the background and the sparkling ones stood out. She pulled out her phone and texted Harry. I need you in the entryway with a large ladder. Then as she waited, she walked around the tree marking each ornament that sparkled.

"What do you need with the ladder?" Harry asked as he set it up beside the tree.

"Hold it still," she told him, "I'm going up."

"Is it safe for you...?"

"Yes, I can do everything I've always done until the spring. Then I'll be happy to be babied a little." She scrambled up the ladder, pausing in different spots to remove an ornament and put it in her pocket. When she'd finished one side, she had him move the ladder to the other side. Finally, she asked him to go find the tool kit that was in the kitchen closet. "I need a needle-nose pliers and maybe a flat-head screwdriver."

He got the tool kit and brought it into the library, which thankfully was empty at the moment. She walked over to the leather-topped table under the massive windows and sat. One at a time, she removed from her pockets the ornaments she'd taken from the tree.

Harry stood behind her looking down at what she was doing, After removing all the hooks from the ornaments, she laid out the pieces.and started moving the pieces around, as if working a jigsaw puzzle. Slowly the groups of pieces took on the shapes of animals. Working deftly, she placed the pieces together. It took almost a half hour to finish the job.

Resting her head against Harry's arm as he gently massaged her stiff shoulders, they stared at a necklace, bracelet, and two pairs of earrings. "I think I'll leave the final attachment of the pieces to the conservators at the museum. I don't want to loosen a stone or scratch a setting. It may have survived centuries, but considering this week, I'll lean toward the side of caution."

"How did you know?"

"I didn't until I was sitting in that comfortable chair you set up for me, my thanks to you and Otto. There had been something bothering me from the beginning about the tree, but I couldn't say what. When I was looking at the photograph album, I saw the photo of Vivian in front of the tree. I realized that the ornaments, including the crystal star, were all the same as they had been more than sixty years ago. They placed the same ornaments in the same position each time it was put up, done by the same company every year. But there was a difference. From the day they set it up, I loved the sparkle. It was only when I saw the old photo that I had a basis of comparison. When I sat here this morning, playing with the train, I noticed the way the light was creating tiny rainbows on the floor. As I watched, it dawned on me that Nelson might have hidden the jewels in plain sight.

"Remember, the Christmas Ball was taking place. He probably took the necklace apart, went into the drawer where the extra hooks are kept, and using the long-armed pincer stick, hung the pieces on the tree. When the company came to take the tree down, they just marked the new ornament places on their master plan and put them away. For sixty years, this part of the treasure was right in front of everyone."

Their phones both beeped. Harry pulled out his phone and noticed a line of vehicles at the gate with Gil in the lead.

"Bring on the parade, Gil," he said, as he pushed the button.

Soon a crowd filled the entry way, the Greek consul, the museum's director for the exhibit and a team of four specialists in packing and transporting the treasures plus two security guards. They were met by the equally large crowd of residents.

Harry welcomed everyone. Then he told them he had news. "Now Kate and I were married a week ago, Saturday. Solving a sixty-year-old murder and theft was definitely not how we planned to spend our time here."

Everyone laughed. "My wish would have been to see none of you at our new vacation home, a place that has been a dream of my wife's to own since childhood. But as she pointed out to me, we would never be allowed to have our honeymoon, until this was solved. So that was what she did.

"Kate has a talent for sorting out impossible situations. My brilliant wife is well-known by law enforcement, especially the FBI, for her skills in finding answers. She has been studying the problem of this crime since the day we arrived. First, she found the statues in a hidden room in the attic, and this morning, she discovered where the jewels were hidden." A gasp swept the room. "We have all been looking at them day after day. But it took Kate's insight to not just look, but see. If you will follow us into the library, I will show you the rest of the treasure."

They all crowded into the library and exclaimed in unison at the sight of the pieces of the necklace, bracelet and earrings laid out but not attached. Beside it was the stack of ornament hooks. "Oh my," Ann said, "the Christmas tree. We have been walking by it and playing under it with the train, and never noticed. Katie, you are amazing."

"Actually, I was really motivated," Kate told her and everyone laughed.

The men and women from the MMA got to work. One pair carefully packed each piece of the necklace for re-assembly, while another took boxes to the attic to pack the statues under Normand Messier's supervision.

The family, FBI agents and police headed to the kitchen. Gil said that he'd get Kate and Harry's statements later in the week, but wanted to get the others out-of-the-way so they could leave. The next two hours was controlled chaos. When the museum truck left under guard, it started a parade. The Greek Consul was effusive in his thanks as was Mr. Messier.

Des and Oliver were next to leave. Oliver was fighting tears. "Kate, I can't tell you how grateful I am for helping me clear my record." Des hugged her and told her he'd let all her friends in the bureau know that she had done it again.

Maeve and Padraig hugged them. "We will be back for New

Year's and more sledding."

Tom, Gram and Gwyn came in for hugs. Gwyn would be storing her motorcycle in the carriage house. She would be staying with Gram and Tom while she lined up work in her field in Connecticut. Kate pointed out they would see each other in another week.

Harry asked Tom to keep an eye on the beginning construction of their house. The foundation should have been poured last week. Tom said, "Leave it in my hands and just enjoy the job of making my sister happy."

When the cars cleared the gate, Harry closed the gate and locked it. When they went back into the kitchen, they found a present from George addressed to Quinn. A note was attached. For the great hedgehog hunter. These are squeakers which my dogs have been taking from their stuffed toys for years. Have your mom sew them into your new hedgehog.

Kate went to her room and got her sewing box. Twenty minutes and one cup of tea later, Quinn was able to walk around the house with a hedgehog which squeaked wherever he bit it.

"Happy honeymoon," Harry said as the proud puppy strutted around going 'squeaky, squeaky.' "It's suppose to snow again tonight. I vote that we go for a walk and reintroduce ourselves to our honeymoon home, and make new memories, and then we can come inside, and cuddle by the fire, as we decide how to spend the week ahead. I talked to Sal and extended our time away. He agreed and said he'd handle it and tell your knitters. We can begin by introducing that baby or babies you carry to every room in the house."

"That's a wonderful idea, but babies?"

"It was your vision," he said. They called the dogs and headed out for a walk before the snow began.

Made in the USA
Las Vegas, NV
26 March 2021

20236884R00173